necking

necking

Chris Salvatore

POCKET BOOKS
New York   London   Toronto   Sydney

Pocket Books
A Division of Simon & Schuster, Inc.
1230 Avenue of the Americas
New York, NY 10020

First Pocket Books trade paperback edition August 2008

POCKET and colophon are registered trademarks of Simon & Schuster, Inc.

For information about special discounts for bulk purchases,
please contact Simon & Schuster Special Sales
at 1-800-456-6798 or business@simonandschuster.com.

Designed by Carla Jayne Little

Manufactured in the United States of America

Library of Congress Cataloging-in-Publication Data is available.

10 9 8 7 6 5 4 3 2 1

ISBN-13: 978-1-4165-6020-3
ISBN-10:   1-4165-6020-3

First this is for my family. Their love of books was contagious and they created the monster I am today (although my dad is not allowed to read the sex scenes in this book). I feel that it might be on the edge of crazy to thank my cat, Jimmy, who sat on my lap while I wrote this book. He's not exactly my muse, but more like a heating pad.

To all my friends in the business and otherwise, there are too many of you to thank for all your inspiration and encouragement. However, do look for your names throughout the book and know that I never stopped thinking about you.

Thank you to Paige, Micki, Danielle, and Jessica for all your hard work and your excitement. And thank you also to all my authors throughout the years. You've taught me to appreciate all sides of the business and a special thanks to Lois and Nelson—ironically, you both taught me to stop being such a nice girl.

necking

Prologue

So, We're Pretending It Never Happened, Right?

I swam up to the bar. "I'll have a Belvedere vodka, please."

"Yes, miss. How would you like it?"

"Just in a glass, thank you. Oh, and a Red Stripe for my friend here." My best friend, Lola, had floated over to me on her raft. I clicked my red plastic cup with her can and we drank up.

Lola wiped her mouth with the back of her hand. "Feeling better?"

We had checked into the resort less than an hour ago.

"Would you bite my head off if I told you that I missed him already?"

"Probably. But I wouldn't expect anything else." Lola's always brutally honest and never puts up with any of my bullshit.

"So, tell me the whole story and don't leave anything out. I mean, I get that he's totally hot. But you, more than anyone else, should know better. You could see from day one he's pure poison. So spill it."

"Okay. But I don't come out looking too good."

She gave an exasperated sigh and I followed her out of the pool and onto the deck chairs that lined the sunny side of the patio. "Come on," she impatiently coaxed. "You've known him for over a year now. . . ."

"Nineteen months and three weeks."

She rolled her eyes. "Okay, nineteen months and three weeks. What changed?"

It was a fair question. I was attracted to this guy from the moment we met: he's funny, smart, and yes, totally hot. *And* he was totally poison, *and* a client and I certainly did know better. Until recently, I was able to at least pretend that I was resisting him. But after last week, I was falling so hard for this guy—a guy whom Lola had to take me fifteen hundred miles away from to try to talk some sense into me.

The incident that started it all happened a little over a week ago, about 3:30 a.m. on a very hot August night. We were hanging out with mutual friends at a club and I had had one too many drinks. I went outside with him to clear my head and get out of the club's extreme air-conditioning while he had a cigarette.

I was very tipsy—okay, totally drunk off my ass—and I just wanted to be near him. To be close enough to smell him. He always smelled so damn good. That night, he smelled like worn leather.

He offered me a cigarette.

"No thanks, those things will kill ya."

He shrugged and lit one up, giving me a lopsided grin as he exhaled. "You're a real wiseass tonight."

"Tonight? Have we met?" I held out my hand to him. He grabbed my hand and put his arm around my shoulders, pulling me into his chest before kissing my forehead.

Now, I know that doesn't seem like such a big deal, especially for a guy who had women lining up just to talk to him, but when his arm came in contact with my bare shoulders and his lips touched my skin, we both jumped back. It burned.

Up until that night, handshakes and air kisses were about all the physical contact, and let me tell you, nothing like this ever happened before.

Although my skin burned in the places where he touched me, I was chilled to the bone.

He quickly pulled his arm away and whispered, "Wow."

"'Wow' is right." I shivered.

He looked right into my eyes, which I rarely allowed, but he had such a concerned expression on his face that I permitted it. "Are you cold?"

I nodded. As late as it was, it was easily eighty degrees and downright balmy. There was no reason for me to be cold.

"Funny." He gave me an ironic smile. "For the first time—in a long time—I'm a little hot."

We quickly put more distance between us and I made a lame, slurred excuse to leave. Even as drunk and as confused as I was, I didn't think it was a good idea to stay so close to him after that.

You see, I'm a publicist for a rather unusual company with a rather unusual list of clients. As a result, I've always needed very strict rules about interacting with the people I work with. There was never to be any physical contact other than handshakes and air kisses, especially with my "special" or, as Lola calls them, my "poison" clients. And he was a very special and very poison client.

Our professional relationship had so far survived our flirty friendship, and I allowed him more liberties simply because I had had a major, embarrassing crush on him since the day I met him. Me and most of the female population of Manhattan, I'm sure.

I went home that night and tried to convince myself that my reaction was all in my head. We had touched each other before and nothing like this had happened. It couldn't make this much of a difference just because it was his first *affectionate* gesture toward me. I'd just had too much to drink, or maybe I was coming down with a flu—my non-air-conditioned apartment was an oven, yet I still had the chills.

I was still stewing about it the next morning, but consoled myself that it was natural to react the way I did. After all, I was only human and totally vulnerable to the charms of such a beautiful creature—and damn it if he wasn't the most beautiful creature I'd ever laid eyes on . . . but I digress. However, someone like little ol' me wasn't supposed to be able to make someone like him respond like that. I'm damn cute, but he really could have any woman he wants. There was no need for him to come sniffing around an off-limits coworker.

"Okay, so what happened next? You can't tell me he didn't call the next day." Lola was sharp.

"Of course he called." Though he kept me waiting until after I got home from work. I had just finished running, sweating out the toxins from the stupid amount of alcohol I had consumed the night before, and I was stretching in the park when my cell phone rang.

"Hey. Want to meet for coffee?" he asked.

"I just finished a pretty intense run." Look at me, totally not seeming like I wanted to see him. "Where and when?" D'oh. Sometimes I couldn't stop myself from being an idiot.

"Does 'now' work for you? I'm at the diner on your corner."

Presumptuous, wasn't he? Of course I was already making my way over to the water fountain to splash some cold water on my face, then checked my reflection in a car's side mirror. I looked okay in the sweaty jock-chick kind of way. I was glad I was wearing the cute shorts that showed off my ass.

"I can be there in a few minutes, but I gotta warn you, I stink."

He laughed. "Good."

It wasn't good. Seeing him looking so cool and delicious would only add to my "glow," as my mother would say, and I already felt like a piglet.

I saw him the second I walked into the diner. As stunning as he was, he had a way of fading into the background, but I always picked him out. I had a gift for debunking that whole *Where's Waldo?* thing he tried to pull off.

I slid into the booth. He already had a coffee in front of him.

"I ordered you a large grapefruit juice. You like that after your runs, right?"

How the hell did he remember that? "How the hell did you remember that?"

"I'm very wise."

"'Wiseass' is more like it." I took a napkin from the dispenser and wiped my embarrassingly sweaty forehead. Well, if I wanted to keep a distance, this was a good way to do it. And I was proving to him that I didn't care what I looked like when I met him. This was all good.

"Listen, about last night . . ." He trailed off and began stirring his coffee. "I probably shouldn't have started anything like that. I mean, we work together, you were drinking, I was getting carried away, and . . ." He added sugar to his coffee. It was just something to do with his hands; he hated sugar.

"Okay, good. We're on the same page, then. Here I thought

it was just the whiskey talking, or maybe I was coming down with 'stupid' fever—one that impairs my judgment and makes me do things that are incredibly dumb."

"Yeah, not one of my better decisions, either." He looked up with the tiniest hint of a smile. "But it felt good, didn't it?"

"So it was that good for you too, huh?" I winked at him.

He chuckled softly. "You don't want to know." He shook his head. "I don't know what made me touch you like that. And I don't know why you, of all people, let me. You're smarter than that, and I'm old enough to know better." He looked away for a second, and it looked like he was going to say something else, but thought better of it. He turned back to meet my gaze with those awesome killer eyes. "I don't know why I even allowed myself to think about you in that way for a second."

We both knew it could never work between us. It would have been impossible for him to blend into my world, and I couldn't ever imagine making the necessary sacrifices for me to blend into his.

I looked away from his eyes—I didn't want to acknowledge what I saw there, nor did I trust myself to resist him. He was way too sexy for his own good.

"I don't know," I answered. "But I find myself thinking about you that way, too."

He let out an exasperated breath. "That's a mistake, baby. I'm a monster."

I laughed at the understatement. "You won't get any argument here."

He gave me a crooked little smile that made my heart skip a beat. "Who's the wiseass now?" He sighed heavily. "Still, you should be flattered. It's not often that I think about someone this way—lucky you, huh?"

"Aren't we awfully full of ourselves? My mother warned me about guys like you."

"Like me specifically?" He looked incredulous.

"Yep. Told me that if I didn't behave, the monsters would come out from under my bed and get me while I slept."

"Sounds like a delightful childhood memory."

I shook my head. "It was rather disappointing, actually. I kept camping out under my bed every night, hoping to meet the monsters."

He smiled at that. "You're a freak."

"You know we have to stop."

"Don't worry, I'll be good. I know something about restraint."

"So, we're pretending it never happened, right?" I asked.

"That's my plan."

He *was* good after that, but I was a wreck. I couldn't stop thinking about our reaction that night; I became obsessed. I found excuses to be near him. Found reasons to call him.

I had a big project with him in the coming months, and if I was going to survive it, I needed help. So I called in the reserves, my best friend Lola, and took off to the islands for a much-needed vacation.

I looked at her over the top of my drink.

Lola was digesting my story and thinking about the next step. "I think you may be overreacting, Chickpea. You're simply attracted to forbidden fruit. He's the bad boy your mother would never approve of, and how hot is that?"

"That's a good point. But . . ."

"Trust me on this." She tipped her head back to get the last drop of beer from her can. It's been a while since you've had any action, and you just need to get laid. Just pick some harmless guy here and get your hormones back to normal. He won't seem so appealing then."

She scanned the beach and zeroed in on two very attractive

men getting off their rented Jet Skis. "How about those two? Let's get their attention and make them drool." She sat up and stretched in a way that immediately caught the eyes of the two guys in question. "And you"—she looked pointedly at me over her sunglasses—"you, my dear, need to pay attention to how good it feels right now to be sipping vodka in the Caribbean sunlight."

She had a point there.

1

Speculation

"No, I'm sorry, but Ms. Nightshade isn't available tomorrow morning. Can we tape the interview in the afternoon and air it the next day?" The details that went into an author's book tour were tedious at best. "Or better yet, why don't you come down to the signing with a crew? You can get some great B-roll, interview a few of the fans you know, capture the whole Nightshade fan phenomenon. Then I'll set up Jackie Stewart's interview at a restaurant or a club—something more interesting than Bella's hotel suite."

I was pitching my author to an NCN producer named Diane and she was considering it. I pictured her as young, mousy, a big fan of the Von Rastenbourg family novels. She probably never got into hip restaurants or swank clubs. I sweetened the pot. "How about we set up the actual interview at Sweat? It'd be the perfect setting—candles, lots of red velvet, beautiful people . . ."

I knew I had her. I sat back in my chair, biding my time while she swallowed my purple Kool-Aid. If you weren't Paris or the Olsen twins, or of course my client the esteemed Ms. Nightshade, you weren't allowed anywhere near the velvet rope at Sweat.

Diane could barely keep the excitement out of her voice when she agreed. "Great. I'll tell the bookstore to expect you and the camera crew at about seven o'clock for a setup, and tell Sweat to put the crew and Jackie Stewart on the list as Ms. Nightshade's entourage."

All in a day's work.

I should probably introduce myself. My name is Giovanna Felice, book publicist at Speculation. Speculation is a science fiction and fantasy book-publishing house. We publish novels about aliens, elves, and all sorts of things that go bump in the night. Over the last ten years, my specialty has been horror. I suppose it's because of my rapport with the authors and my ability to deal with the scary megafans.

Like any publicist, I have to handle the egos, the bizarre requests for specialty items, the always-annoying travel arrangements, and contend with a million details at once. But working with the *Fangoria* set creates a unique set of additional problems. Although 99 percent of the fans are delightful, I also get to deal with psychos who tried everything from presenting my authors with dead cats to actually trying to bite them.

Tonight's event was with Belladonna Nightshade, a novelist who wrote about the Von Rastenbourg vampire family. The characters were ancient, sage, painfully elegant vampires who ran around in lace and velvet. They agonized about the bitterness of immortality and the heartbreak of being so beautiful, all the while slipping into the bedrooms of attractive mortals and vacillating over whether or not to make *them* beautiful, tragic vampires, too. I know, it sounds trite, but she was a really good writer and the fans couldn't get enough of it.

Her latest and second in the series, *The Honor of Lady Von Rastenbourg,* was already number five on the *New York Times* bestseller list and the author's tour hadn't even started yet. Tonight's event was bound to push it to number one. We got hundreds of book-buying fans at every signing. We used to do her events at midnight as a gimmick, but so many fans showed up that they sometimes lasted until 4:00 a.m. Now the book signings begin at sunset. It was still gimmicky and it got us out of there in time for the inevitable afterparty with her adoring entourage. To be honest, it got harder and harder to tell the difference between the fans and her "people." I used to be able simply to check for fangs, but a clear lack of ethics among dental professionals had made that trick useless. Now I had to check for an actual pulse.

In case you haven't guessed by now, Ms. Belladonna Night-shade really is a vampire, though pretends to be a mortal who caters to the growing trend in vampire novels. You know what they say: write what you know. She wasn't my only vampire author, but she was my favorite.

It was four p.m. and in addition to the NCN interview with Jackie Stewart I'd just booked, I wanted to try to get Bill Hoffmann from the *New York Post*'s "Page Six" to come down to the club tonight, too. I put my headset back on and called him.

My assistant instant-messaged me that Jonathan, Belladonna's "manager," right-hand vampire, and my total obsession, was on line two. I told her to have him hold, and quickly left a message for Bill.

I always took Jonathan's calls—pathetic, huh? I'd been back from my intervention/vacation for less than seventy-two hours and already I was dying to hear from him. Okay, so now you see why Lola was trying to talk me out of him. And now you see why it can never work between us. Still, my heart raced when I saw his phone number on my caller ID.

"Hey, Johnny, you're up early."

Contrary to popular belief, vampires can be awake at any time, but they usually sleep during the day since they can't be in the sunlight without experiencing considerable pain. So while I could have Belladonna do her interviews live in the morning, getting her there while avoiding the sunlight was a logistical nightmare. I did have her do live morning radio interviews from her hotel with the curtains drawn, and occasionally I'd go through the logistical sunlight nightmare if the interview was network and couldn't accommodate my request to pretape. That threw off the suspicious few who got the idea she really was a vampire. And now you're beginning to see what a *Twilight Zone* episode my life had become.

I checked my e-mail while Jonathan started complaining about the quality of the sheets in the hotel and the terrible room service. I knew he really didn't give a damn about the sheets, and since when did vampires care about room service? He was pissed off about something and wasn't coming clean with me.

He had a deep, rumbling, baritone that I could listen to all day, and normally I'd be happy listening to him bitch and moan in his sexy, velvety voice. But I didn't have time for it this afternoon. "Listen, Johnny, just shut up and guess what I've got lined up for us tonight?"

"What?" He seemed irritated that I'd interrupted his tirade.

"NCN news! That's right, Johnny-boy, Jackie Stewart—the big time. It's the next best thing to Diane Sawyer—like she'd be caught dead at Sweat, which is where Bella will be doing the interview. Thank you very much."

I got ready for the inevitable praise for my skill as über-publicist.

"First of all, don't get me all excited with thoughts about icing Diane Sawyer, and second, Gia, you're a fucking rock star!"

This is one of the things I loved about him. I had no idea how old he really was, but he spoke like he was from this century, and unlike some of his more dramatic cohorts, he wasn't always so damn serious.

"That's a really good get. Can I do something for you in return?" I heard a smile/leer in his voice, and figured he was getting over whatever bug had crawled up his ass earlier.

"I'm not looking for a master or for everlasting life at the moment, but you'll be the first to know if I change my mind." I twirled my pen and leaned back in my chair again. Regardless of my ridiculous crush, I always loved working with him. And I'd missed him. "For now, I'll settle for you not bitching about the hotel since it's costing Speculation a friggin' fortune. Come on—room service and bad sheets? You can do better that that."

Yeah, I was a flirt, but I was feeling a little more confident after my intervention/vacation, and I truly wasn't interested in giving up daylight. Not that I still wasn't tempted to have Jonathan give me just a little love bite. Imagine every sexy vampire stereotype you can think of, and that's Johnny. I once told him he looked like he had just stepped out of central casting, and he shot back "where do you think Hollywood got that look?" Which was a good point. He had dark hair, pale skin, brooding dark eyes, full lips, broad shoulders, and a lean, slender physique. He usually wore leather pants that clung to his hips just right, with the clichéd silk shirt unbuttoned just a little too much. I'd harped on the absurdity of his wardrobe so much that I think he now wore these outfits just to get a rise out of me. He had a standard Goth choppy haircut, but what most Goths don't realize is that only real vampires could pull off that sort of thing. And did I mention he was funny? He kept me laughing all the time.

Anyhow, that was my Johnny. I was the only one who called him that, because he reminded me of Johnny Depp in a *Pirates of the Caribbean* kind of way. Who knew, he may have been a pirate once. He never talked about his past, and that would certainly explain the goofy silk shirts.

He was completely delicious, and even if it did take all my strength after a few drinks not to present my neck to him, one thing about these Old World types was that he respected me, and I knew I could trust him never to take advantage of me. So for now, he was just my eye candy. My incredibly sexy, cool, bloodless eye candy.

"So what time do you want us downstairs?" he asked me.

"Be in the garage at six. I'll call you from the limo and I'm taking you to the back entrance of Books Inc., so you'll have some time to decompress before the event." I spun around in my chair and checked my elaborate wall calendar. The sun sets at seven oh seven tonight, so it'll be dark by the time we get there."

Being a publicist at Speculation required that, in addition to monitoring the sunsets and full moons, I had to make sure every hotel had an enclosed garage that could be accessed from the hotel without passing a sunny window. But that wasn't a problem—due to paparazzi and obsessed fans, it was a standard request among normal celebrities.

"Hey, Johnny." I couldn't keep the smile out of my voice.
"Yeah?"

"What do you get when you cross a snowman with a vampire?"

He laughed. "Frostbite. You're trying to trip *me* up with fuckin' vampire jokes? I wasn't exactly born yesterday."

"Nobody likes a wiseass." I was sure he could hear me smiling.

"Okay, fellow wiseass, so what do you call a blonde with half a brain?"

"Must we do blonde jokes?" I tried to sound exasperated, but I loved this goofy part of our flirtation.

"Oh, it's fine for you to make fun of my people, but blondes are off-limits?"

"I'm not so sure your crowd are really considered *people*, but I'll cut you some slack." I gave in. "Okay, I'll bite."

"Promise?"

I gave him another dramatically exasperated sigh. "Okay, so what do you call a blonde with half a brain?"

"A golden retriever."

"On that note, I'll see you tonight." I hung up on him and smiled. He always made me smile.

I had to be out of the office by 5:30 and I still needed to check on the bookstore security and call my guy at Sweat, but I had time to check in on Lola.

In addition to being the best friend a girl could ever have (who else would fly me down to Jamaica and talk me down from ruining my life?), Lola was a very talented writer and I really enjoyed working with her. She wrote werewolf novels for Speculation and, yes, she was also a werewolf. We had returned from our vacation just in time for the new moon. Both new moons and full moons had special meanings for werewolves, and I was worried about her. She sometimes had a hard time recovering.

"Hello?" Her voice was raspy and weak.

"Hey, Lola, how're you feeling?"

"Hungover, without the fond fuzzy memories. But I'll be fine in a few hours. What are you up to, Chickpea?"

"Eh, same shit, different day." I was rifling through my

purse, looking for the special red-ink pens I had bought for Bella's event tonight. The fans got off on that kind of thing.

"You've got that Bella signing in Long Island tonight, right? How's that going? Is she demanding AB negative in the limo?"

Lola was so normal, so grounded, so honest. She and I were instant friends since the first book we worked on together six years ago. She really understood the business, and appreciated all that went into going that extra mile.

"No, nothing like that. You know how it is with the vampires—it's not the details, it's the late hours."

She laughed. "Have you talked to Jonathan since you've been back?"

I loved her, but she had the annoying knack of knowing me a little too well.

"Yeah, and I'm fine. Don't worry; I'm not enlisting in the army of the undead anytime soon."

Werewolves had a heightened sense of . . . well, everything. Smell, sight, and sound, which included an acute perception of emotions. Until she asked about Johnny, I hadn't even noticed my pulse was racing; she had probably heard it over the phone.

"Listen, Giovanna my love, you didn't just call to check up on me, you needed me to talk you down again. Don't try to fool me. Despite that whole week on the beach trying to deprogram you, you're still totally into him. He's turning on the ol' bloodsucking charm, and you're already falling for it. Did I miss anything?"

Lola could be a real pain in the ass. "I hate you, Bitch." The nickname was always said with total affection, I assure you.

She laughed at me. Typical. "You're going out with them after your event tonight, aren't you?"

"You know I have to."

"Don't sound like it's such a fucking chore; you know you love it. Tell me where and when, and I'll meet you there and hold your hand."

"I don't need you to hold my hand, and you know you're not the most popular cat with some of that crowd." Traditionally, vampires and other beings (especially werewolves) didn't always get along. Luckily, most werewolves stayed in the wilderness and the vampires tended to gravitate to the cities, for obvious feeding benefits. Most of my immediate vampire friends were cool with Lola, but who knew who else would be at the club tonight?

"Bella isn't threatened by me since I've always been a midlist author, and Jonathan likes me. All her other minions can kiss my hairy werewolf ass."

I gave her the details about the club and she agreed to meet me there.

Speculation Publishing was a great place to work if you a) liked to read a lot, b) could keep a grip on reality once you realized that half of your clients were the real deal, and c) could keep your mouth shut about the fact that half of your clients *were* the real deal.

It was time to get the heck out of there. I grabbed my publicist's bag of tricks: extra pens, Post-its, digital camera, sewing kit, wooden stake, silver bullets—don't be so sure that I'm kidding. Then I went to the ladies' room to freshen up my makeup before heading down to the limo. It had nothing to do with seeing Johnny; I was primping because of the NCN cameras. Even if Johnny was off-limits, I could still look good enough to raise the dead.

2

Did It Hurt?

We arrived at the bookstore shortly after sunset, met the NCN camera crew in the parking lot, then slipped into the stockroom through the back of the store, unnoticed by the fans. There I briefed the crew, including the producer, Diane— I was right, she was totally mousy and I felt sorry for her. I went over which scenes would make for good B-roll and what to look for in a superfan. Then I made sure the bookstore manager and the security detail they'd hired were all on the same page.

Finally, I peeked out from the bookstore stockroom. There they were. The fans never disappointed me. There had to be at least 550 people crammed into the store, and more were coming in droves. Books Inc. was a great independent bookstore located in an affluent area of Long Island that reported its sales to all the bestseller lists—we loved them.

Bella's fans were always a mixture of heavy-metal types, working class, affluent businesspeople, and the Goth kids who decked themselves out in the vampire-chic uniform. I would bet there wasn't a scrap of black leather or velvet left in the tristate area. Red nails, black hair, red lipstick, studded leather, silver, multiple piercings, crystals. Same crowd, different day. Don't get me wrong, I loved each and every one of them. They were the stuff jobs are made of. Particularly mine. (Parents, don't despair. Although your daughter dresses like Morticia, she's really smart and she reads all the time, and that alone could land her a job someday. Hey, it worked for me).

At a few minutes before eight I made sure Belladonna had everything she needed, straightened my suit jacket, and made my way to the podium for a few announcements before introducing the guest of honor.

"Good evening, ladies and gentlemen. Ms. Nightshade will be out momentarily, but before she arrives, I want to go over a few procedures. I know many of you have been to Ms. Nightshade's events before, but please bear with me while I go over just a few things.

"You've all been given a card with a letter on it: A through— I think we're up to T. After Ms. Nightshade's reading, the book signing will take place upstairs. We will be calling you up in groups by letter. So if you have, say, G, feel free to go to the café and grab a bite . . . just as long as it's not a bite out of another paying customer." I'm rewarded with polite chuckles.

I caught Johnny's eye. He was standing in the stacks, smiling at me out of one side of his mouth, showing just a hint of his right fang. He was wearing leather pants again and a deep blue silk shirt, with his incredibly supple leather suit jacket sleeves pushed up to the elbows. Damn it, I hated it when he was this sexy. How was I supposed to do my job when he was looking at me like that?

"And speaking of biting," I continued, "there will be no biting or bloodletting of any kind tonight. Ms. Nightshade signs books with her own pen and with her own ink. No one's blood will be substituted for ink." I looked around the room for the Renaissance fair types and saw just a handful. "I only see a few costumes out there, but please remember that all weapons must remain sheathed at all times or they will be confiscated.

"Ms. Nightshade will personalize all of your books and add her own special message to them before signing them. Please don't request anything other than a name to be inscribed— she's not here to write another novel, and she wants to get a chance to meet all of you."

I glanced over to where Johnny had been standing and of course he was nowhere to be seen. F-ing unreliable vampires. By the way, that thing you heard about vampires being seen only when they want to be seen, and being able to fade into the shadows? Well, that's totally true, and it's very annoying. At times, Belladonna had to make a conscious effort to move in a mortal fashion.

I started my introduction. "Ms. Belladonna Nightshade is a *New York Times* bestselling author. The *Horror Revue* has called her 'a combination of Shelley, Stoker, and Rice with a dash of Jackie Collins.' Her first book is sold in over one hundred countries, and her latest and most eagerly awaited, *The Honor of Lady Von Rastenbourg*, is already selling out in stores everywhere. Ladies and gentlemen, I give you the brilliant and enchanting Ms. Belladonna Nightshade."

Thunderous applause and screaming. One girl in the front row howled. A group in the rear was actually chanting "Bella, Bella."

Then Belladonna Nightshade herself emerged in a black silk, long-sleeved evening gown. Her upswept shiny black hair, along with the dress's portrait collar, accentuated her long neck. With a theatrical flair, she opened up a leather-bound book that looked a heck of a lot like the *Necronomicon* and began to read from *The Honor* in a strong and haunting voice, occasionally looking up to make eye contact with the audience. She was wonderful. She instantly had them in the palm of her well-manicured hand. She really made my job easy. She was the show; I just had to make sure the media was there to get it all.

I stepped back toward the stockroom door, and Johnny asked, "So, are you going to tell me where you've you been?"

"Jeez, Johnny, I've been up at the podium—where have you been?" Look at me, sarcastic and flip with a creature of the night. Lola was wrong. I didn't need any hand-holding; I had this situation totally under control. I was über-publicist and über-flirt tonight.

"I meant last week. I called you at the office and your assistant said you were on vacation. You didn't tell me you were going away." His voice was tense.

"Oh, and you're the only one who's allowed to be mysterious?" I leaned back to nudge him with my elbow, but he avoided the contact. Vampires were only touched when they wanted to be. Now I knew what had been eating at him before. But what could I say? *I needed some distance from you so I could stop fantasizing about you day and night*? I don't think so.

"I needed some downtime before this tour. Our mutual boss's schedule can be demanding and I knew I wouldn't have the chance to get away for a while. So Lola suggested a week in Jamaica before the new moon." It was half the truth, but I'm sure he realized that our recent close encounter a few weeks ago had added to my stress.

Still standing behind me, he leaned his head over my shoulder. "You're tan." My answer must have satisfied him, because he didn't seem angry anymore.

"Do you like that?"

His lips were an inch from my ear. "It's turning me on."

I felt his breath on my neck. My breath started to come faster and I knew he was listening to my heartbeat. This time when I leaned back, my arm made contact with his stomach. His flesh was as hard as marble and just as cool to the touch, even through the fabric of his shirt. What was I doing? Weren't we supposed to be behaving ourselves?

He leaned even closer. "I'd like to see your tan lines later."

I smiled. I shivered. I could do this. It was just a harmless little game, right? And I knew just how to get him back. "It was a clothing-optional beach. You won't find a tan line on me, baby."

He groaned. Well, growled, really. It started in the back of his throat and continued down until I felt it roll through his stomach. Now I wasn't so sure either of us knew this was just a game.

I covered up with a laugh and a teasing poke in his side. "Don't they feed you as part of your contract?"

"Yes, but oddly enough, I'm hungry again. Now, why do you think that is?" He hiked up the sleeve of my suit jacket and held his arm against mine. Mine, tan and sun-warmed. His, cold and pale. I know it's impossible, but I could swear that the hair on his arm was actually caressing my skin of its own accord. He began to look up and I turned away quickly to avoid his eyes. That thing about a vampire hypnotizing you? That's also true. Normally I could handle it, but I knew my resistance was low tonight.

"Bella's almost finished. I've gotta go."

He hooked two fingers in the crook of my elbow to stop me from walking away. It was a subtle but impossibly strong gesture. "Just one more thing. I need you to answer a question for me."

"Okay. *Whatever the hell you want. Take me here behind the stacks.* But no, I was being professional.

"Did it hurt?" His breath moved the hair just behind my ear and it was making me weak.

"Did what hurt?" I whispered back.

He inhaled deeply and for a moment I was afraid he was going to say something corny about my hair smelling like sunshine, and a Caribbean breeze which of course I took painstaking efforts to ensure that it did. But no, he said, "Did it hurt when you cut yourself shaving this morning?"

My heart began to pound and I felt the small nick on my right ankle begin to pulse.

Applause. Bella was finished with her reading. I quickly stepped away toward the podium, and felt the stickiness of blood smear the back of my boot. He must have smelled it, damn it.

Now for the exciting part of my job. Hold open the book to the title page, read from the Post-it note, and say to my author, "This is Jessica and she has two books to be signed tonight."

Then Bella starts in. "Jessica, what a beautiful ring you're wearing. Is that handcrafted?"

"Yes, I got it at last year's Renaissance festival."

"It's so becoming." She was a dream author.

A perky blonde bookstore employee in sensible shoes asked if she could trade places with me, sounding like she really wanted to help. I gestured toward a fan who had to weigh three hundred pounds and resembled Meat Loaf in the *Rocky Horror Picture Show.* "Okay, I said, "what will you do if that guy tries to bite her?"

"That really happens?" At my nod she chewed on her lip, then stood up straighter and said with more confidence than

I'm sure she felt, "I'll be fine, security is only ten feet away."
It was the right answer.

I made sure Bella had everything she needed and let the
perky girl take over. As Bella's manager, Johnny was supposed
to be there, but he hated talking to the fans. Since I didn't see
him in the immediate vicinity, I thought I'd sneak away and
make a phone call.

Hanging around with vampires and werewolves for a living gave me some insight as to how to slink along unnoticed,
and I escaped from the crowd. To my supernatural friends my
attempts seemed clumsy, and Johnny found them downright
comical. But I found I had improved my vanishing act consid-
erably among the mortal crowd.

I slipped out into the September evening. It was beginning
to smell like fall already. I used to love everything about the
long days of summer, but lately I found I had been looking
forward to the longer nights . . . Okay, it was clearly time for
that phone call.

"Lo, it's me."

"Hey, there; don't tell me the signing is over already? I'm
still shopping in Soho." I could hear the sound of Lola sorting
through a rack of hangers.

"Far from it, it's just getting started. What are you buy-
ing?"

"Jeans. I'm at Jeffrey's."

"They're expensive. You must have gotten a pretty big advance on your book."

"Yeah, they told me they'd just cut your salary to cover it."

"This was just what I needed. A perfectly normal conversation that didn't involve my bleeding ankle. This might distract
me for about ten seconds. "So do you think you can meet me
here instead of the club?"

"Giovanna Maria Louisa Felice. I'm not trekking all the way out to the Island only to come back to Manhattan to go to Sweat with you and your loser vampire friends. What has Jonathan done already that's got you so worked up that you require supervision? Honestly, I can't leave you alone for a second with him."

Even over a cell phone, she could tell from my breathing pattern if I lied. So I told her about our conversation, about my tan, my shaving nick, our arms touching.

"Lo, I'm losing it. I'm more into him than ever. I should know better—I should be able to see through him."

"Oh, don't be so hard on yourself. He's a professional predator. His job is to hunt and seduce his prey. You're just being human. Hell, I'm not human and *I* find him sexy as hell."

She was right, of course—seduction was what vampires did best. I smiled, feeling a little less panicked, but still pretty damn defenseless. I was glad she'd have my back tonight.

"Listen, you be strong and remember what we talked about last week. I've got half my ass in these jeans and need both hands now. I'll be waiting for you at Sweat, I gotta jet." She hung up.

Jonathan was standing at the door to the bookstore when I turned around. It was useless worrying about how much of my conversation he'd heard, since vampires have that incredible hearing.

He called out, "You'd better come in, the NCN chick has some questions."

I put my phone in my purse, but made no move to walk past him.

He came closer and blocked my way. "Sorry. I guess I made you a little uncomfortable in there." His hands were in his pockets as if he was trying to physically restrain himself. "It's just been a while since I've seen you, and you look even better than I remembered, and you smell . . ." He breathed in deeply. "Well, you smell a hell of a lot better than I remember. Must be that perfume you're wearing on your right ankle." He gave me a sheepish smile.

His words threw me for a loop. Apologies were rarely the order of the day with him, and second, what did a girl say when a guy complimented her on her bleeding ankle? I came back with, "Don't sweat it. You know what they say: no blood, no foul."

He gave me that wicked, heart-stopping smile. "That was a good one."

"Thanks, I've been saving it for a while."

He gave me sly wink.

"Why, Jonathan, if I didn't know any better, I'd think you were coming on to me. We're supposed to be pretending we're not attracted to each other, remember?" I batted my eyelashes, then pushed past him.

Inside, I found the producer and pointed out a few extreme fans to the camera crew. Fans with fangs made for good TV.

It was after midnight when the last fan left the store. Ka-ching! There were close to 750 fans by the end of the night, and many had bought multiple copies of *The Honor*. Belladonna, gracious as always, invited Diane the producer to ride with us in our limo to the club, while the camera crew would follow behind in the van with the equipment. It would probably be the highlight of her life.

We all headed to the limo—me, the producer, Bella, and her hair and makeup person, a tall West Indian vampire named Antonia who was really Bella's best friend. Jonathan was already there when I entered. He patted the seat next to him and melted into the shadows so that only Bella, Antonia, and I knew he was there. I tried to carry on a coherent conversation with the producer while Johnny pressed his thigh against mine and slowly tortured me all the way back to Manhattan.

Sweat was what all New York City clubs wanted to be. Dark, hard to find, exclusive, packed with celebrities who said they didn't want to be seen, and peppered with gossip columnists. It was strictly A list. In fact, I'm not sure Bella's entire entourage would even be allowed in if it weren't a Wednesday.

Jackie Stewart was waiting for Bella at the bar. The crew ran ahead and set up a lighting package for the interview in the VIP room while Antonia touched up Bella's makeup. Antonia was worth every penny—it wasn't easy to keep Bella from looking translucent under the lights.

All this fuss and the actual interview took less than fifteen minutes, start to finish. Jackie excused herself, pleading her need for "beauty sleep," and the mousy producer lasted only another half hour. Bill Hoffmann and a "Page Six" photographer had come and gone so fast, I almost missed them. They vanished when Bill realized that Bella was the biggest celebrity at Sweat on a Wednesday night. But I did manage to corner him and make sure he got the title of the book right for the item.

It was close to three a.m. when Bella reached over and grabbed my hand. "Get a drink dear, you deserve it."

She smiled—thank God she was happy with the night. Even after such a successful night like this, I still worried about screwing something up. I guess that's what made me good at my job.

"This has been a great night. You're off the clock."

She had always liked my work, and had even joked about changing me so I could be her publicist forever. I laughed it off.

We had discussed her future several times and agreed that

her career as a novelist would have to end after about ten years. Basically, as soon as it became apparent that she wasn't aging. She wanted to fade away, but I suggested a dramatic fake death to boost the sale of her backlist titles. I wasn't necessarily kidding, either—I know it would be what the publisher would want.

I smiled gratefully, ditched my suit jacket and stashed it with my bag under Bella's table, then headed downstairs to the regular bar. I was never a big fan of the VIP rooms; I found them boring and I preferred the dance floor. I spotted Lola dancing with two hot guys who looked pretty human. She liked humans, and she liked hot humans in pairs even more. I don't know if it was because she was a werewolf or if was just her way, but Lola had an incredibly active sex drive.

At the bar I ordered a Rain vodka martini straight up. Johnny had mentioned before that he didn't much care for the smell of vermouth on me, and I thought it might slow him down.

As I reached for my drink, the guy next to me sniffed the inside of my elbow. Weird, yes, but hey, this was New York. He wasn't a vampire—way too warm. After working at Speculation for ten years, I was pretty good at picking out the undead in a crowded club. Probably a wannabe—they came to this club a lot. I quickly drank my martini.

Joining Lola on the dance floor, I squeezed her hand and shouted over the music, "Thanks for coming."

"Wouldn't miss it. How was the signing?"

I gave her a thumbs-up and started dancing with one of her guys.

"Where's lover boy?" she asked.

"I haven't seen him since the limo. God, Lola, I've gotta do something about him, he's driving me crazy."

The elbow-sniffer at the bar began making a beeline for Lola. I excused myself to the two humans and went to get another martini. Hey, I work hard, I play hard. And tonight I was in the mood to play very hard. Let's call it stress.

I looked over my glass and looked right into Johnny's eyes. Damn it—the one the thing I was trying to avoid all night. I hated it when he snuck up on me like that.

"You've been avoiding me." He stroked one of my fingers holding the glass. "I've been forced to hang out with Bella's hangers-on and the posers."

"I haven't been avoiding you, I've been working." I removed his hand from mine and fished an olive out of my glass so that both hands would be busy. "Bella just had a very important interview. She needed me."

"So do I." He took my hand. "Dance with me?"

"Johnny, we're . . ."

"I know, we're not interested in each other that way, we're just friends, now finish your damn drink and dance with me."

I downed my drink and let him lead me to the dance floor. He was a good dancer. I guess if I knew I was going to live forever, I'd take the time to learn how to dance well, too.

I looked around the room. Sweat was a "friendly" club—which meant that all beings were welcome, so long as they behaved themselves and made the appearance of getting along. Tonight, several vampires I knew were getting lucky. The dance floor was a regular banquet.

Vampires don't have to kill their victims. They could snack on just about anyone, and the prey was rarely aware of it—unless, of course, that was the vampire's intention. Vampire bites heal remarkably fast and the side effects usually just resemble a hangover. The real challenge on the vampire's part was finding the strength to stop after just a taste.

So how did I know Jonathan had never taken advantage of me? I just did. He was the type to get off on full consent.

I knew I looked good. The Jamaican sun had streaked my

dark blonde hair and I kept it twisted up with a clip—to be honest with myself, I was showing off my neck on purpose. I had on a black pencil skirt and high heeled black leather boots that added a good four inches to my five feet three inches height, and my white tank top made my tan stand out even more. I guess I never thought about it, but a tan really could be considered a turn-on with this crowd—I was downright exotic. I wondered if vampires ever used tanning beds? Probably not.

On the dance floor he teased me, seeming inadvertently to touch me briefly on my arms and the small of my back, although I knew he never moved *accidentally*, and he knew exactly what his touch did to me. How could someone with such cold skin burn me? Tonight he couldn't seem to stop brushing up against me while dancing, and I couldn't stop letting him. I wasn't sure if it was the martinis or his touch, but something was making me very dizzy.

I looked over and saw a mutual vampire friend and resident bad boy, Billy, about three couples over. If Lola thought Jonathan was poison, then Billy was downright corrosive. I'd called him Billy when I met him because his platinum blond punk haircut reminded me of Billy Idol, and he liked the nickname so much, he never told me his real name. He was looking at me over the shoulder of a redhead. He had one hand up her skirt while he was sucking her neck hard. That's how a lot of them did it—they confused their victim with sex and the poor thing didn't even realize it was being fanged. Some actually reached orgasm when the vampire removed his/her fangs. And yes, they would do it on a crowded dance floor. Especially Billy, who was shameless.

Billy winked at me and motioned with his eyebrows that I should allow Jonathan to do the same. I gave him the finger and stuck my tongue out at him. Like Jonathan, he was funny and not so damn serious and brooding and dramatic, like so many of the vampires I knew. However, Billy didn't play around when it came to food. He was very committed to the lifestyle and very hungry all the time.

Out of nowhere, Jonathan grabbed my hip and pulled me back toward him, settling his thumb in the depression in the front. "Flirting with that one is a dangerous game."

He was giving me that half smile again, the one that showed his right fang. Very sexy. I swallowed hard. His hand was caressing my hip, and the other was now on my waist. Even through my clothes, I felt it in other places that were pretty dangerous.

"If I can handle you, I can handle him." I tilted my head with a defiant grin. I wasn't sure I was actually handling Johnny right now, but we both knew I had no intention of going down that road with Billy. He was a good guy to have as a friend, but legendary as a temperamental and sometimes cruel master.

Jonathan grinned, clearly enjoying himself. "You know, all my friends say you're a tease."

I gave him the finger, too. "All your friends suck."

He grabbed at my hand so fast, I didn't see it coming. Taking my middle finger, he put it gently between his front teeth. Mouth contact. This was major.

You know how Julia Roberts wouldn't let Richard Gere kiss her on the lips in *Pretty Woman* because the contact was too intimate? Well, it's kind of like that with vampires. Mouth contact with *any* part of another person's body, even without biting, could be a very special gift. It was a step you couldn't take back. Like virginity.

I don't think he even realized what he was doing, let alone what he was doing to me when his tongue brushed against my finger. But he got the picture when he saw the pure shock on my face. More than any mortal, I knew exactly what the significance of that action was.

I stopped dancing, pulled my hand away, and turned my head so he wouldn't see my eyes. I had no idea how to feel. Though I should be horrified, I felt supercharged, almost ecstatic from the contact. Could he hear my heartbeat over the music?

"Hey, there's Lola, I want to get the scoop on that guy she's dancing with. Be right back." I slipped away toward Lola, who was getting pretty lucky on the dance floor with the elbow sniffer, and pulled her into the ladies' room.

"Hey chickpea, thanks for the break." She checked under the stalls for feet, then splashed some cool water on her throat, and began cleaning up her swollen lipstick-smeared lips.

"Looks like I interrupted something good." Her dark eyes were glassy and she was panting. "He's a werewolf too, right?"

"You're getting way too good at your job. How'd you guess?"

"He sniffed my elbow at the bar."

"A dead giveaway."

While she continued to fix her face, I stared at my finger. I wanted to sneak it into my mouth to see what his saliva tasted like—it wasn't like it was his blood or anything. It was surprisingly warm, and replaying the scene in my mind made me throb deep inside.

"So how's it going with hot stuff? You two looked pretty cozy on the dance floor. And I see our Billy found a new friend."

As if on cue, the redhead came into the bathroom looking dazed. Her neck wound had already healed and now barely resembled a hickey. She was stumbling around and bounced off the wall and into the nearest stall to pee. We heard her ricocheting around in there and we both stifled giggles.

Lola whispered, "Damn, I knew he was good, but I didn't know he was that good. Maybe he's worth a try?"

"She came on the dance floor," I mouthed back. You didn't have to whisper with werewolves.

"Shut up!"

"Yeah-huh."

Lola raised her eyebrows approvingly. "Well, that doesn't suck."

The redhead staggered up to the sink and tried to repair her makeup, but her motor skills were seriously impaired. She pulled on the skin around her neck, examined the pinkness, shrugged, and left.

The second the door closed, I said, "I have news. Something's happened. I got mouthed," I blurted.

Was that even a real word? I was a freakin' English major, for crying out loud, and that was the best I could come up with?

"Johnny had my finger"—I held it up—"in his very sexy mouth for about thirty seconds." It still felt so good; I couldn't stop grinning.

"*What?* Gia, snap out of it." She grabbed my chin and looked into my eyes to make sure I was lucid. "How stupid *are* you? How did it happen? Did you make eye contact? Did he trick you into it?"

"No, no, nothing like that." My euphoria began to fade. She was such a killjoy. I explained the situation and she calmed down a bit, but still frowned.

"You can't go back you know. Your cherry's been popped."

"I know. But you're overreacting. It was a total accident, not a vampire-seduction kind of thing. I'm really kinda disappointed, to be honest. It's like losing your virginity in the back seat of a car, after you've imagined a fancy hotel room with rose petals on silk sheets. But regardless, it happened. So now what do I do?"

"It'll be okay. It's not like it was Billy." She put her arm around me and squeezed. "Listen—you're feeling good right now, but think about it. The next time he might accidentally do more than suck your finger. Go home and sleep it off, okay? He's just turned on by your shaving nick, and you're just being human."

"But maybe I don't want to sleep it off."

"Chill, sister. You've been drinking and you're falling for his tricks."

"You know Johnny better than that. He's not trying to trick me. We both liked it. Maybe we can make this work . . ."

"Okay, okay, stop. Listen, I'm not going to try to talk you out of this here. This is something you have to think about when you're sober. You're pretty vulnerable right now, and you really, really should go home. Johnny can't help what he is, but you have the sense to leave, so leave."

She stepped back to check herself out in the mirror one more time, pushed her cleavage together, and tossed her dark brown hair over her shoulder. Lola's temper always dissipated as quickly as it flared. "Now get the hell out of here and leave me to my werewolf dance partner."

"Bitch," I said, sniffing. But she was right. What could she do now? The horse was out of the barn.

I left Lola to her elbow-sniffer and made my way to the bar for a Red Bull to clear my head. Jonathan wasn't on the dance floor, but Billy and his redhead were back at it again. Since I had to work tomorrow, I downed my drink fast and made my way up to the VIP room to get my things and say good-bye to Bella.

She was still in the VIP room, sitting with Antonia and a few tragically hip vampire men—the little blond one with the big, sad, blue eyes who never spoke; the tall, sexy, black one with the shaved head and amazing tattoo; and the hot British one who reminded me of Sting. Bella certainly had good taste in friends. I admit, that was a bad choice of words.

"Gia, dear, are you okay?"

"Yeah, I just came to get my things. I'm heading out of here. Do you need anything else?"

"No, I'm fine." Bella gave Antonia a look, and she and the small crowd moved to another area. We all knew they could still hear every word of our conversation, but they moved as a courtesy.

When we were alone, Bella reached out and took my hand. "Are you sure you don't want to sit down for a moment? You don't look too good."

I knew she meant well, but I wasn't in the mood for another dead-on assessment. Sometimes a girl likes to keep her secrets.

"Do you want to ask me anything?"

What could that mean? "I'm fine—really. I've just been up for about twenty hours straight and I didn't have any dinner. And I have an early day tomorrow."

"Are you positive that's all there is to it? Your breathing is very labored. Oh—hello, Jonathan."

She looked past my shoulder, where he had come up behind me. I hadn't known he was there, but apparently my lungs did.

"Giovanna is leaving. Will you make sure she gets home safely?"

Jonathan gave Bella a curt little bow. "My pleasure."

He always treated Bella with deference. They were both very quiet about the nature of their relationship, as they were about their personal histories and their ages. Sometimes Jonathan seemed very old to me, even older than Bella. Yet she was the diva and he the manager. After working with them both for almost two years, I still didn't have a clue about what their deal was.

I air-kissed Bella, reminded her about her radio interview at 8:20 a.m., and then Jonathan and I made our way out of the club.

"You okay?" His hand was on my elbow as he guided me out the door and past the velvet rope.

"Yeah, I'll be fine. We're not doing a very good job of pretending we're not totally into each other, huh?"

"Yeah. I'm really sorry about that." We stood by the wall under the club's awning, a lot like the time when he first touched me a few weeks ago. The tension was unbearable, and I know he wanted to touch me again. I wanted that, too.

He lit up a cigarette and drew in a heavy drag. "I didn't want it to be that way."

Huh? My mind snapped to attention. "Wait a minute. *What* way?" My voice went up an octave and I started to sweat. "You mean you were planning this? You *wanted* that whole mouth thing to happen? I thought it was an accident!" I began to get panicky. "Jonathan, I—"

"No, it's not like that! Jeez, this isn't going well at all." He tossed his cigarette into the street and ran his hands through his hair, looking frustrated. "I didn't plan it. I didn't want it to happen. But I can't lie and tell you I've stopped thinking about you that way. It's just that you look really good tonight." He brought one hand up to stroke my cheek. "And your skin is so warm." It was; he was making me flush.

We both leaned back against the wall, exhausted by this damned frustrating attraction.

He wearily put one arm around me and kissed my head. "Your hair smells nice, too."

"Please don't say it smells like sunshine."

He laughed that deep, beautiful resonant laugh that I loved

and I felt it move inside my chest. "And just how the fuck would I know what sunshine smells like?" He had a point. "It just smells nice and not so much like vermouth." I was wondering how long it was going to take him to complain about that. With an obvious effort, he pulled away. "You'd better go. Take the limo home and send it back for us."

"I'd rather take a cab."

He stepped out to the curb and held out his hand, and a cab pulled up within seconds. As he helped me into the cab, he said, "I'll call you tomorrow. Maybe we'll have a drink before the book signing."

Without giving me a chance to respond, he closed the door. He gave the driver my address, a twenty-dollar bill, and some specific instructions while looking directly into his eyes. The driver pulled away and I sank into the seat.

3

Should We Toast Something Stupid, Like Sunsets?

I woke up to the alarm at seven, still in my clothes, sprawled on top of my bedspread. I peeled off my rumpled mess of a suit and stepped into the shower, feeling icky all over. I had gotten only two hours' sleep, hadn't eaten since lunch the day before, was a little hungover, and was very confused. And why the hell was my ankle stinging like that? I looked down and saw it was covered in dried blood. Did I cut myself that badly yesterday? No wonder I was turning him on so much last night.

I had to get him out of my mind and get my act together.

I went to work, but my head was still on last night. I basically moved things from one side of my desk to the other until lunchtime, then headed to the gym for a run on the treadmill.

I listened to loud, angry music. I sweated, I showered, but I didn't feel any better.

As I left the gym, my cell phone rang. It was Lola. "Hey Bi-ach, how'd your date go last night?" I asked.

"Oh, is it supposed to be over? He's in the shower."

"Slut."

"No, just in heat. Amazingly, this guy is from up by my country house. He actually followed my scent all the way down to the club. And they call it puppy love . . ."

Lola had a country house in upstate New York where she could run free when she changed. It was a very private place she had inherited from her grandmother, way up in the Catskill Mountains. But she was more of a city girl and stayed mostly in her Upper West Side apartment.

"Sounds like you had some night," I said.

"Yeah, baby! I don't know why I never did this before. Humans blow. From now on, it's werewolves-only for this girl."

I laughed. She sounded great.

"How about you? Did you get home alright last night?"

"Yeah, my prince of darkness was a real prince and made sure I got home safely." I left it at that. "Listen, I know your man can hear every word we're saying, so I'll let you go. I have another book signing with Bella at Union Square tonight, so if you two feel like coming out with us afterwards, I can see if I approve."

"He already approves of you. Said you smell like good people."

Well, that was nice to know.

The day dragged by. I checked the RSVP message line for last-minute responses to Bella's publication party tomorrow night, played a few games of Spider solitaire, and generally goofed off. I had tons of work I should have been doing, but I just couldn't focus.

Then a familiar instant message name popped up on my screen.

BiteMe: "How's my favorite human today?"

Johnny was checking in—always the gentleman. I answered back immediately.

PitchAndMoan: "Loose and full of juice."

BiteMe: "Bragging?"

We did this a lot. We could have these stupid IM sessions for days.

PitchAndMoan: "Ha ha. Are you sure you couldn't get Prick as a screen name?"

BiteMe: "And are you sure you couldn't get "WiseAss" for yourself?"

PitchAndMoan: "You're up early, Johnny-boy. Did thoughts of me keep you up all night?"

BiteMe: "Kind of. We got sort of carried away there, didn't we?"

PitchAndMoan: "Do you hear me complaining?"

BiteMe: "f-ing tease."

PitchAndMoan: "☺"

BiteMe: "Why do vampires make good interior designers?"

PitchAndMoan: "I give up."

BiteMe: "They specialize in 'fang' shui."

PitchAndMoan: "Yawn. That was awful—where did you hear that one?"

BiteMe: "It's worse than you think: I made it up myself."

He was holding up his part of the deal, pretending, which made me feel a little better.

PitchAndMoan: "So really, what are you doing up already? You should be getting your beauty sleep; we've got work to-night."

BiteMe: "I can't sleep. I even tried the bathtub."

No vampires that I knew slept in coffins. But both Bella and Johnny had told me that when they were in a hotel where they felt uncomfortable with the door lock, they locked themselves in the bathroom and slept in the tub. Vampires were most vulnerable when they slept. Bella had recently gotten herself a big bear of a mutt named Blitz; she slept better with him standing guard.

PitchAndMoan: "You should try to get some rest. Maybe you can borrow Blitz. Do you need a wake-up call?"

BiteMe: "No, I'll be okay."

PitchAndMoan: "Well, I've got work to do before the event tonight, so I'll catch you later." I doubted I'd really get much work done, but he needed some sleep.

BiteMe: "I'll call you."

I couldn't resist one more, though.

PitchAndMoan: "BTW, why did the blonde nurse take a red pen to the hospital?"

BiteMe: "I think I know where this is going."

PitchAndMoan: "In case she had to draw blood."

BiteMe: "I love the way you combined both of our interests."

PitchAndMoan: "Gotta go publicize. Ciao."

I got back to work. Well, I got back to moving things around my desk and playing Spider solitaire.

I kept replaying last night in my head, and I wasn't sure which way to go with it. This morning I wasn't able to decide between professional and conservative versus sexy and provocative, so I was wearing a pinstriped pantsuit with a very low-cut top and f-me shoes.

The phone rang at about 5:30 as I was shutting down my computer to head home and stare into my closet for a better outfit.

"Publicity; this is Giovanna."

"It's me. I meant to call you earlier but I finally drifted off, then I overslept." Johnny's voice was even deeper when he was half asleep, more velvety. "So can you meet me for a drink before we pick up Bella?"

I spun my chair around and looked out the window. Still bright daylight. "What did you have in mind, the hotel bar?"

"Actually, I was thinking about my room."

Gulp. "Do you think that's wise? I mean, after last night . . . Can we be trusted on our own?"

Did I just hear him wince on the phone? "I deserved that. Yeah, it did kind of get out of hand and I should've known better. I'll make it up to you. Please, I'd like to see you."

That was what I wanted, too. Could he hypnotize me over the phone? "Don't be so hard on yourself. I should have known better, too, after working here for ten years. I'm sure we can both be adults about this."

"Great. I'll even mix your martini myself—vermouth and all."

"Sounds like an offer I can't refuse." I had my purse in hand and was halfway out the door.

I walked the five blocks from my office to the hotel as fast as my high-heeled pumps could carry me.

I knocked at his door and heard him say, "Come in."

I opened the door and was nearly blinded by the light. His suite faced southwest and he'd thrown all the curtains open to a spectacular view of the early-evening sun.

"Nice view, huh?" Johnny sat at the far edge of the sofa in the corner, his knees pulled to one side to keep his body completely in the shade. "I've always loved sunset. Even before . . ." He trailed off. "Go take a look. The view's even better when you're closer."

I walked over to the window. He was right, the view was really something, but I didn't have any idea what he was up to.

"You look so beautiful in the sunlight."

I smiled. What woman didn't want to be told she was beautiful? He, on the other hand, looked pitiful all huddled in the shady corner of the room. I raised my eyebrows at him questioningly.

"I wanted to see you standing in the sun. I thought if I could keep this image in my mind, maybe it'd be easier for me to keep my hands off you."

Please don't was on the tip of my tongue, but I kept quiet. He seemed to be in an odd mood and I didn't know where he was going with this.

"I ordered us some champagne." He smiled guiltily. "I didn't get a lot of sleep, and I don't think I could have handled the vermouth—I don't know why it turns my stomach like that." He gave me his half smile because he knew how it affected me.

I went to the table and poured us two glasses. Vampires can eat and drink, though they don't get a lot of enjoyment out of it. They just do it sometimes for social reasons.

"Maybe you still remember your martini hangovers from your human days," I teased.

"I don't think so. Martinis weren't exactly the height of fashion back in the Stone Age." He winked at me.

I walked over to the couch and sat next to him—me in the sunlight, Johnny in the darkness—and handed him a glass. "Should we toast something stupid, like sunsets?"

"Nah." He examined the bubbles in his glass. "Let's just toast the opportunity to work together again."

Keeping it work related was a good idea—we did have an event in a few hours, and that *might* keep me from thinking about ripping off his clothes. On the other hand . . . Oh, what the hell. I dove in.

"Johnny, about last night. We obviously both want some-

thing more. The question is, how? You know I'm not interested in changing, and you've said several times that you would
never change me. Is there another way? I mean, can we . . ."

"Gia, I don't want you to get the wrong idea about the way
I feel about you. It's not that I wouldn't love to change you—I
think about having you that way constantly, but I could never
put you through all that. Have any of your clients ever told you
what it's like?"

I shook my head. "It's not just leaving your family and
friends behind forever, and getting used to a new diet—though
those are hard enough. But there's also a weird isolation from
the human race. Most of our social contact is limited to our own
kind, and you're a publicist; being unable to socialize would be
torture for you. But worst of all . . . you know, sometimes it
doesn't work out." He looked away. "Even if you didn't tire
of me in ten years, you could in fifty or a hundred. I mean, it
is forever. You could become resentful—or worse, you could
come to hate me. And I couldn't bear that."

Even though I could never imagine ever tiring of him, it
was an excellent point.

I looked at him. He was waiting for me to respond.

"I couldn't ever hate you, Johnny. No matter what." I was
already way too deep in love with him. "And no one is changing anyone here. Can't we find another way? Can't we at least
date the human way, and . . . ?"

He knew exactly what I was asking, and gave me a rueful
smile. "We aren't big on human sex. Vampire sex is different.
When we get aroused, we get *too* excited. We lose control. We
get aggressive."

That sent a chill down my spine. I knew exactly what he
meant by *aggressive*, and it scared the hell out of me. Vampires
are strong. Much, much stronger and faster than humans. If he
ever lost control, he could easily kill me just with his strength.

But let's not forget about those teeth. Even if he could restrain himself from accidentally crushing every bone in my body with his bare hands, could he resist taking my last drop of blood in the heat of the moment? If he ever drank from me and was very excited, could he stop? In the ten years since I started in this business, I had seen the accidental death of many a human. Sometimes vampires just got carried away.

He was right. There was no other way. We could go on casually flirting and teasing, but there was no next level. He would always have to stop before it got to that point.

We sat there watching the sunset together. Somewhere along the line, we joined hands. His was cool and hard, mine was warm and soft. The difference felt overwhelmingly sad, and I started tearing up. Why did we torture ourselves like this? This could never work. It was either change and be with him, or remain human and try to live without him. We were hopeless. He couldn't even reach over to hold me now—I was in the light, where he couldn't touch me.

I stood up and walked out of the room, tears running down my face, knowing he couldn't come after me. I didn't know what to do next, or where I was going. I just wanted to be somewhere no one would see me crying.

As I headed toward the elevator, a door opened—Bella's. She took my hand and led me inside, then closed the door.

Her blackout curtains were drawn shut and the lamps created soft light. She put her arms around me and hugged me, stroking my hair comfortingly.

By now I was sobbing inconsolably, shaking uncontrollably. I knew Jonathan could hear me through the walls, but the more I tried to stop, the harder I cried, wet and sloppy and hiccupping like a five-year-old. I didn't cry often, and I wasn't very good at it.

Eventually my wracking sobs subsided and Bella led me

to the sofa. As she pulled the chair around so she could face me, Blitz insinuated his head under my hand. I scratched him behind his ears, feeling my breathing even out. That thing about vampires being able to control certain animals is true. Bella told him, "Sit with Gia," and he rested his heavy head in my lap.

Bella produced a hot cup of tea from somewhere. "Here. Hot tea loosens the throat."

Those were my words. I've said them to countless authors, including Bella, before their appearances. I sipped the tea while stroking Blitz's head, which soothed me.

"Talk to me," Bella invited.

I wanted to, though I was somewhat embarrassed. She'd clearly heard everything Jonathan and I had said to each other in the room next door, otherwise she wouldn't have known to collect me from the hallway.

When I looked at her calmly sitting across from me, I wanted to tell her that I was tired of this hopeless attraction I had for Jonathan. I wanted to tell her that I was sick of thinking about him all the time when I knew a relationship with him could go nowhere. I wanted to tell her that I needed to live a normal life, get married, have children, grow old, vacation in the sun, not eat people . . . Instead, I sobbed, "I love him. I love him more than I thought possible."

She nodded sympathetically. "I know you do. I know he cares for you, too." She folded her hands in her lap. "I also know he respects you. I can tell that he's been behaving himself. He's discreet with you and I never smell him on you. Has he ever even kissed you?"

"Not on the lips. But it's getting harder." I looked down at my teacup. "We've been having more and more accidents."

"We rarely have those." She said this with a disapproving glance at the wall adjoining Jonathan's room.

"I know, but sometimes we just get carried away. We think we can stop, and so far, we've been able to. But it's getting harder. The pull is getting stronger."

"He *is* lovable, isn't he?"

At first I thought it was just my fascination with the supernatural that attracted me to him. But after ten years of doing everything from organizing travel arrangements for a coven of witches to establishing a livestock connection in every city for my authors who require live meals, I get over novelty pretty fast.

"Now we can't even be in the same room without some kind of physical contact. If he were human, I'd just have sex with him to get him out of my system and get on with my life."

Bella raised an eyebrow, looking just like Jonathan when he did that. She was almost as tall as him, and had many of his other features, too.

"Bella, I've never asked, and you don't have to tell me, but how do you know Johnny?" She looked down at her lap and refolded her hands. "I'm sorry, . . ."

"No, it's okay. I look a little like him, and naturally you have questions. Besides, I've been wanting to ask a favor of you that would require your knowing a little more about my background, and this seems like as good a time as any." She back into her chair with her legs crossed. "I can't tell you everything—he should tell you his part of the story. We both like to keep our lives private, and I don't know how much he'd want you to know. But at least I can tell you my part." She took a moment, then told me her story in a low voice.

"Jonathan and I are cousins. He was born two years before me. Our mothers were sisters, and our fathers were good friends. We grew up in the same house, brought up side by side like brother and sister. We've always loved each other very much.

"However, as we matured, my love for him changed. It was an unnatural feeling for me to have toward a blood relative. No longer could I think of him as my cousin. I was totally and completely preoccupied with him. I knew he saw me watching him all the time, but I suppose he thought it was just hero worship or maybe a silly crush—not the all-consuming attraction that had taken over my life. To this day, he's never given any indication that he felt any of those feelings in return, nor has he ever acknowledged that he knew how I felt then. He has always been a gentleman, if nothing else.

"Eventually, when I realized he would never return my love the way I wanted him to, I reluctantly accepted it. We remained close after we became adults, even after our lives took very different paths. I was married off to a man of my father's choice. I didn't love him the way I loved Jonathan, but I did care for him. It wasn't a bad marriage. We got along well with each other but never had any children. It saddened me greatly at the time, but not a day goes by now that I'm not thankful for that blessing.

She paused for a moment.

"When I was thirty-two years old, my husband and I were out walking one night, returning from our anniversary dinner, when we were attacked. They were monsters, Gia. Eight of them. I later learned that this was planned, that they had decided to change me that night and not kill me. Many times I wished they had. The leader held me and made watch as they devoured my husband. They literally tore his body apart in front of me. I'll never forget that image. After there was almost nothing left of the man I married, the leader leaned in and bit my throat.

"I stayed with their coven for over a year. I had to. I had

nowhere else to go and I didn't know how to live this new life. Besides, the leader would barely let me leave his side. It was clear to the group that I was his. He always brought me along to every feeding. It excited him to make me kill, and thrilled him to have me watch him kill.

"My family and friends assumed I was dead. After what was left of my husband was found, they didn't want to believe I had survived an attack like that.

"Then, during one of the rare times I was allowed to be alone, I was approached by a man. Julius, another vampire. He was ancient, but he was changed when he was about my age. He told me he had been waiting for me to be alone to talk to me. He had been watching my coven for months and he seemed to already know my story. He took pity on me and asked if he might take me away from that band of monsters. I immediately agreed. I hated my existence and would take any chance to be free of them, no matter what the risk.

"Julius saved me. He taught me his gentler way of life. He taught me that I didn't have to kill to eat, and showed me how to keep my new strength in check. He protected me from the others, and loved me like I'd never been loved before. It was so different from what I had felt for my husband, or even Jonathan. He was my soul mate. He was my twin flame.

"Ironically, I'd never felt more alive. I was happy with my new life and didn't want to look back. Yet I did want to do one more thing before leaving the mortals behind forever. I wanted to tell Jonathan that I was alright. Julius agreed that I needed at least that bit of closure.

"I hadn't seen any member of my family since I was changed two years before, and I didn't even know if he still lived in the same house. I saw a light on in the upstairs window and took a chance. I opened the door and smelled him instantly. I was so relieved that he was still there.

"As I made my way past the dozing housekeeper and up-stairs, a different smell took over: sickness. My Jonathan was dying. I entered his room and saw him propped up in bed, reading a book and sipping bourbon. I ran to his arms and we hugged and cried a long time. I buried my face in his shoulder. He had just shaved, but even the scent of soap and his unique smell couldn't cover the overwhelmingly putrid odor of his sickness. He had recently injured himself, and his left leg was now gangrenous. The surgeons were coming in the morning to amputate.

"I had to save him. He was too beautiful to die.

"I told him everything. How I was changed, how I lived, what would happen to him if I changed him. I gave him a choice. He took it.

"I bit him on the throat, and thought I would die from the ecstasy of his taste. I had been feeding for years by then and he didn't taste at all like I expected. Even though I had found true love with Julius, Jonathan would always hold a special place in my heart, and the feeling of his blood coursing through me was intense. I broke away when I began to taste the rot. I took his straight razor from the table and slit my wrist. I had never done this before, so I was clumsy and blood sprayed the bedding and the wall behind the bed. I held it to his lips and he drank. I felt it pull on my heart.

"When I guessed he had had enough, I pulled away and we both watched my wrist heal. When he saw what was happening to me, he reached down to uncover his leg. We both watched as color returned to his leg, then foot, then toes. When he could wiggle his toes, he smiled. He threw off his covers excitedly and got up to dress.

"He was completely naked, and so beautiful and so totally self-assured. Though he was scarred in many places, the im-perfections only made him more perfect.

"He dressed quickly and gathered a few things to take with him. When he glanced in the mirror, he was surprised to see his reflection. I explained that there were many misconceptions about our kind. Then we left that world forever.

"I took him to my new home and introduced him to Julius. We tried to prepare Jonathan for the time when the inevitable remorse would set in, but his exuberance at being well again overshadowed all our warnings. He was so grateful for this new chance, so excited to get out and see the world through his new eyes, that I think he had the easiest transition in vampire history. It was as if he was meant to be one of us.

"He even stayed the same Jonathan. The change often alters a person's personality, but he stayed the same funny, charming Jonathan."

She paused again, clearly considering how much more she would tell me.

"Twelve years ago, Julius died—in one of the only ways we can die, in a fire. Most assumed it was suicide. It was hard for me to remember how much life he had seen when I looked at his youthful face, but I could always see it when I looked into his eyes. Perhaps he had grown tired of living, as some said, but my heart told me he would never leave my side willingly.

"I took it badly. I stopped feeding. I grew thin and despondent and often wished to follow him. It took years, but Jonathan was always there for me, he got me through it. It was he who suggested that I begin writing. And he who suggested this awful pen name." She smiled. "I eventually came out my depression, and turned in my first manuscript. You know my story from there."

She took a deep breath, as if steeling herself for something big. "Now I need to ask you about that favor." I need a mortal I can trust for this." She gave me a searching look.

That look alarmed me. "What about Chloe?" I asked.

Chloe was sort of a group slave, a modern-day Renfield without the flies. Several of the vampires in Bella's circle needed someone to do things for them that they couldn't or didn't want to do, from light housekeeping to body disposal. Each member that shared her had drunk from her, but she was never allowed to taste blood. That way she could walk in the daylight. If I thought about it too long, it sickened me.

But Chloe didn't mind any task assigned her, so she was the obvious choice for whatever Bella wanted.

"Let me clarify. I don't need just any mortal—I need you." She looked directly into my eyes—not in scary-vampire-hypnotizing way, but with a very serious expression. "I want this to be kept just between the two of us. That means no Lola, no Jonathan, nobody. I can't use Chloe because she has a loyalty to too many of us, and if questioned by one of the others, she'll talk. Besides, you have certain skills and resources that she doesn't have."

Now I was really intrigued. "Okay, Bella. I'll help if I can."

She wrung her hands. I can't tell you how disarming it was to see the most confident being I've ever met look so troubled. She took a deep breath and lowered her voice to barely a whisper. "I want you to find the vampire who changed me." She let that sink in. "I want you to find out where he is, how many he has in his coven, and when he's most likely to be alone."

She paused for a second, then rushed on. "He's very smart and I hear he manages to do quite a bit of business during the daytime. He goes by several names, depending on what he's up to, but I'll give you all that information along with a description later . . . if you agree. Right now, I just want you to think about this. It won't be easy. In fact, it could be dangerous—and you'd have to call upon your other underworld clients."

"Bella, I—"

"Don't answer me now. Just think about it and tell no one."

I nodded.

She looked at the clock. It was 6:30. "Go down to the limo and wait for us there. You need some time alone. Blitz, let her go." The dog lifted his head from my knee and went to Bella's side.

Like the dog, I did as I was told. I took my time getting down to the garage, thinking about Bella's story. It explained a lot. Why sometimes Jonathan seemed older; why they looked alike; why he helped her with her career.

I also thought about her request. She was keen to spot the fact that I was more connected to the entire underworld than the actual beings were, since they rarely mixed outside of their own small circles. I had the advantage of a Rolodex full of vampires from covens all over the world, not to mention witches, werewolves, and other supernatural beings that would never be caught dead in each other's company. As far as I knew, Speculation was the only publishing house that dealt with "real" clients and I couldn't think of another industry other than maybe some Hollywood agents that had the opportunity to intermingle with the kind of clients I had. I was probably one of the most connected beings in the world.

In the limo, I checked my voice mail. Lola and her new boyfriend Max would come by the bookstore around 11:30, three more people RSVPed to Bella's publication party on Friday, and lucky me, Johnny had left a message, too.

"Hey, Gia." A long pause. "I don't know what to say. It seems like all I do lately is apologize to you. I feel really awful about upsetting you like that. Let's both take some time and cool off, and we'll deal with it after Bella's party tomorrow, okay? Pretend it never happened—hmmm, where have I heard that line before?" I heard a hopeful smile in his voice.

"I'd like to take you to dinner after the party—like a real human date. We can talk then. Let me know tonight."

Cool off? He had no blood in his veins, how much cooler could he be? I, on the other hand, needed some serious cooling. Just the sound of his voice had my heart racing.

But putting this off was a good suggestion—I had way too much work to do between now and the start of Bella's tour to let this distract me. I'd go out with them all tonight and blow off some steam, making sure I was close to Lola so she could keep me focused. I'd deal with the Johnny situation Friday night. He'd be going on tour with Bella the next day, so it would be good to talk just before he left. Then we'd have some time apart to think about things. Maybe my head would be clearer by the time he got back.

Before I knew it, they were piling into the limo: Bella, Johnny, Antonia, and to my surprise, Billy. He flopped down on the seat next to me, a welcome distraction—at least I wouldn't have to think about not touching Johnny. I hugged him hello. "Hey, killer, what are you doing here? Slumming?"

He gave me a Billy Idol sneer. "My date's a big Belladonna Nightshade fan. I thought I'd meet her at the store and impress her by arriving with the author."

"Not that cute little redhead from last night? You sure she can walk today? Lola and I saw her in the ladies' room and she could barely function."

"I know." He grinned like the cat that ate the redheaded canary.

"Why didn't you ask her to come with us? There's plenty of room, and it'd be nice to have another human in the car once in a while."

"Nah, I'm not out to her yet. I don't want to scare her away."

"It's hard for you *not* to be scary," I shot back.

He laughed; he got off on being told he was scary.

"Do I scare you?" He looked hopeful.

"Only with your breath—somebody get this creature a mint!"

He laughed and hugged me. "Damn it, I friggin' love this human!"

Now *this* was harmless flirting. How had I ever confused what Johnny and I did with this? I wasn't attracted to Billy at all; when he kissed me on the cheek occasionally it meant absolutely nothing to me. Of course I knew he'd eat me alive in a hot second if he was hungry enough, but it would take a lot for him to cross Jonathan. Not many vampires messed with Jonathan. He was well liked, respected, and held a high rank within his group.

He was kind of a legend as the vampire who hadn't killed anyone in many, many years—the exact number varied with whoever was telling me the story, and since vampires tended to be very dramatic, I was certain the story was embellished. But whatever the number, he was known for his self-control when it came to feeding. His self-control around me was an entirely different story.

It was sometimes hard to hang out with vampires. Like I said, they liked drama, and as a result, I was constantly being told about killing, body disposal, and messy police investigations. But even if they did enhance their stories, one thing that I had to keep in mind was that vampires *were* deadly. It wasn't all romance and velvet, and I was often the only one in the room with a pulse.

As for my other clients, they weren't exactly harmless, either. Mess up a warlock's book tour and you might find your ass covered with boils—not that I'd know anything about that. Even Lola and I had strict ground rules about our contact with each other when it came to her "time of the month." And don't get me started on the aliens. How many publicists do you know who have portable ultraviolet lights and a supply of freeze-dried insects in their offices for their clients?

Getting back to the limo, it was clear that Billy was smitten with his redhead du jour; he couldn't stop talking to me about how hot she was. I expected her to be completely enslaved by the end of the week. She appeared to be weak-minded and he'd tire of her before long. He went through that type pretty quickly—chewed 'em up and spit 'em out. If she was lucky, she'd live to be confused about the missing weeks of her life. If she was unlucky, she'd wash up in the Harlem River. Billy didn't have much of a conscience.

4

Too Beautiful to Die

The book signing went very much like the previous night's. Since this event was close to the Speculation offices, many of my coworkers, including my boss and our publisher, came. I stayed at Bella's side the entire evening, refusing the store employees' offers to help. I looked like über-publicist in front of the company bigwigs, and it gave me a great excuse to avoid a certain very sexy vampire who hovered in my peripheral vision. At 11:45, Lola and her boyfriend showed up. By 12:30, all the Speculation folks had gone home and we were wrapping up the last of the line.

There were three people left when I felt a light tap on my shoulder. By the jolt of electricity that shot through my body, I knew it was Jonathan.

"Can I see you for a second?"

Without looking up, Bella waved me away, and a bookstore employee stepped into my place.

I hadn't had time to process what we had talked about in the hotel room, but when I saw Jonathan smiling that dangerous, gorgeous, crooked smile, all I wanted was to return to last night, when we were just a sexed-up couple on a dance floor.

I followed him behind some bookshelves and tried to keep my voice light. "So, let me guess, you'll want a rare steak tomorrow night?"

He turned around and shot me another of those killer smiles. "You know, it's not cool to joke about *stakes* with us vampires. Besides, all I want right now is you." He grabbed me and held me tightly around the waist, then worked his hands under my suit jacket and up my back. Apparently he wanted to turn back the clock, too.

He nuzzled my head and hummed—yes, hummed—with contentment. "You smell amazing." His nose was buried in my hair. "I've wanted to hold you like this since you walked out of my room. It's been torture watching you all night." He was swaying gently, almost dancing with me as he whispered into my ear. "I got all serious and feeling sorry for myself when I saw how pretty you were in the sunlight, then the sunset got me all nostalgic . . . Sorry for being so doom and gloom." He kissed my hair and breathed in my scent.

All I could think was, *He thinks I'm pretty!* What was I, thirteen? "It broke my heart when you left so upset, and I felt even worse when I heard you crying in Bella's room. I've never heard you cry before."

"There's no crying in publicity. But I wasn't exactly publicizing with you, was I?"

I felt him chuckle, then he kissed my hair again. "Good point." He was still rocking me side to side. "So I know what you're thinking, and yeah, I should be leaving you alone. But

I just have to be near you now." He moaned softly, his hands under my shirt now, caressing my bare back. He'd touched me there before and I couldn't imagine how I'd ever breathe again if he stopped. If he wasn't holding on to me, I'm sure I would have fallen over. "I'm so fucking confused. I don't know what the hell is going on. I can't sleep, I can't eat, I—"

I laughed at that. "Well, on behalf of the population of New York City, thank you for your new diet."

Look at how good I was, keeping control—until I realize that he'd backed me up to a wall.

Luckily, one of the store employees had managed to sneak up on us, startling even Jonathan. I must really have it goin' on if I can completely distract a vampire.

"Excuse me?"

She was about twenty-one, probably a college student and used to walking in on makeout sessions. We pulled away from each other, and I smoothed down my hair and straightened my jacket.

"Ms. Nightshade asks that you both meet her downstairs at the limo."

"Do you know if my friend Lola is with them?" I asked.

"The tall, thin woman with the gorgeous brown hair? With a brown-haired guy who's kinda shaggy?"

I nodded.

"Yeah, they're all together." That was a pretty good description of Lola and Max. I had a feeling he wasn't as civilized as Lola. I guess I should have known by the way he sniffed people at bars. Maybe *he* thought my hair smelled like sunshine and a warm Caribbean breeze. I'd have to ask him later.

The chauffeur opened the door for us, and we were met with an uncomfortable silence. Apparently like we'd interrupted an interesting conversation about ourselves. Most gave us polite but curious stares.

Except for Billy, who had his arm around his redhead (who, by the looks of it, had already been tasted several times tonight). His eyes went directly to my chest. "Whoa, check out the rack on Gia! Girl, you should never keep those beauties in a bra."

Okay, so I was a small girl with a D cup and apparently my bra was MIA, but did I need this? "Billy, what are you, thirteen?"

"One hundred thirteen this month!"

"Billy!" Bella scolded, and swatted him on the knee. "You've got to be more careful."

"You're right. Damage-control time." He leaned in and took another taste from the poor girl's neck while he kneaded her right breast. He pulled away, lips bloodied. "I'll bet yours are better, Gia."

"Fuck you." Quite a witty comeback, no? "Remind me again why we let him hang out with us?"

The redhead rested her head on Billy's shoulder while he licked his lips. She had an insipid grin on her face and her hand was inside Billy's pants. A leap forward for the women's movement. But at least the attention was on those two now and not me and Jonathan.

I looked over to Lola and Max. While Lola was used to this and was accepted by this crowd, I wanted to see how Max was faring. I needn't have worried; they were smooching in the other corner.

We ended up at a club where Billy was a regular, this time I stayed in the VIP lounge. I wanted to talk to Lola and, unlike 90 percent of the room, I did not have superhuman hearing, so I needed a relatively quiet place. Besides, the club was less than half human, and too many of my nonhuman friends were treating it like a supermarket. I wasn't as freaked out by that as I used to be, but I didn't necessarily want to see it, either.

Johnny ordered me a martini, and I considered that a sign that he was going to try to stay away from me for the time being. He and Max went outside to smoke—hey, when cancer can't kill you, you can afford to look cool and indulge an otherwise addictive habit.

Lola and I settled into a banquette. "So, you and Max can't seem to keep your paws off each other."

"Me?" She laughed and it sounded a hell of a lot like a bark. "I'm not the one who came into the limo braless!" Where *was* my bra, anyway? "But yeah, I'm totally into him. He's a bit scruffy, since he's just been running wild longer than I have—he was bitten when he was a child. But I intend to class up his shape-shifting ass. I'm taking him for a haircut tomorrow. What time is your party?"

"Just after sunset, when else?" I ate an olive. I always liked a drink with vermouth and a snack—martinis, manhattans, etc. "So the sex is fabulous. How's the rest of him?"

"The rest of him is great. He's got an awesome body. He's taller than me, which is not so easy to find." Lola was easily five feet eleven. "He's kind, interesting, funny, has a job—the whole package."

Max didn't look like the type to hold down a job. "What does he do?"

"He does freelance photography: weddings, babies—totally disproving the myth that we actually eat babies." She was talking very fast and was very animated; she really seemed to be head over heels with him. "And the sex is the best I've ever had. Who knew I liked to have the scruff of my neck bitten? Well, he did, of course." She sighed and took a long pull from her beer.

I was really happy for her. Up until now she had dated

only humans, and it had been hard for her to have a long-term relationship. She couldn't tell people the truth about her condition, since most guys would think lycanthropy was an STD and she didn't like lying about why she had to disappear twice a month.

"So, speaking of sex, let's get back to your bra."

I caught her up on everything, from last night's chat outside the club to my mauling behind the stacks a half hour ago, and all the angst in between. Including our decision to take a break from thinking about the heavy shit until the night before he went out on the book tour. I didn't mention my talk with Bella. Normally I advise people never to tell a publicist a secret, but when it was important, I was like a vault.

"So after all that, you're going out on a real date with him tomorrow night? Just the two of you?"

"Yep, but I'm having second thoughts." We ordered another round from the waiter. "I know this relationship is a dead end. What can we possibly talk about that will change the outcome? It's not like we can have a one-night stand and move on with our lives." I took a big sip of my martini and hoped it would start numbing the anxiety I'd been feeling all evening. "They go out on tour Saturday, and part of me feels that if we decide to break it off, I want one last fling with him. One last night of pretending this could work," I clarified. "But while he's on the road with Bella, I can have some space to think about it all. I just don't know."

Lola appeared as if she wasn't listening to me, but I knew better. She was not only listening to my whining, but to several other conversations in the club like a loyal and protective predator. She turned back to me. "Go on the date. It sounds to me like you two have some important things to discuss, and you have a serious decision ahead of you."

"What the hell does that mean?"

"It sounds to me like you're considering a more permanent commitment."

"Don't be stupid, Lola."

"Yeah, I'm the stupid one. G, you're in love."

"So what?" I didn't bother denying it, even though it was the first time I'd acknowledged it, even to myself. Sometimes I hated that sixth sense of hers. How did she know before I did how crazy I was for him?

"Just because I love him doesn't mean I'm going to give up my life for him—literally. I'm a happy human." I was getting pissed now. "Didn't you always say that given the choice, you'd prefer to be human?"

"Yeah, but I wasn't given the choice, so that's a pretty safe thing for me to say." She took another pull from her beer. "And we're talking about two very different changes here. Apples and oranges, if you will."

She was right. Like Bella, Lola wasn't given a choice about her transformation. But unlike Bella, Lola was a slave to the moon. Bella could survive without succumbing completely to her most basic desires; she didn't *need* to kill. Lola had no option when it came to her time of the month. She involuntarily shape-shifted, then killed and fed on mammals—and nothing could change that.

"And let's not forget," she continued, "you haven't been a 'happy human' since the day you met him."

Well, that sobered me up.

"Come on, don't look so sad." She took my hand in hers. "You don't have to make your decision now. Go on the date. You'll be in a public place, so you'll be fine."

"You're right. He just has this way of weakening my resistance, and he's way too attractive for his own good—or mine."

"Yeah, he looks awesome tonight." Her eyes darted across the room and found Jonathan talking to one of Bella's hangers-on. The she-vamp looked him up and down and I swear I saw her lick her lips. In all fairness, he did look awesome tonight. He was wearing jeans for a change, along with a black T-shirt and that incredibly supple black leather jacket. He'd said that he hadn't eaten in days, and I could totally see it tonight. His face was thinner, paler; I could see the veins under his skin; his eyes were set more deeply into his face, and he had purplish circles underneath them. Strange how this look worked for him. Well, it was working for me, anyway.

The sound of Lola sucking in her breath brought me back to our conversation. She was now watching Billy and the redhead going at it across the room. "You know, that Billy's been looking pretty good to me lately, too."

"Lola, you *are* in heat!" I slapped her thigh. "Listen, Bitch, just because he can make Little Miss Dumber-than-a-Bag-of-Hammers over there come anytime, anywhere, doesn't mean you're his type."

"You mean because I'm actually wearing a bra?"

"Does it matter?"

"I like that punk-rocker thing he's got going on. He just may be *my* type—if I went for vampires." She wiped the corner of her mouth with her finger. Drooling?

"Lola, anything male is your type right now."

She shrugged and sat back again. She knew I was right. "So what's *your* type, other than tall dark vampires?"

I thought about it. It had been a while since I had thought about anyone other than Johnny. "Oh, I don't know. I wouldn't kick Hugh Jackman out of bed."

"Ooooh, this is getting very interesting. Wolverine or Van Helsing?" She elbowed me. "I didn't know you had a fur fetish. Maybe I should keep Max on a shorter leash around you."

"Hah! I hadn't thought of that." I nudged her back. "Anyway, I was thinking more along the lines of his Peter Allen role."

"Freak."

Just then Jonathan and Max returned, and I immediately wanted to climb inside his jacket. *Good going, Gia.* I'd lasted a whole 1.5 seconds before having a sexual thought about him. But at least we weren't making out like the wild dogs next to me; Max's knee nearly knocked over my drink. I righted my glass and said, "Easy there, Max, or I'll have to turn the hose on you two."

I turned back to Johnny and caught him staring at the pulse in my neck. With a human guy I'd say something like, "Hey buddy, eyes up here," but that wouldn't have been any safer. I adjusted my hair to cover my jugular. "Johnny, I was thinking about tomorrow night."

"Huh?"

Did I just manage to hypnotize a vampire? I did it with my throat, not my eyes, of course, but still. Damn, I was good.

"I was thinking I might take a rain check and we should do dinner when you get back from the tour. You know, give us both a chance to think."

"We'll have plenty of time to think while I'm on tour." He had somehow gotten ahold of my hand when I wasn't paying attention, and he was stroking each finger individually. "Besides, if I don't have you near me every possible minute from now until the day I leave, I'll be totally miserable."

He put his arm around me and I snuggled into his chest. He stroked my arm with one hand and held my hands in his other. Although his skin was cold, I could feel through my suit jacket the heat that his touch generated. It nearly distracted me from the eyes I sensed watching us—Bella, Billy, and a few others I couldn't name. I kept my gaze on our hands in my lap.

"In fact," he continued, "why don't you call in sick and sleep with me tomorrow? Just sleep, nothing else. I haven't slept well lately, and maybe with you next to me . . ."

I gave him a look of total disbelief. "First of all: *No f-ing way!* I wasn't born yesterday. And second, on a more practical note, you want me to call in sick and then show up to the party where all the company brass will be? Yeah, that'll go over well. Give me a friggin' break."

Still, his offer was incredibly tempting. I'd never fantasized about sleeping with him—well, literally sleeping with him—but it sounded awfully nice. If my whole body trembled from him just holding my hands, what would it feel like to lie next to him?

"You can't blame me for trying, right? I'm supposed to be a very charming creature, able to lure you into all kinds of dangerous situations."

"Jonathan—"

"Uh-oh, I'm getting *Jonathan*. I must be in some deep shit."

I smacked his shoulder. "Come on, be serious."

"I thought you liked me because I'm *not* serious."

"No, I like you because you're not serious *all the time*. You're incorrigible."

"Fuckin' English major, showing off with big words." He said it under his breath, but I knew what he was doing. He just wanted me to say yes. Men were all the same—human or not.

"Johnny, I know what you're up to, and rest assured, it's working. But you have to promise me that if we go to dinner tomorrow night, it will just be dinner. We're getting too careless."

I was surprised to realize that I was rubbing his inner thigh as I said this. I pulled my hand away and tried not to notice that he was smirking at me. He captured my hand again and simply held it.

Then he took my chin in his other hand and looked directly into my eyes. I loved looking into his eyes, but rarely allowed myself the indulgence. Their dark beauty always surprised me. How could they be so black and so rich at the same time? I supposed that irresistible beauty was part of their danger.

"Say you'll come to dinner with me."

I nodded. I didn't care if he used his vampire power to make me agree; I didn't want to be away from him, either.

"We'll talk about this"—he gestured with his chin to our still intertwined hands—"then."

I brought his hand to my lips and kissed his knuckles. I breathed in his scent, and knew the whole room must have heard what it did to my pulse. "I think I need to get up now. I'm a little . . . I just need to step away from you for a second."

He nodded. He was getting a little carried away, too.

I called over my shoulder, "You coming to the LR with me, Bitch?"

"Sure." Lola untangled herself from Max. He looked disappointed until she said, "Meet me outside and we'll head over to my apartment."

In a hot second, Max had gathered his things and was saying his good-byes. It was kind of sweet, in a horny teenager kind of way.

I leaned in toward Lola. "I swear his tail is wagging."

She barked out a laugh.

Different ladies' room, same drill. Lola cleaned up her face while I tried to even out my breathing and ignore the voice of reason in the back of my mind.

"Everyone was looking at us, weren't they?" I asked. Although Lola had been practically buried under Max for the last half hour, I knew she was aware of what was going on in the lounge.

"Yeah, but screw 'em. They're just not used to their kind showing anything resembling respect toward humans." She slung her purse over her shoulder. "Be careful, Chickpea, and don't stay too late. I'm not comfortable with this crowd tonight. Now, I've got a hot date—I'm outta here like Vladimir."

"That's a good one—I may use it later."

We hugged good-bye, and she practically ran out of the club to meet Max. Her tail was wagging, too.

I shook my head and started back up the narrow staircase to the VIP room. Billy was coming down the stairs and he blocked my way. "Very cute, Billy. Let me by."

He was leering down at me, and I saw that his teeth were stained with fresh blood, and a trickle ran down the side of his mouth. The redhead probably wouldn't last until morning. He was reckless, showing me his bloody teeth like that—anyone could have seen him. He was breathing hard and had a scary, frenzied look on his face. I had always thought those "crazy eyes" were an act with him, but at this moment I wasn't so sure. His eyes were red and opened unnaturally wide.

"You know, I can end all that suffering for you in about ten seconds." He sucked some blood off his bottom lip.

"Thanks, but I'll pass." I had an awful feeling about this. Isn't that what they always say in movies, before the bad thing happens?

I tried to get by him, but he pushed me hard into the dark corner by the restrooms. The impact knocked the breath from my lungs. Now I was really scared. He started feeling me up clumsily, running his hands roughly over my ass, my chest, my neck, everywhere.

"Come on, I won't kill you. I'll just change you, and then you and Johnny-boy can be together. Guilt free. Let me do this for you. Just this once." He pushed into me. "My treat."

I was shaking with fear. I had never seen him like this. I had never seen any of my vampire friends like this. I knew what they were capable of, but for the most part they behaved themselves around me.

His hands were on either side of my head now, and his hips were grinding into mine. He was desperately trying to make eye contact, but I knew to look away. He licked my face, and I could smell the redhead's blood that was still on his tongue and now smeared across my cheek. He breathed in, and I knew he was reveling in the scent of my panic.

Struggling would be useless, and might even get him more excited. I had to do *something*.

I glanced over his shoulder and pretended to see someone. More disoriented than usual, he took the bait. When he turned to see what I was looking at, I ducked under his arm and ran up the stairs to the VIP room, where I'd be safe. I wiped at my cheek, thankful that I was crying, since the tears washed away the redhead's blood.

When I got to the lounge, I sneaked a glance at the redhead. She was curled up on a bench, her breathing shallow.

Bella saw the fresh tears in my eyes, and assumed that the sight of the poor girl had upset me. "You know how it is, Gia. It's in our nature," she said gently.

I nodded and looked around the room. I didn't see Johnny, but I knew if I started to leave, he'd magically appear at my shoulder. Where was he two minutes ago, when I needed him?

Shaking, I managed to make the rounds, saying good night. Billy was nowhere to be seen, but I didn't expect him to be. He was incredibly hungry and had likely moved on to the dance floor to prowl for prey.

I grabbed my purse and, as I predicted, Johnny appeared.

"Are you alright?" he asked.

"I'm fine. I'm leaving."

He stiffened. Could he smell my fear, the blood, my tears, or all of the above?

"I'll get you a cab." Always the gentleman.

It was raining outside, and we stood under the awning for a few minutes, looking in different directions and not talking. I didn't know what he was thinking about, but I was desperately trying to convince myself that my confrontation with Billy hadn't really happened.

I broke the silence by asking him for a cigarette. I hadn't smoked in years, but suddenly I felt like doing something destructive. That is, even more destructive than playing with vampires after a few martinis.

He pulled out his cigarettes and offered me one. "These things will kill ya, you know?" He threw my line back at him.

"Yeah, so will your friends." He smiled.

I didn't. My close encounter with Billy still had me trembling. Bella had said the favor she'd asked of me might put me in danger. How much more dangerous could looking for her enemy be than hanging out with her friends?

After lighting my cigarette, Johnny put the pack and lighter back in his pocket and kept his hands there.

The cigarette smoke felt incredible. It burned my lungs and reminded me how good it felt to be human. I sucked in another long drag.

"Jeez, Gia, I thought you didn't smoke?"

"I quit years ago, before I knew you."

"Don't tell me I drove you back to it. Those things really *will* kill you." He looked genuinely concerned.

"Nah. I'm just having one hell of a week."

"Okay." He put his arm rather stiffly around my shoulders. "Because I want you breathing around me as long as possible." He slid his other arm around my waist, then kissed my head. "Besides, you're too beautiful to die."

Too beautiful to die. Bella had said the same thing about him.

The magnitude of his words struck me, and at that moment

I finally understood *his* side. It wasn't that he just wanted me carnally, or whatever vampires wanted. It wasn't even that he loved me and wanted to spend eternity with me—although that wasn't out of the question, either.

He didn't want to watch me suffer mortality.

He wanted to change me because he didn't want to watch me age and eventually die. It was almost a protective thing: kill her to keep her safe.

My cigarette fell to the ground. I pulled down the neck of his shirt and I kissed his chest where his heart should have been beating, wanting to give him mine, then and there. An emotional wreck, I mumbled into his chest, "Where's a damn cab when you need it?"

He stepped into the rain and hailed me a cab.

On the ride to the Upper East Side I kept looking out the window, convinced someone was following me. Though I was pretty sure Billy was too fucked up to stalk me, I ran from the cab to my apartment.

I didn't see a lot of sleep in my future.

5

It's in His Nature

Work was hectic that Friday. My assistant didn't show up for work—again. This made fourteen sick days within four months. We had to talk. I'd just had most frightening night of my life and was out until five a.m., and *I* managed to get here. But my assistant was home sick with Lyme disease or chronic fatigue or SAD, or some other condition she couldn't really prove she had.

She couldn't have picked a worse day to do it, either. This was the night of Bella's publication party and the day before she went on tour. And to top it all off, my soon-to-be-ex-assistant had gotten the entire guest list wrong—I'd have to retype most of it from memory. Only a privileged few at Speculation knew the truth about our 'unique' authors—the publisher, my boss, and a handful of editors—so I had to personally be sure we had all our i's dotted and t's crossed.

The party was being held at a luxurious apartment on Central Park West. The owner was one of New York's most affluent vampires and an old, dear friend of Bella's. A lot of important people were going to be there, including my boss and the publisher.

And Bella's book wasn't the only thing on my plate. The World Fantasy Convention was coming up in November and although that was almost two months away, you can just imagine how much work that entailed since so many of my authors attended it. I had to book flights for several witches who became highly offended when I suggested broomsticks to save some money—no sense of humor.

I also had to figure out how to get my Filtanian author (from a galaxy far, far away) through airport security, since he had a metal skeleton. How did Wolverine manage? Maybe adamantium didn't show up on scanners. I was tempted to call Stan Lee or Chris Claremont on that one.

I also had two vampires coming in from Alaska who preferred to sleep in their native soil (a preference, not a requirement), and did I mention they also traveled with their own supply of blood? So now I had to find a hotel that would accept the delivery of several sizable crates of dirt and had rooms equipped with large refrigerators.

And on top of all that, I was still considering Bella's proposition. After last night, did I really want to take more risks? She'd also said I'd have to call upon some of my clients, and I wasn't sure how I felt about that. Would finding this creep put my clients in jeopardy? I couldn't do that.

My phone was ringing so much that I finally had to ask my boss if I could borrow her assistant, Elizabeth, to help me with the volume. Then I went into the kitchen to get myself some nice chamomile tea. I needed to chill out before I took someone's head off.

I wasn't gone for more than a minute when Elizabeth came running into the kitchen, totally panicked.

"I'm so glad I found you." She tried to catch her breath. "Your friend. The author, Lola. She's on the phone. She's crying and yelling at me. She made me find you."

Lola crying? That had to be a first. Lola was a rock. I ran back to my desk, slamming my office door behind me. "Lo, it's me." She sniffed and whimpered in response. "What is it? What's wrong?"

"Billy's dead," she said through gritted teeth, sounding pissed.

I gripped the desk. This couldn't be happening. I had an awful feeling growing in my stomach. "What happened?"

"He was killed last night. Chloe found him this morning when she brought up his laundry. He was in bed with a wooden stake through his heart. She said it was driven straight through to the mattress."

Shit. Not good. Something told me to ask, "And the redhead?"

"Dead. But it looks like Billy finished her off before he was killed."

I was only half listening to her. Could Johnny have found out? Did he smell Billy's scent on me, or the redhead's blood, or was it a combination?

Lola was taking this hard, like any of my special clients would. There were very few things that could make a werewolf feel vulnerable. If there was someone in our midst who could kill a vampire, that was one of those things. "Billy could be a bastard sometimes, but who could have done this? Gia, who would have done this?"

"Johnny," I whispered. Johnny had found out what he did to me and killed him for it. Did Billy deserve to die? Good question. He was a serial killer. A stalking, preying, manipulative machine, and if you had asked me last night when I was scared out of my mind, I'd say yes. But few had the skill or strength to kill him.

"Spill it. What do you know?"

I told her about my encounter with Billy after she had left with Max. About his crazy eyes. About how he had cornered me, then tried to tempt me. About how he had licked me, and about how I escaped.

"Holy shit. Was he in a haze?"

When a vampire's blood lust took over, it was similar to a shark's feeding frenzy or a drug-induced mania. The total inability to act rationally. Lots of things could trigger it—not feeding enough, feeding too much, extreme anger, frustration, or any severe emotion. While in a haze, the vampire felt he could never feed enough, which often resulted in an ugly pile of bodies. It was a dangerous state to be in, and most worked hard to keep evenly satiated to exercise a measure of control. Some had more control over this state than others, but it was always an extremely difficult instinct to fight.

"Yeah, I think so. His eyes were wide and red. Then there was all that shit he said about ending my suffering that didn't make any sense, so he was pretty out there."

"Of course it makes sense, Gia—he was coming on to you."

"Don't be stupid. He was just so incredibly hungry, he was rambling nonsense."

"No, don't *you* be stupid, Gia. He wanted your consent way more than he wanted your blood. Billy had such a huge crush on you that if this was the only way he could get you, he'd take it. Even at the risk of pissing off Jonathan. Think about it. If you gave your consent, none of the others would blame him. It would just be Jonathan that he'd have to face."

Billy had a thing for me? How the hell did I miss that? But now that she said it, it made sense. The teasing, the flirting, the special attention he paid me. He often looked at me while he sucked another, and there was that constant hunger whenever I was around. And then that final offer. Even in his haze, or maybe because of his haze, he had summoned the courage to seduce me using the one thing he knew I loved possibly more than my mortal life. He had offered me a way out. A guilt-free life with Johnny. That was one hell of a lure.

"Gia?"

"Yeah. Just digesting it all."

"You can't tell me you didn't know." I didn't answer. "My God, Gia, you really are in a fucking dreamworld! I'll bet that's why all the vampires were staring last night. They wanted to see how Billy reacted to Jonathan's first public display of affection toward you. Jonathan was marking his territory, and I'll bet that's what set Billy over the edge. But I doubt anyone expected him to go that far."

She was right. She had put it in werewolf terms, but she was right. Before last night, Jonathan and I had kept all of our interactions pretty low-key. He was usually professional with me unless we were either in a private place or in a large, faceless crowd. His arm around me in plain sight of his group of vampires was a public declaration.

"Listen, Lola. I've gotta wade through all this shit and get my act together before tonight. I have a ton of crap to do before setting up the party at five."

"You really think Jonathan killed Billy?"

"Yeah. He must have realized what Billy did and killed him before morning. Keep it on the DL, okay?"

"Who am I gonna tell? I'm not exactly on the vampire phone tree like you are. The only reason I knew about this is because Bella called me and asked me to break the news to you." I heard her suck in her breath. "Shit, do you think Jonathan killed the redhead, too?"

necking

"Don't be ridiculous; he hasn't killed anyone in years. Killing Billy—that was a murder with a weapon, he didn't feed on him. And you said yourself that the redhead was probably Billy's victim."

"Yeah, but think about it, Gia. Jonathan doesn't look like he's eaten in days. You can't tell me you haven't noticed."

Of course I had noticed, and I was a little worried about him. But he wouldn't have finished her off, right? Yet that same sinking feeling that told me Johnny had killed Billy was back, and confirming that he had killed the redhead, too.

My first instinct was to protect Johnny. "I think you're wrong there. She was barely breathing when I got back to the VIP lounge. I don't think she would have survived the ride home from the club, let alone one more feeding from Billy." It was mostly true and I wasn't totally sure Johnny killed her, so I hoped Lola would buy it.

Lola considered that. "Good point. I'll let you go, but call me if you need to talk."

I hung up and realized I was crying again. I had never cried so much in my life. I reached into my drawer for a tissue. Instead, I slashed my index finger on a box cutter. "Fuck!" Now I was going to attend a vampire party smelling like fresh blood. I cleaned up my mascara, then searched for a Band-Aid for my finger.

There was a timid knock on my door. "Yes?"

A nervous-looking Elizabeth poked her head into my office. I was sure she had heard my little expletive through my door. "The posters for the party are in here and the messenger is ready to take them over to the apartment."

"Of course, come in."

Elizabeth busied herself with collecting the three-by-four-foot posters. "Giovanna?" She looked very worried. "Are you—I mean, is Lola—I mean, are you both alright?"

77

"Thank you, we'll be fine. We just found out a friend of ours died last night."

She put her hand to her chest. "Oh, I'm so sorry. Did you know him well?"

Good question. "No, but I thought I did."

When she had left and closed the door behind her, I called Johnny at the hotel. It was 3:30 and I wasn't sure if he was awake yet. The hotel phone went straight to voice mail. Damn it. I needed to talk to him *now*. I called his cell phone.

"Hello." The deep-sleepy, sexy, gravelly voice.

"It's me. Sorry I woke you."

"Don't be sorry, it's good to hear your voice." I heard him light up a cigarette. Since he was just a social smoker, it was a habit left over from his mortal life, not an addiction. I mean, how could a vampire be addicted to nicotine? Either way, I thought he must really be stressed to light up first thing.

I blurted, "Did you hear about Billy?"

"Yeah." He yawned. "I killed him." Just like that.

It was strange. I'd thought I'd be outraged, angry, or sad. I was utterly surprised that hearing him confirm my suspicions actually calmed me down. I must be totally numb. But through that numbness, I remembered Bella's words: *It's in our nature.* Still, I needed to know why. "Did you have to?"

"Mm-hm." I heard him take another drag. "It'll sound stupid to you, but yeah, I had to kill him."

"Try me."

"Okay, but you'll think it's archaic."

Of course I would. Everything these vampires did was archaic.

"Billy was lower than me in rank. I was older. He was young, but he had been around long enough to understand the rules. He knew you were off-limits, and that touching you meant certain death, but he couldn't help himself. If I let him get away with it, it would have shown weakness, and that would send a bad message to the others. A vampire's seniority is sometimes the only thing that makes him feel safe. I know it seems old-fashioned, but it's just how we work."

He waited for me to reply, but I didn't. I was thinking about it. He was right. Billy had left him no choice.

"And just so you don't think it's just a stupid male macho thing, you should know the rules are the same for all of us. Bella would have done the same thing if she were in my position."

"And the redhead? That was you, too, right?"

"Yeah." He exhaled heavily. Guiltily. "You're not mad, are you?"

Was I? No, not exactly. *It was in his nature.* Scary. When did I start accepting my clients' lifestyles as no big deal? I was about to tell him this when another totally unexpected emotion overtook me. Jealousy. I was jealous of the redhead's final moments with him. She had gotten to experience a closeness with him that I never would. I must really be losing it, if I was jealous of a dead woman.

"Gia?"

"I'm here. And I'm not mad. Tell me everything. How did it happen? You smelled him on me, didn't you?"

"Mm-hm. It was all over my shirt after you kissed my chest. In a way, it kept me focused. Your scent mingled with his and the girl's—literally right under my nose." Another drag and he continued. "After you left, Billy fed pretty heavily at the club and was too full to even care where he was or what he was doing. We needed to get him home. So me and some of the others loaded him and the girl into the limo and got them back to his apartment. We put him to bed with the redhead, then left.

I came back on my own just before dawn. I walked in, killed him, and was about to walk out when I just felt so tired. I sat on the edge of the bed and thought about you, and how he must have scared you half to death. I was so angry with myself for not seeing it coming and not being there to protect you.

"The redhead was lying next to him. She was moaning, weak, near death. Gia, you've got to understand. I can't say I did a humane thing by taking her life, but I can't say it was inhumane, either. I hadn't been able to eat for so long and I was so fucking hungry. She would be dead within the next few hours anyway, even if I never touched her. I haven't killed for food in almost a century, but I just—I just . . ." He trailed off.

"How did it feel?" I had been told that nothing was as fulfilling to a vampire as killing for food, that it was better than sex.

"Truthfully? Weird. With Billy, it was the same as it always was when I killed another vampire. I used a wooden stake—not my hands, not my teeth. It was very impersonal."

What did he mean, *always*?

"I had almost forgotten what it was like to take a life for food. It's different every time, but I'd forgotten how creepy it could be. Sometimes I see their memories, sometimes I sense inner peace, and sometimes I feel their last emotions."

"And what did she feel?" I needed to know.

"Relief. She was tired of the half-life she was living and disappointed in herself. She was really falling for Billy, and she was heartbroken when she learned he didn't feel the same way about her. Are you sorry he's dead?"

"I'm sorry things worked out the way they did, but I understand that you didn't really have a choice."

"And the girl? Are you upset that I killed her?"

I could do one of two things: obsess over the deaths of a man who should have been dead years ago and a woman who was 90 percent dead when Johnny got to her, or accept it and let Johnny know that I understood.

Why wasn't I a basket case after learning that the man I

loved had murdered two people? Had I become callous after working with ghouls all these years? I didn't want to think so. Frankly, I was ashamed of myself.

"Hey, Gia, you still there?" I had been silent too long.

I let out a long breath. "Yeah, I'm just getting used to it all."

"What does that mean?"

"Well, it's not like any of this is a surprise, but . . . Well, I'm having some trouble with the way I feel about it."

"I'm sorry, baby, I forget sometimes what it's like to be human. This has got to be a bitch for you. I should watch what I say to you."

"No, no, it's not that." How could I put this? "What I'm having trouble with is how *not* upset I am."

He sucked in air through his teeth. "Shit. Then I *really* should watch what I say to you. You should never get used to us, Gia."

"I know." I looked at the clock. Damn, where did the afternoon go? "Listen Johnny, I've got to get ready for this party."

"Hold on. Are you going to be okay? Really?"

"Yeah." I gave a sardonic laugh. "Apparently I am."

"Prove it."

I thought for a moment. "Do you know why vampires kill mosquitoes?"

He gave a very small chuckle, "Yeah. Too much competition. Very subtle."

Okay, but at least he knew I got it. "On that note, I really do have to cut you short. Are you sure *you're* going to be okay?"

"You're consoling *me* after I just told you I killed two people? Gia, you're an amazing woman. Freaky, odd, and confusing, but amazing." He yawned. "We're still on for tonight, right? I made reservations for us at Harry's."

"Yeah, the party's from seven thirty to ten, so I should be done by ten thirty. Will that work for you?"

"Yeah. See you soon."

"Wait, Johnny." Should I even ask him? I had thought I had done the right thing by keeping what Billy had done to me to myself, but . . . "Are you mad that I didn't tell you about Billy?"

Silence.

Uh-oh, long silence. Shit. I knew I should have kept my mouth shut.

"Giovanna. If possible, it made me love you even more. It showed me just how much you understand the way things work with us. You did the right thing. See you tonight."

He loved me! I played it real cool and hung up without saying good-bye, hoping he thought that was another one of my endearing human qualities. This was too much to process.

Let's recap: a) my boyfriend—for lack of a better classification—just told me that he had killed two people, b) I shocked the hell out of myself by realizing I had come to accept a lifestyle that should scare the hell out of me, and c) Johnny just told me he loved me.

I'd have to get my shit together pretty damn fast if I wanted to get through the next few hours. Why couldn't I have the kind of job where I didn't have to be so "on" all the time? Then I could drop everything and go tell him that I loved him, too. Hold him and tell him that I couldn't live without him. Okay—bad choice of words, but that's how I felt.

I called the caterer and the liquor store and the bartender for the party and all were on schedule. Elizabeth agreed to go over early and help the doorman with the guest list. I called the key media people on the guest list who hadn't RSVP'd and found out that four of the five were coming. We're never upset if they don't RSVP; frankly, we don't expect it. We're simply delighted when they *do* show up.

Slipping into the ladies' room, I washed my face, put on

makeup, and changed into something black, tight, and low-cut—my sexiest little black dress. I had picked it out that morning—a lifetime ago, thinking about my big date. I wore my hair up again, and put on pretty rhinestone drop earrings with a matching bracelet. I had my nails painted blood-red for the occasion. I looked damn good. I'd say I was dressed to kill, but the thought left me a little nauseous.

The party was on Central Park West, so I walked through Central Park. When I found a secluded bench, I sat and stared off into space, clutching my evening bag like a life preserver.

This new acceptance of mine didn't come from Johnny telling me he loved me. No, it came from somewhere else. From a decision I hadn't even realized I'd made, though Lola had.

My next step was unexpectedly but completely clear. I wanted to be with Johnny, regardless of what he was and because of who he was. Lola was absolutely right last night when she said I was looking to make a more permanent commitment.

I wanted to be with him forever. What had taken me so long to realize it? If you'd put a gun to my head yesterday and asked me what I wanted out of life, I would have told you marriage, family, a normal life. Suddenly all those things were unimportant. My life wasn't worth living at all, if I wasn't with him. Now, I couldn't imagine my future without changing.

I thought about telling him tonight, but wanted to get used to the idea first. It still scared me. At the very least, though, I'd have to tell him that I was thinking about it. He'd know something was up the second he saw me, due to that freaky vampire sixth sense.

I looked at my watch. Showtime. Time to go smile, shake hands, and publicize my ass off.

6

Oh Yes, I Think It Was Sunshine

The apartment where Bella's party was being held was fabulous. Floor-to-ceiling windows showed Central Park lit by lamps along the pathways. The turnout was better than I expected. Many of the higher-ups from Speculation were there, as were many of Bella's friends, a few other Speculation authors, and a smattering of media. The author, the publisher, and my immediate boss Lois were thrilled with whole party. Good—my performance review was coming up, and I could use a raise.

Bella tapped a glass to get the crowd's attention. "Thank you, all of you, for coming. I'm so happy to bring Lady Von Rastenbourg and her family back to my readers. Of course, I couldn't have done it without my own family. A special thank you to my publisher. George, you have never made a bad decision on my behalf. You and your entire company, from the sales force to the production department, have been a dream to work with. And thanks to the publicity department, especially Giovanna Felice, who has managed to get me on the *New York Times* bestseller list with both books. Gia, I couldn't even manage to find a bookstore, let alone go on tour, without you. And last but not least, my manager, Jonathan. Not many of you know this, but it was Jonathan who convinced me to write in the first place. Without him, Lady Von Rastenbourg would not exist." She raised her champagne glass. "To you all!"

I hadn't seen Jonathan until then, and he looked amazing. He was wearing a dark gray suit and a black shirt with an open collar. His hair looked freshly cut and was combed back with casual elegance. I'd never seen him dressed up before, and man, he looked hot. Had he dressed up for our first date? Impressive. He also had . . . color. He had filled out. He had . . . eaten. I didn't want to think about that.

"He cleans up pretty good, huh?" Lola had come up beside me. "How're you holding up?"

"Good. We talked." I took a sip of wine. "You were right about Billy and the redhead, by the way."

"You seem pretty calm about that."

I shrugged. "You know what they say. It's in their nature."

"Oh, so you're okay with going out on a date tonight with a guy who committed two murders last night?" I couldn't tell if she was being sarcastic or serious.

My stance instantly became defensive. "Murders? Aren't you being a little harsh? He *ended the breathing* of a man who should have been pushing up daisies ages ago, and finished off a woman who wouldn't have survived until morning." Saying it out loud felt weird. It's not like I didn't believe what I was saying, but I just sounded so flip.

She nodded. "Point taken."

I think she may have been proud of the way I was handling it. I had a feeling that her comment about murder was a test, especially since she'd know if I was lying.

Max came over and talked to us for a while, as did Bella, and my boss. A surprising number of Bella's friends came over to congratulate me on a successful party. I seemed to be quite the celebrity among her friends. Or maybe I was just an oddity—the token human who understood them. Either way, I was holding court with most of the undead for half the party. I still hadn't had a chance to talk to Jonathan, but I caught his eye from time to time while he chatted with other guests.

By 10:30, the place had pretty much cleared out. I was talking to the owner of the apartment when I felt my scarf being draped over my shoulders, and my heartbeat instantly increased. Jonathan had come up behind me.

"If you will please excuse me." His voice washed over me and I was sure it had the same effect on our hostess. "Mrs. Seward, it's been a lovely evening. I hate to leave, but Ms. Felice and I have another engagement."

He reached to take her hand, but she offered the inside of her wrist instead. Vampires were freaky sometimes. He gave her wrist a lingering kiss and I swear, what blood she possessed rushed straight to her cheeks. Apparently he had the same effect on all women, dead or alive.

It was a warm September night, and Jonathan and I decided to walk to Harry's, one of our favorite restaurants. The head chef, Ron, was also a vampire and pretty good friends with Jonathan. Vampires made excellent chefs on the overnights. They didn't get tired, had all the raw meat they could eat, and they never let their taste preferences get in the way of the food. Besides, they got to scope out prey at the bar nightly. Not a bad gig for a creature of the night.

We walked hand in hand in silence. I was thinking about what hints I could drop to let him know what I had decided, and wondering what was going on in his head.

We arrived a good twenty minutes before our reservation. When we were at the restaurant door, my cell phone rang. "It's Bella, I'll be quick," I said as I flipped open the phone.

"I'll order you a martini and wait for you at the bar."

"I'm more in the mood for a bourbon." I winked and turned away to take the call. "Hi, Bella—were you happy with the party?" At least that part of my message to him was loud and clear—no vermouth tonight. He raised his eyebrows and gave me my favorite half smile—he could be an evil tease.

"I just wanted to tell you what a wonderful job you've done. The party was fabulous, and I couldn't be happier with the way this book tour has started out."

"Thank you."

"Do you have a second? I didn't get a chance to talk to you all evening, and wanted to make sure you were okay with everything that's happened since last night."

"Thanks Bella, I'm fine. I even feel like I should have seen it coming—I mean, what was going on was obvious, and Billy really pushed the limits."

She made a sound of approval. "And the girl? How are you dealing with that?"

"She was near death anyway—Billy had seen to that. And Johnny had to eat." I half expected that dreadful feeling I used to get when I talked about these things, but instead, I just felt glad it was over. I was more frightened by the shady character digging through the garbage can on the corner, than the vampire waiting inside the restaurant. I wasn't the same Gia I used to be.

"You see a lot, Giovanna. I'm impressed, but I don't know if I'm happy about this change in you. I love your human edge, but I guess ten years with our kind has finally changed you."

She paused. "That *is* the only thing that is going to change in you, right?"

Vampires could be so damn perceptive. "I'm still a hundred percent human. I'm just starting to see things differently these days."

"That's not what I asked, Gia. Be careful how you answer me."

"What?" I feigned ignorance to someone who knew I was lying. Damn, I had guts.

"I'll let you get away with it this time, but please be careful of where that thinking can lead. There are no trial runs here. You'd better be sure you know what you're looking for." Bella, it seemed, knew exactly where my head was. After all, she was pretty good at recognizing the signs of being totally in love with Jonathan, being that she had been there herself. She was always one step ahead of me.

"You're preaching to the choir, Bella. I promise I won't do anything rash. I'll take my time with this."

"Good." She paused, then changed the subject. "Have you thought about that favor I asked of you yesterday?"

Not much, who had the time? But Bella was my friend. I wanted to help her, and I was one of the only people in the world who could do this favor for her. And from what I heard about the vampire that changed her, the world would be a better place without him. "Yes, I'll help you, Bella. But the minute this puts one of my unsuspecting contacts in danger, I'm pulling the plug."

"I totally understand, and do the same for yourself. If you sense things are getting out of hand, tell me and we'll call it off." She breathed a big sigh of relief. "You have no idea what this means to me. I'll call you from the road with more details—and of course, I'll compensate you for your help."

I told her that wasn't necessary, but she wouldn't take no for an answer.

"Now go inside and have a lovely dinner with my cousin. He can only be so patient."

I snapped the phone shut, then opened it again and turned it off. I wasn't a publicist now. Tonight I was a beautiful enchantress on a mission to seduce a man. I adjusted myself a bit in the reflection of the store window next door. I knew I looked good; even the man with his hand inside the garbage can couldn't take his eyes off me. Now *that's* a testament to beauty.

Johnny was standing at the bar, holding a high-backed bar stool out for me, shamelessly giving me my favorite half smile. Two glasses of bourbon sat in front of him on the bar. I took the offered seat and he moved to kiss me on the cheek. I allowed it. He was warm for a change. He dragged his lips up to my ear, and my nose brushed up against his suit jacket. He smelled incredible—like soap, some product the hairdresser used in his hair. Something uniquely belonging to him.

I took his hand and kissed his knuckles. "You smell wonderful!"

"Well, you smell like . . ."

"Don't tell me—sunshine?"

"What is it with you and fucking sunshine? How can someone smell sunshine?" He squeezed my hand in his.

"Duh, I'm dating a friggin' vampire, what do you think? I'm trying to turn you on. Besides, how do you know sunshine *doesn't* have a smell?"

He kissed my forehead and inhaled deeply again. "So you smell wonderful, let's leave it at that."

I felt a pulsing in my hand and suddenly realized just why I smelled so good to him. The cut on my finger had bled through the bandage and onto his palm. No wonder I got so much attention from the bloodsuckers at the party.

He followed my eyes, saw the blood, and inhaled.

"Go ahead." I inclined my head toward our hands. "Consider it a trial taste." I flashed him a wicked grin.

"Do you think I should?" His smile was fading.

Why was he so concerned? Would he become overwhelmingly bloodthirsty and attack me right on the bar?

"Maybe I should excuse myself and go take care of this."

Was he kidding? I shrugged. "Oh, so you'll leave me here to go hide in a stall and lick your palm? You'd rather look like you're jerking off in the men's room than let me see how this affects you?"

His smile came back. He liked it when I talked dirty. "Suit yourself." He pretended to cover a cough and sucked his palm clean. When he took his hand away, I noticed that in his excitement, he had punctured his own skin. As it healed before my eyes, he actually sighed contentedly.

"Was it good for you?"

He rubbed at his eyes. "Well, I could use a cigarette, if that's what you mean."

"So you approve of the vintage?"

He laughed. "Yes, it was an amusing little vintage. Busy, but never precocious, He went to take a sip of bourbon, then put it down.

I assumed he wanted to savor my taste still on his tongue. "Of course, there was a certain playful quality I couldn't quite put my finger on . . . Oh yes, I think it was sunshine."

I pushed him. "Freak."

I stared down at my hand in my lap. My finger was still throbbing and I wondered if it was just throbbing on its own, or if he was doing it. It was a deep cut and I probably could have used a stitch or two. He had turned his head to see if he could catch the maître d's eye to see if our table was ready, and I had a dangerous idea.

I unwrapped my Band-Aid and casually held his glass, dangling my index finger over the bourbon.

"Gia, don't." He had turned back and saw what I was up to.

"I know you prefer your bourbon straight, but a mixed drink from time to time won't hurt you." Devious grins between the two of us. I'm sure the other bar patrons were thinking we should get a room. Fuck them. Three drops fell into the glass. I swirled the liquid around, grabbed a cocktail napkin for my finger, and handed him the drink. "Go ahead. See what I would taste like drunk."

"You're the worst kind of flirt." He picked up the glass and brought it to his nose, smelling the mixture. "Should I sip and savor, or down this all in one gulp?"

"Hmmm, take a sip first, then decide."

He sipped . . . considered the effect . . . then pounded the rest back. I had him. He was my slave. Well, for the time being. He moved his hand from the back of my chair to my shoulder and I felt the heat of his touch shoot through me down to my toes. So much for him being my slave. Right now, I'd probably sign over my co-op to him. He was my kryptonite.

He slammed the glass down on the bar and I jumped. He was staring straight ahead, his mouth slightly open and his eyes dark and glassy. He seemed to have trouble controlling something, because his right hand was balled into a fist at his side.

"So that sucked, huh?"

That seemed to jar him back to the present. "What? Yeah, suck." He shook his head. "What are you talking about?"

"Ha-ha! You're in my power. Should I ask you for some ridiculous favor right now while you're all fucked up?"

He laughed deeply and tilted my head back with his hand. "My friends are right, you *are* a tease. I may have to punish you later."

"Not if I get to you first. Besides, your friends suck."

"That joke is tired."

"Who's joking?" Since he appeared to have regained his composure, I asked, "So, what was it like?"

He laughed again. "I don't want to say." He thought for a minute. "Well . . . No, I can't tell you. It's too embarrassing." Was he blushing?

"Come on, don't be shy." I nudged him. "Tell me, what did it feel like?"

The bartender had taken Jonathan's slammed glass as a signal for a refill, and we waited while he poured more whiskey and set a bowl of nuts between us. Jonathan swirled the liquid in the glass. "Well, all I can say is you should be happy that I took the opportunity I had last night. Otherwise, you may have been in big trouble right now."

"The redhead? You're saying that if you didn't feed on her, what? That you'd throw me down on Harry's bar and suck the hell out of me?" I laughed incredulously at the idea. "What's that, the vampire equivalent of whacking off before a big date?"

"Kind of," he said defensively. "And what's with all the references to masturbation?"

"Hey, I live alone." I tossed back my drink, satisfied that I rocked his world, but greedily wanted to do it again.

I slipped my finger into his drink, wincing at the sting from the alcohol. The cut bled freely into the liquid, changing the color from golden to amber. I removed my finger and sucked off the bourbon, then rewrapped it in my napkin. "That was purely for medicinal purposes. I needed to clean the wound."

He cleared his throat. "Naturally." He sounded like he was trying to keep his tone casual, but he was clearly worried about what I just did. "That's a significantly stronger cocktail you've just made me. I may need a designated driver after this one."

"We didn't drive here." I started picking at the nuts on the bar.

"You're driving me crazy, woman." He picked up the glass and held it to the light. "That has a nice color."

"Did you know I'm a regular blood donor?"

"No, really?" He turned to me as if I had just said something fascinating. We were pretending this was a normal conversation between two human beings.

"Absolutely. I'm B positive."

"I always knew you were my type."

"I'm part of the gallon club at the New York Blood Center."

"Yeah, baby, talk dirty to me." He turned back to look at the drink.

"Yep. A pint every two months."

"Pints are good."

"I could fill up one of those pint glasses behind the bar and still operate heavy machinery." I pointed to his glass. That's merely a drop in the bucket."

I put an arm around his waist, under his jacket. "Try to sip this one. It may go right to your head."

"I'm counting on it." He leaned his hip against my thigh and draped his arm over my shoulders, then took a small sip. Although he'd said he was going to take it slowly, he grabbed the glass with both hands and drank from it hungrily. He was sucking at the last drops of the liquid and making a deep, sinister growling noise at the back of his throat I had never heard before. All his muscles had tensed. For the first time since I met him, I was truly frightened.

What did I do now? Should I make a stupid joke? Touch him reassuringly? Run out the door? I peered around to see his eyes. Glassy again. I was worried about him—and me. I put my free hand on his arm and said softly, "Johnny, are you okay?"

No answer.

"Johnny?" I rubbed his back in what I hoped was a calming motion. "Johnny, say something."

He turned to me, and if I thought I was frightened before, now I was downright terrified. He looked positively menacing. His pupils were completely dilated; his lips were parted and shiny with . . . drool? Was he really salivating? He was shaking, and so was I.

"Do we need to leave?"

He nodded, his jaw clenched now.

I threw down some cash on the bar. I kept my arm around him and guided him out of the restaurant. Apparently I'm too intoxicating for my own good.

Outside, he broke away from me and staggered to the wall. He leaned against it and slid down until he was sitting on the ground with his head between his knees, hands over his face.

I squatted down to his level. "Johnny, what can I do?"

He looked up at me as if he didn't know who I was. It scared the shit out of me. He was grimacing as if in pain, and his fangs gleamed in the streetlight.

"Johnny, let me get you back to the hotel. We can walk from here. Or do you need to take a cab?"

Still no answer.

Maybe he couldn't walk. I stood up to hail a cab.

His hand shot out to grab my arm and pulled me down to the ground in less than a second. Some weird sound of surprise came out of my mouth. His grip was strong and it hurt. He pulled me close to his face and looked right into my eyes with his wide-eyed stare. His brow furrowed as he tried to focus on who I was.

"It's me, Johnny. It's Gia." I couldn't break his stare—no mortal could have.

He finally blinked and shook his head.

His voice came out strained and raspy. "Run away, Gia."

7

Gia, You've Got It Bad for Monsters

What had I done? The evening had started out so play-
fully. I was starting to lay the groundwork for our heavy
conversation, and we were having such a good time. *You always
go one step too far.* I could hear my mother's voice in my head.
She was right. I got power hungry and it bit me in the ass—and
tonight it almost bit me in a worse place.

I ran. I was originally going to go home, but although he'd
never been invited there before, I wasn't sure if it was safe for
me to go there. Should I go to Bella at the hotel? What if he
showed up and she handed me over to him? Her loyalty to him
far outweighed our friendship. But she'd never do that, right?

Holy shit, I was panicking.

Lola.

Lola lived on West 119th Street up by Columbia University.

I hailed a cab and cursed every red light. I kept looking out the back window, afraid he was following me—not that I would have known, since he's accustomed to blending into the shadows.

Lola could protect me, right? What could be safer than a werewolf's den? I felt like crying, but I was in survival mode and that kept me in check.

I buzzed Lola from the intercom downstairs. I should have called her to tell her I was çoming. What if she wasn't home? I buzzed again.

"Hello?" she asked.

"Lola, it's me, Gia. Let me in. Hurry."

She buzzed me in immediately and I ran up the five flights of stairs. What if Jonathan knew where she lived? Would he dare to take on Lola and Max? I ran faster. When I got to the top floor, Lola was in her doorway wrapped in a sheet; Max stood behind her in his unbuttoned jeans.

"Gia, what's—"

I ran into her arms.

She held me and led me to the couch as Max locked the door behind us. "Gia, my God, calm down. What is it? What's wrong?"

I got out a "J" sound through my chattering teeth.

"Jonathan?"

I nodded.

"Is he alright?"

I shrugged. I was shaking violently and still couldn't get out the words. I had held it together the best I could while getting to her apartment, but now that I was in my haven, I broke down. I took a deep breath. I had to say something. "Protect me" was all I could manage.

Max was now back at Lola's side; his jeans were closed and he was wearing an open button-down shirt. If he was anything like Lola, this was about as modest as he was going to get.

He looked confused. "I thought you said Jonathan was an alright guy?"

"He is," replied Lola. "He's not the one you need us to protect you from, is he, Gia?"

I nodded again.

She looked disgusted "Jeez, Gia, what did you do?"

That snapped me out of it. Now I was kind of pissed off. "Why would you assume it was me that did this? Like *he*'s so perfect? He could have said no. He didn't have to drink it. He's an adult—in fact, he's been one for a long fucking time! You can't blame this on me!"

"Ssssshhhhh, baby, no one's blaming you." She knelt in front of me and took me in her arms, rocking me, stroking my hair, and sniffing me. "I hardly smell him on you. He barely touched you tonight. Calm down and tell me what happened. You may be overreacting, honey. Max, bring me some booze."

I took some deep breaths and Max handed me a big tumbler of vodka with ice. I took a big drink, then exhaled.

When I was no longer in danger of hyperventilating, Lola started again. "Now, tell me. Did you two have a fight?"

"No." I shook my head. I was calm enough now to be coherent. "I let him taste me."

I held up my bloody finger. I had lost the napkin somewhere along the way, and blood was running down my hand.

"Max." Before she could finish, he was there with a dish towel, wrapping my finger and applying pressure.

"We were just playing. My cut bled on his hand and he tasted it."

Lola looked like she was about to interrupt and lecture me on how stupid I was, but I didn't let her.

"It was no big deal, Lo. He had fed the night before, so it's not like he was hungry. It was like tasting dessert after a full meal—he could take it or leave it." She gave me a dubious look. "Okay, bad analogy." I took another big drink of the vodka and felt the alcohol burn my throat.

"And . . ."

"And he liked it. He liked it lot."

"No shit. Then what?" You could always count on Lola to cut through the BS.

"So I let it drip a few times into his whiskey."

Max sucked air through his teeth, and Lola shook her head disapprovingly at me. "You're fucking brilliant, Gia."

"No, you don't understand. He was fine after that, he—"

"There's more?" Lola rolled her eyes. "What the fuck were you thinking? Why didn't you just draw a friggin' target on your neck? What's wrong with you? Were you *trying* to drive him to the brink of insanity? For crying out loud, Gia, you were baiting a monster!"

"No, it wasn't like that at all. We were having fun. You know, joking around." Even to myself, I sounded like an afterschool special on date rape.

"Tell me." She was sitting on the floor now, running her hands through her hair from anxiety. Her sheet had fallen down around her waist, but she didn't even notice.

"You know, I'm going to come out looking pretty bad in this," I said.

"Tell me." Her tone was insistent.

"I stirred his drink with my finger, let it bleed into it for a good minute."

She was right. I did bait him.

"My God, I'm an idiot! I made him a Giovanna cocktail." I told them the rest of the story, ending with his plea for me to run.

"Gentleman Jonathan." Lola shook her head. "You're damn lucky to be alive."

She knew something about the uncontrollable urges of the supernatural; she also knew that I should know better. She saw this as 90 percent my fault. She got up and let the sheet fall to the ground, totally unself-conscious about her nudity.

"You can crash on the couch. I've never invited Jonathan or any of his friends into my apartment, so he can't get to you here."

Satisfied that I was safe for the moment and knowing nothing else could be done until tomorrow, she said, "Max and I are going to finish having sex. See you in the morning. Come, Max." She left the room.

"You know, he could have said no," I called after her.

"Good night, Gia." Max padded off behind her.

I took off my pumps and cuddled up under an afghan on the sofa. Even if I could have slept, the growling and yapping from the next room would have made it impossible. Instead, I wept. Again.

I woke up at around eight a.m. to the sound of Lola using the toaster in the kitchen. She was wearing Max's shirt from the night before, buttoned only halfway, and socks. All the werewolves I had ever met shared this lack of modesty. After all, what use did they have for clothes?

She sensed my eyes on her without turning around. "Did you get any sleep?"

"I think I nodded off around dawn." I tried to get up, but was stopped by a stabbing pain in my left arm. I yelped and I looked down and saw that my arm was swollen, discolored, and had an alarmingly clear imprint in deep purple of Jonathan's hand. My right hand was still wrapped in the dish towel and, to my absolute horror, I had bled through it completely.

Lola had walked over to me. "Those look pretty bad. The arm is sprained, at the very least, and you're losing a lot of blood out of that little cut." She took a bite of a Pop-Tart. "You'll have to see someone."

"I can't go to a hospital. They'll ask too many questions. Besides, I look like a battered woman. It's too embarrassing."

"I wasn't talking about a hospital, genius. I'll take you to my guy. Let's get you dressed."

She helped me up and I followed her to her bedroom. Max was naked and curled up in her sheets, his legs twitching in a dream.

Lola was a lot taller than me and had bigger feet, so she helped me into the only clothes that would fit me: sweatpants, a T-shirt, a jean jacket, and flip-flops.

Downstairs, she hailed a cab. "Where are we going?" I asked as she helped me into the backseat.

"Little Odessa. Dr. Laktarnik will fix you up, no questions asked." She gave the cab driver the address in Brooklyn.

We rode in silence, since she didn't want the driver to accidentally overhear anything incriminating. We passed a lot of streets called Brighton this and Brighton that, and ended up in front of a two-family house a few blocks from the beach.

The door was answered by a woman who looked right out of central casting. She was about seventy years old and wore a housecoat, bedroom slippers, and a head scarf. "Follow me," she said in a heavy Russian accent, then led us through the living area that smelled like cabbage and was decorated in dark, heavy, Old World furniture and plush velvet drapes and furniture. She opened a door and announced, "You've got customers," then closed the door behind us.

An older man with thick white hair, wearing a sweater with elbow patches, sat behind a huge mahogany desk. He took off his glasses and came around to greet us. "Hello, Miss Lola, love. How are you? How's the foot?" His accent was less pronounced than the woman's and he seemed very robust for his age.

"Tip-top, Doc. Thanks for asking." She pushed me forward. "This is my friend, Giovanna, who's a human." Okay, so obviously I wasn't at a normal doctor's office. Funny, in my line of work I was introduced this way a lot. "She's got a cut that won't heal and a bruised arm, probably a sprain. You can move your fingers, right, Gia?"

I nodded.

The doctor came forward. "Let's have a look." He gently took my arm in his hands and made a few *hmmm* noises, then peeled away the bloody dish towel to look at my finger. He grabbed my face and looked into my eyes. "Spending some time with vampires, no?"

"How did you know?"

"Let's take care of the cut first. This will hurt a lot."

Great—just what I wanted to hear. It didn't exactly tickle now.

He busied himself with putting on gloves and arranging instruments, including a very sinister-looking hypodermic needle and a prehistoric-looking needle and thread, along with a pile of smelly wet leaves.

"Miss Lola, I'll need you to hold her down. I don't have the strength."

I didn't like the sound of that. I sat on the doctor's sofa and Lola put her arms around me.

He switched on a lamp and came toward me with the syringe. "This will dull the pain."

I wanted to be brave, but inadvertently started to squirm. I had never considered that Lola would be so strong, but it was as if I was being restrained by steel bands. It was like she had some kind of supernatural strength—duh. I made myself laugh. I figured the shot must have been a local anesthetic, because it burned but eventually subsided.

The doctor cleaned the wound, then stitched it up with that ugly black thread. He wrapped it in the smelly leaves, and then in a clean white bandage.

"That will take about two weeks to heal. I'll give you some of these herbs so you can change the dressing daily. Make sure you drink the tea I give you and a lot of pineapple juice in the next few weeks. You'll have a bad scar. It will never heal well." He took off his gloves. "Now let's see that arm. Miss Lola, you may let go of her now."

When he held my left arm, I winced and made a little pitiful sound. He asked me to wiggle my fingers while he poked and prodded. It hurt like hell. "This vampire likes you, I think." He dug his fingers in along the bone. "This vampire likes you a lot, I think."

Through gritted teeth I asked, "What makes you say that?" How could he confuse this kind of injury with a mark of affection?

He took my chin in his hand and looked directly into my eyes again, then sat back on the edge of his desk and raised one finger. "First of all, he could have crushed your arm, but didn't." He raised another finger. "Second, you're not dead— or even bitten. I can tell by looking into your eyes—you can always tell by the eyes."

"Or the smell," Lola chimed in.

The doctor nodded in agreement and raised a third finger. "And lastly, he drew your blood by sheer will. Even the blood vessels in your arm aren't healing properly. That can only be caused by an extreme attraction, and that's why you can't stop bleeding. This vampire loves you too much," he said matter-of-factly. "It will get worse. You should avoid all future contact with him or you will eventually bleed to death."

Well, that was right to the point. Was that what happened with my shaving cut earlier in the week? It still wasn't completely healed, either. He stood and began wrapping my arm in more smelly wet leaves, then in an Ace bandage.

"Change this dressing once a week. Wear the bandage on top of it to keep it warm and to hide the marks. It may take up to a month to fade enough for you to feel comfortable with others seeing it. Right now it looks like you have a very bad husband. I'll give you a sling, and some herbs to take as a tea twice a day. You'll need to come back in two weeks for me to remove the stitches."

He rummaged around in a cabinet and made up a few packets. While he was working, he asked, "So, how is everything with you, Miss Lola?"

"Things are going really well, Doc. I have a new boyfriend."

He inhaled deeply. "Another werewolf, yes?" With his acute sense of smell, I wondered what *he* was.

"That's right."

"Good for you, Miss Lola." He turned around and put the packets into a large envelope. "Stick with your own kind. It's for the best." He gestured to me. "You, young lady, could learn from her. It's better if you stay with your own kind. That will be three thousand, five hundred dollars."

Lola opened her wallet and counted out four thousand dollars. "There's a little something extra in there for you. Thanks, Doc."

After we left his home office, she asked, "Do you feel up to the subway? It'll be hard to get a cab here."

I said I did, and we headed for my neighborhood. On the train we both stared at the floor, lost in our own thoughts. If I had to guess, I'd say Lola was thinking about Max. Me? Well, take a wild guess.

He had drawn blood from me without even trying. Dr. Laktarnik said it had happened because he loved me too much. I looked down at my still throbbing finger. Huh—some kind of macabre declaration of love. I got the impression that the doctor didn't consider this a common occurrence. I had a library of reference books on the supernatural at home; I'd have to look it up later.

We didn't get to the Upper East Side until almost two o'clock, and by then it was buzzing with the brunch crowd. Lola and I went to the diner down the block from my apartment and found a quiet booth where we could talk.

"Who was that guy?" I finally asked after we both ordered huge breakfasts, with big glasses of pineapple juice, of course. "I thought I was the one with all the underworld connections."

She shrugged. "He's the kind of guy who finds you, not the other way around. He helps out people like me. Not just werewolves, but any being that needs medical attention. Except vampires, of course; that would be too dangerous. He's part of the underworld's underworld."

He might be an important person for me to know, given my new side job. I got the feeling he didn't much care for vampires, so he could be a useful connection for Bella's project.

I turned my attention back to Lola. "I thought werewolves healed incredibly fast. Why did you need him for your foot?"

She stalled a bit before she answered. "I've known him for years. I stepped on some glass about two months ago during my time of the month, and it was especially hard to remove because with the injury, my foot retained some elements of its paw."

That must have been a sight. "Where did he learn all that stuff? He really knows his vampire injuries."

"He's a warlock from the old country. He's seen it all. Especially when it comes to vampires."

"You took me to a witch doctor?" I laughed.

"Like you could have done better? Eat your eggs and drink that pineapple juice. You've lost a lot of blood."

"Where did you find him? Or when did he find you?"

He took care of me after I was bitten."

Lola had never really told me how she was bitten, just bits and pieces. "Are you ever going to tell me about that?" I asked.

She took some toast off my plate and dipped it into my eggs. "It's not any big secret, it's just something I don't like remembering. Drink your pineapple juice."

I complied, hoping that my obedience would coax her into telling me her story. After a couple of minutes, she finally did.

"You know it was twenty years ago, and that I was twenty-three when it happened. I had just broken up with some asshole, and I went up to my country house for a weekend pity party. I drank too much tequila and smoked too much weed, and I thought a walk would clear my head.

"I was walking along the road when a car came along, so I stepped off to the side of the road. I felt something sharp dig into my ankle, and a really big dog pulled me off the road and into a ditch. It was dragging me deeper when another car came by. The dog saw the headlights and ran away; I climbed out of the ditch and went home.

"The next day, the bite looked awful. It was raw and it smelled bad, so I figured it was infected. I went to the hospital to see if I needed a rabies shot or something. They asked if I had any symptoms like headache or light sensitivity, and I told them that I was too hungover to tell. They gave me five shots and I went back to the city Sunday night.

"When I got to my apartment, there was a note under my door. It said something to the effect of 'Your blood tests indicate that you may have contracted a contagious blood disease;

please contact me at once for testing. Signed, Dr. Gregori Laktarnik.' This was the very beginning of the AIDS epidemic and I was scared shitless. I called him and he told me to come to his office right away so, I trekked out to Brooklyn immediately.

"When I got there, he told me that the hospital upstate had contacted him about my bite since he was on a list for certain 'red flag' readings on blood tests. When I got there, he looked at my eyes, examined my bite, then pricked my finger. He put my blood under a microscope. When he stood up, he said, 'I have bad news for you. You've contracted lycanthropy. There is no treatment and no cure, but I can teach you how to manage.'

"Well, I had no idea what the hell lycanthropy was. He handed me an over-xeroxed pamphlet with a picture of a wolf and the full moon on it. It was called something lame like 'Living a Normal Life as a Werewolf.'

"I was like, 'Yeah, riiiiiight.' He told me to come back in two weeks for the new moon, and explained that I had to be just as careful at that time of the month as with the full moon. I was in total shock and total denial, so I just agreed and walked out of the office.

"I tried to put him out of my mind, but read that damn pamphlet anyway. It warned me about being in populated areas when I changed, told me about the slowed aging process and the rapid healing abilities—all that shit. Two weeks later, he called me at work—I was still writing my restaurant review column for the *Village Voice* then. He reminded me that I had to come to his home that night, before sunset. I still thought I didn't believe him, but fear of the 'what if' won out.

"His wife let me in and led me to the basement instead of to his office. I entered the room and saw a cage in one corner. Well, 'what if' or not, I was about to hightail it out of there. I turned to leave and Dr. Laktarnik was blocking the door, aiming a pistol at my heart. He said, 'Go through at least one cycle. Then if you still want me to shoot you, I will.' I told him I thought this was all bullshit, but that sounded kind of hollow, considering I came to the appointment. He assured me that I had no choice at this point and even if he was wrong, a silver bullet to the heart of a human would still kill me. I got into the cage. Tied to the bars was a small goat happily eating from a tray of pellets on the floor. I didn't want to think about what the goat was for.

"The doctor sat in a chair opposite the cage. He instructed me to remove my clothes and handed me a blanket to wrap myself in before the transition happened. He detailed what my transformation would entail, including how much it would hurt the first time. I listened carefully—he told me a lot more than the pamphlet had. He also told me that I could probably live a somewhat normal life, and told me what precautions I would have to take to ensure I never infected another. He said that if he ever learned I had bitten someone, that he'd be required to find me and kill me.

"I don't remember any more about my first shape-shifting than I remember about any others—it was just a blur bracketed with brief recollections of extreme pain. The morning after, I felt terrible, sore all over. I looked at what was left of the goat and threw up. Then I realized what I had just vomited, and threw up again. It was bad.

"Dr. and Mrs. Laktarnik gave me a place to shower and a big human breakfast and sent me on my way. I went to him for the next few months while I was getting acclimated. Sometimes there were others who shared the cage with me, but they kept to themselves and none of them were new. I supposed they were tourists looking for a safe house or something.

"When he felt I could control my cravings for human meat, he said I could spend my transitions up at my country house.

He told me I might run into a pack in that area, but as long as I acted submissive, I should be able to hold my own—unless I wanted to join them. I didn't. Other than Max and the one that bit me, I've never met another werewolf outside of his office.

"Like I said, I don't like remembering it."

"That must have been really scary."

She shrugged and continued to pick potatoes from my plate. "Hey, look to your left. You know that Goth chick?"

Lola inclined her head toward a woman in a black leather jacket and skirt, with purple and white hose and platform boots. I supposed I could have seen her at one of Bella's book signings, but if I did, she would have blended into the crowd.

"Nope. Should I?"

"She's a slave. I can smell the vampire spit on her through that horrid clove cigarette smoke in her hair."

Yuck, slaves creeped me out. I always tried to avoid Chloe. There was something about a person willing to be kept in a half-life state for the *privilege* of serving bloodsuckers that was—if possible—even more wrong than being a vampire itself. I looked at her again so I could ask Jonathan if he knew her. Except I probably wasn't speaking to him again.

I changed the subject back to werewolves. "Was Max ever with a pack?"

"Yeah, he even knows the bastard that bit me."

Lola didn't seem to think that a slave in a restaurant was a big deal, so I decided that I wouldn't give it any more thought, either. I probably passed them on the street every day, but didn't have Lola with me to sniff them out for me or Johnny to make jokes about them. Now that the excitement over dealing with my injuries was over, I had to get used to the fact that I had lost him. The sadness was like a brick lodged in my chest.

"Max didn't like the whole hierarchy thing," Lola continued, and I was glad to have my thoughts interrupted. "Said it was too much pressure. He was on his own for a few years before he caught my scent, and you know the rest."

"I owe you some serious cash, and then some. I'll write you a check as soon as I can use my finger again."

She waved it off. "All in a day's work."

I picked at my food, in no mood to eat. Now that it was daylight, and I was safe and all cleaned up, I was miserable, not to mention very worried about Jonathan. Did he find a safe place before sunup? Was he able to recover enough to find his way back to his hotel?

Lola asked why I looked so worried, then assured me that he'd be fine and told me to check my cell phone for messages.

I had forgotten that I had turned off my phone.

Sure enough, there was a missed call from Johnny, but no message. The call came in at 8:13 a.m., well after sunrise. So at least I knew he was safe.

Lola was eating every morsel of food on the table. I guess all that sex had built up her appetite, and between bites, she talked about Max.

"He's just so perfect for me, you know? I know the human side of us should take it slow, but the other side of me wants him to myself forever. We're going to run together during our next *time*. Even though he doesn't live with the pack by my house anymore, he still runs with them from time to time. He's going to introduce me." She gave me a meaningful look. "Don't worry, I'm not going to try to kill the savage that bit me. He was killed years ago by some other vengeful were-wolf."

Lola then started telling me about meeting the family of her true love, so why was I so tight-lipped about Johnny with her? Why didn't I tell her that he told me he loved me? Why didn't I tell her that she'd been right all along about us? Was I afraid she wouldn't approve? That after last night, she wouldn't like me seeing him anymore?

After hearing what the doctor had said, I knew I couldn't wait much longer. She should know what I had decided. In fact, I wanted to hear myself say it out loud.

"Lola. I'm going to do it. I'm going to change."

She stopped eating and looked at me as if she didn't quite believe that I believed what I was saying.

"I love him, Lo, and I don't think I can resist him much longer." I held up my bandaged finger. "And I can't keep leading him on like this. The doctor's right: I'll bleed to death."

"Are you sure about this? Just the other night, you said that you wanted a normal life."

"I used to want that, but that's all changed now. What good is a normal life if I don't feel my life is worth living without him? He'd watch me get old and die, and I'd live out my life thinking about how every day brings me closer to the end of our time together. We can't go on with our relationship as it stands right now. I can't let myself become that"—I gestured to the Goth-girl slave at the counter—"and I can't end it, either. I love him too much. I don't care how I get him—but I want him."

She reached across the table to take my hand and did the good-friend thing. "Chickpea, don't rush into this. You had one hell of a scare last night, you've had very little sleep, and you're pretty heavily medicated right now. Think about this some more. There's no going back, you know." She sniffed the air, trying to pick up any odors of fear or anxiety on me.

"Lola, I know what you're thinking, but you were right all along: I think I made this decision a long time ago; it just took me a while to realize it. I accept what he is, how he survives, and I still love him."

She still looked leery, like she thought I was delusional from blood loss.

"I'll tell you what. I won't tell him until he gets back from the book tour. That will give me time to get used to it. How's that?" I squeezed her hand. "Be happy for me, okay?"

"I am, Gia." She smiled. "This certainly gives new meaning to the phrase 'can't live with him, can't live without him.'" I gave her the finger. "Just promise me that I'll be the maid of honor at your midnight wedding, or whatever vampires do. And then you can be godmother to my puppies." She winked. Since werewolves were sterile, this was her way of saying she'd be there for me.

In my apartment, Lola made me my first dose of disgusting tea. "The doc said those herbs will knock you out, so settle in on the couch and get some rest." She covered me with a blanket, put on the TV, and made sure my phone was within reach. Publicists can't sleep without their phones; they're our security blankies. "Are you sure you don't want me to stay?"

I assured her I was fine, and fell asleep before she even left the apartment.

At 9:45 that night, my phone rang. "Hello?" I was groggy and grouchy.

"Gia, it's me." Jonathan's voice was hoarse.

"Johnny, are you okay? Where are you?" I struggled to sit up, forgetting about my sore arm, and fell back with a grunt.

"I'm fine, I'm just outside Atlanta. Did I wake you up?"

"Yeah." Why was he in Atlanta? Oh yeah, the book tour. "How was the trip?"

Bella and her crew traveled on a tour bus, which worked out very well for them. The windows were blacked out and it had several comfortable compartments that locked from the inside. Speculation had it was custom built—not just for Bella, but for other beings that needed it. It was a low-profile way to travel and it enabled our special authors to avoid going through airport security.

One time we had an author who was also a guitarist in an alt rock band. He had a reputation for trashing hotel rooms, and if you plotted the history of this habit, you'd see it coincided with the full and new moons. Book publishing didn't have the same kind of budget as the music business, so we had him take the bus out for his tours. I had the upholstery covered with plastic, called my livestock guy in each city, and locked him up with a goat, sheep, or pig for the night. No one knew he was a werewolf, we saved tons of cash on hotel damage, and we just had to hose out what was left of the animal in the morning. At the end of the day, everyone was happy.

"The trip was fine. Uneventful."

I was fully awake now and wondered why we were making small talk. "Johnny, are you alright? What happened to you?"

Big exhale. He was smoking again. "I don't know, Gia. I guess I'd say I bit off more than I could chew, but I don't know if I could survive your criticism for a line like that." That *was* an unfortunate choice of words, even for us. "I really should have been able to handle it, but I went into a deep haze—it's never been that bad, and it's never come on me that fast. I didn't see it coming and I couldn't control it. That tiny amount shouldn't have done anything to me, especially since I had just fed the night before. I don't know how I got so deep into a bad haze like that." He was clearly upset.

What did that mean? "Where did you go after I left?"

"We were lucky we were at Harry's. Ron heard the whole thing from his kitchen and came outside just as you were running down the street. He figured you were on your way to safety. He gave me some raw meat to slake my immediate thirst, then took me out after his shift to . . . you know."

"Johnny, you can say it. He took you out to feed and get the haze out of your system. It's okay, remember? I know what you are."

He was quiet for a while. "Gia, did I . . . I don't remember much about last night. Ron said he heard you scream. Did I hurt you?"

"I don't remember screaming."

"Answer my question." His tone was insistent.

"You squeezed my arm pretty hard, but that's it. Then you told me to run."

"Is it broken?"

"Just sprained and bruised. Lola took me to her doctor in Brooklyn." I didn't mention my finger, because technically, I cut myself and there was no sense in making him feel even guiltier.

"The witch doctor? He's supposed to be good, especially with vampire-related injuries. You'll heal in no time." Did everyone know about this doctor except me? And here I thought I was so connected. "Gia, I'm really sorry that I hurt you. When I think about what could have happened, I get sick. I was so worried about you all night."

"Really, Johnny, I'm fine now. You did the right thing by telling me to go. I stayed at Lola's last night, and now I'm safe at home watching old movies."

He sighed heavily. He sounded exhausted. "We played too hard last night."

"I know. And I always go one step too far."

"You're really okay?"

"I promise."

"Good." His voice changed and became lighthearted again. "Well, one good thing came out of it. I found your bloody finger napkin in my pocket today. I'll take it out and smell it when I get lonely on this tour." He was trying to get a rise out of me, and it worked.

"Eeew! What is that, some kind of vampire porn?

He was laughing triumphantly. He got me good. "When will you fly out to see me, so I don't have to resort to my porn?"

At that moment, I realized that I was lying to myself as well as to Lola. I couldn't wait until he got back; he'd be on the road for weeks. "How about when you're in LA? Bella has all those movie meetings, so you'll be there a while. Maybe we can spend a whole weekend together."

He groaned and I felt it in the pit of my stomach. "LA? That's a month away. I don't know if I can wait that long."

"You'll live." I couldn't keep the smile out of my voice.

"Nobody likes a wiseass." I could hear him smiling, too.

"Well . . . I thought about my upcoming work schedule. "I may be able to swing something connected with a trade show. I could only meet you for dinner or something, though. I have to work my ass off at these shows."

"I'll take it." His voice seemed much lighter. "What movie are you watching?"

I looked up. Lola had set the TV on the classic movie channel. "Looks like *The Thing from Another World*."

"*The Thing*? Damn, Gia, you've got it bad for monsters."

"Tell me about it."

8

Tail

The next two weeks were unbearable. Work sucked and I missed Johnny and Lola. She was so completely preoccupied with Max that we rarely talked anymore. We used to IM each other all the time, but now she hardly turned on her computer.

When I went back to Little Odessa alone to get my stitches removed, Dr. Laktarnik seemed pleased with the way my finger was healing, though it still looked pretty gross to me. The scar was still a raw plum color.

"This looks good. I can see you've been staying away from that vampire and taking my herbs. I'll make you some more to take for the next two weeks. Unless . . ." He looked at me over his glasses. "Are you planning to see this vampire again?"

I looked away. "Yes."

He shook his head. "I'm not condoning this. This is a bad idea." He looked more closely at my face, trying to discern more about the situation. "But I know these things can happen—they don't happen often, but when they do . . . You'll have to make a hard decision before long, young lady."

"I—"

"No, don't tell me." He held up his hands. "If you tell me, I'm obligated to take action."

What the hell did that mean? I knew there were slayers out there, but these days, vampires mostly behaved themselves—forensic science forced them to—so naturally vampire killers were few and far between. Besides, so many slayers wound up being seduced by the other side that most vampires I knew paid them no mind.

I had never met one before. And not that I thought all slayers would look like Sarah Michelle Gellar, but I didn't expect them to be little old men from Brooklyn, either.

He told me, "Until you make this decision, this bleeding will get worse before it gets better. His attraction to you is very strong already, and as it gets stronger you'll be at a higher risk. You will eventually hemorrhage and bleed to death. I will give you more herbs, but that will be only a temporary solution."

Which meant I'd have to take action on my decision in LA. If what the doctor said was true, there was no way I could spend an entire weekend with him and live.

I talked to Johnny on the phone every morning and night. We were like those pathetic couples who make everyone nauseous. True to my word to Lola, I hadn't talked to him about my decision. On one hand, I thought that I should tell him so he could get used to the idea, but on the other, I thought that was something best done in person. He had to know it was coming, though. After I offered him that little mixed drink, he'd have to be totally clueless to miss my intentions.

Pro: spend eternity with Johnny. Con: never see my family, most of my friends, and most of humanity again; never have children; give up my career; give up my life as I knew it, never walk in the daylight; never have a normal life; oh yeah, and I'd have to eat people.

It's not like I wanted to be a vampire; I just wanted to be with Johnny, and this was the only way.

Still, sometimes I worried that was my humanity that attracted my human smell that turned him on, my human flaws he found endearing. What if I was a disappointment to him after being changed? I knew I was just being insecure, but I worried about it nonetheless.

Autumn is one of our busiest times of the year. I had a lot of big fall books (all releasing in time for the Halloween season, naturally), I had countless authors going to various conventions, and I had to attend several trade shows around the country. One good thing that came out of this was that I was able to sneak in a dinner with Johnny while I was attending the Great Lakes Bookseller Association show in Ohio.

It was a weird, disjointed date. He rushed in from Louisville an hour before, and I was dog tired from working Friday straight through to Sunday. I had been up since five, my convention suit was now a wrinkled mess, I had blisters the size of quarters on both heels, and I had just taken a double dose of Dr. Laktarnik's herbs, so I was a little nauseous.

I walked into the restaurant and saw him seated at the table. He looked so good. He was wearing his usual leather and silk, and I was sure he did it just to annoy me.

He was very stiff. He stood up, lightly kissed my cheek, and we immediately began looking at the menus. This was our first time seeing each other after the incident at Harry's, and we seemed to be afraid of both physical contact and eye contact. We must have looked like we were strangers.

"How was the trade show?"

"It was okay. All my authors were human this time, but they still kept me out all night drinking. I swear I haven't slept or been sober since Thursday. How's the tour so far?"

He regaled me with some stories about the fans on tour, the media escorts, and the media bookings. One reporter from Birmingham had insisted on photographing Bella in a coffin for an article, Bella was a sport and did it. A morning show in Nashville insisted on playing "Monster Mash" as a lead-in to their interview. And one radio host in Baltimore gave away plastic fangs at their live broadcast from Bella's book signing.

In turn, I caught him up on Lola's latest escapades. She'd recently challenged a female from Max's old pack who had been sniffing around him lately, and my girl totally kicked the other female's furry ass.

We were both being cautious and didn't get into anything heavy. Since we'd talked on the phone every day, we wound up repeating ourselves. By the time the check came, we seemed to have run out of things to say.

The words on the top of my mind were out of the question: *I love you. Take me. Change me. I need to be with you forever.* I had decided over dinner that I would wait; it would be weird to start that conversation on a four-hour visit, then fly home as if nothing had ever happened. That wouldn't really be healthy for either of us.

As soon as the waitress left with the check, Johnny said, "Well, that was the worst dinner conversation I've ever had. How about you?"

I laughed. "Yeah, that was pretty lame. Want to start over?"

"Yeah, let's take a walk."

We left the restaurant and walked down the block. He held my hand tentatively. My right arm was still tender, so he was extra gentle.

I tried to start a better dialogue. "So, how are you getting back to the bus tonight?"

"I rented a car. But I have to tell you, I'm getting damn of tired of that bus."

I raised one eyebrow. "Is that your attempt at a subtle hint? Am I supposed to invite you back to my hotel room?"

He laughed. Okay, we were finally loosening up a little. "No, I don't think that would be such a good idea. You're looking way too hot for me to be able to hold back."

I threw back my head and laughed at that one. "Come on, Johnny, I look like death warmed over."

"As luck would have it, that's exactly my type." He gave me that wicked grin.

"Freak."

My hotel was just across the street. When he led me around the corner, though I went along willingly. He guided me into an alley. I wasn't afraid, but I was nervous.

He backed me into a doorway in the darkened alley. "I'm sorry, Gia. I'm trying to be good, but I can't do it anymore. I've got to touch you." He put his hand behind my head, stroking my hair, and looked down into my shadowy face. He exhaled a little sigh at the contact. It felt so good to have his hands on my skin again.

"Don't be sorry. I was beginning to think I had lost my touch." I relaxed my head into his hand.

He brought a thumb around to stroke my jaw. It was very dark, but what light there was picked up his teeth when he gave me my favorite little smile. "No, you're doing just fine. But last time, I was afraid that I wouldn't be able to stop." I'm not sure if I want to stop now, but . . ."

He pressed against me and I knew exactly what he meant. I couldn't bear to be away from him, either. I couldn't seem to get close enough and I leaned into him. He was strong, hard, and unyielding, and I was sure it wasn't just his cold skin that was making me shiver.

He moved his thumb up to my lips and parted them. I opened my mouth just a little and let him in. I bit down gently on the skin and with my tongue, I caressed the place where the flesh met the nail. He didn't feel or taste like I expected. He was salty and cool and firm, not icy cold and rigid. He sighed and I took it as encouragement. It may have been a long time since he'd been a mortal man, but I wanted him to feel human tonight. I closed my lips around his thumb and sucked—gently at first, then harder.

He opened his mouth, probably to stop me, but only a squeaky noise came out. He breathed in and pulled his hand away with some effort. He hugged me to him then, but his fists were clenched with an obvious effort to control himself.

While he did that, I tried not to hyperventilate. Okay, so I wasn't telling him about my plans until we were in LA. But if he didn't get the message loud and clear now, then he just wasn't trying.

I finally felt him relax against me. One arm worked its way under my jacket and the other tilted my head into the crook of his neck. Even in my heels, I was still several inches shorter.

"May I kiss you goodnight, if I promise it won't be on the lips?"

"Where did you have in mind?" I winked, knowing he could see it in the dark.

"How about here?" He kissed my forehead.

"You know, I think I'd prefer the lips."

He grinned lasciviously. "Playing dangerously, I see."

I was smiling, too, but licking my lips in anticipation.

"Okay." He seemed to brace himself. "Ready?"

"Mm-hm."

He leaned in and pressed his lips to mine. My heart tried to make its way into my throat, but he quickly pulled away. I was shaking. I was sweating. I was drooling. I had often wondered how it would feel when he actually kissed me properly, and I was positively addled by it. I didn't have a functional brain cell in my head. What I did have was a growing stinging sensation in my heels. My blisters were beginning to bleed. I had to stop this.

"Hey, Johnny."

"Yeah?"

"You'd better go." I didn't want to leave, but I didn't trust myself to stay, either.

I left him in the doorway to watch me as I crossed the street to my hotel. And yeah, shook my ass all the way.

That Monday afternoon, Bella called me from the road with more information about my new project.

"He likes east coast cities and often goes by the name of Daniel," she told me, "but I've also heard him called Donnie and David. He usually sticks to D names."

So I just had to find a vampire with a D name. Piece of cake.

She e-mailed me a composite sketch. Like most vampires I knew, he was very attractive. I wondered if vampires selected only beautiful people to change, or if people became more beautiful after their change. Maybe they evolved from normal-looking humans into a macabre lure to their prey.

Daniel had jet-black hair and blue eyes—black Irish. She'd heard he was last seen in New York a few months ago, and that he had a taste for low-rent prostitutes. That actually gave me a great start. I had an underworld contact at a strip club in

Long Island City, where the activities extended way beyond lap dances, and "low rent" was an understatement.

I asked if I could bring Lola in on this project since she had certain abilities that I didn't: better hearing, better sight, sharp teeth, claws, etc. Bella said that she'd rather I didn't right now, though she might change her mind down the road. She really wanted this to be kept quiet. Fine. I called my guy at the strip club as soon as I hung up with Bella.

I took the N train to Queens after work to meet with Felix, a Mexican/Native American vampire who furnished "dates" for some of my vampire authors. I just had to promise that the ladies would be back at work the next day, albeit a pint or two low. Felix owned a sleazy nudie bar in Long Island City called Tail—how very subtle—where all the girls had questionable reputations, conspicuous bruising, and usually a few untreated diseases. They also were the type of person society wouldn't look too hard for if they went missing. Some were completely human, some were slaves, but they all put out for every kind of man. In addition, Felix had a few vampire strippers on staff. They helped with security and liked the easy feeding.

Felix was only about five feet six, but easily weighed 250 pounds—all pure muscle. He had long, thick black hair that he wore in a ponytail, and his flawless skin was the color of honeyed glass. He wore gold hoop earrings and had a golden razor-sharp right fang that he flashed intentionally.

At 6:30 on a Monday, there weren't a lot of drunken businessmen at the club. Without even asking my name, the bouncer led me straight to the back room. I guessed that very few women showed up in business suits here.

"Gia, it's good to see you again." He hugged me and kissed my cheek, and I restrained myself from recoiling. I'd have to shower ten times to get the feeling of Felix-the-vampire-pimp off of me. "Jesus, you smell like a goddamn pizzeria."

"So I ate a little garlic before coming here—a girl has to take some precautions." Especially since only Bella knew I was here, and she was miles away.

"Don't worry, honey; I don't bite the hand that feeds me. You give me too many clients." That golden fang was the antithesis of sexy.

The room was covered in tacky fake wood paneling from the 1970s and there were framed, signed pictures of half-naked B-grade porn stars on the walls.

I took a chair across from Felix's scarred wooden desk. "Thanks for meeting me, Felix." I gave him a friendly smile. "The club looks good."

"No, it doesn't, but thanks for lying." He winked at me. "So what brings you to the scummy side of town? You said you needed a favor."

I had carefully constructed a story that could closely fit with the truth—after all, Felix was a vampire and he'd know immediately if I was bullshitting him into giving up one of his paying customers. "I need help finding someone. Someone who appreciates your kind of lifestyle." I took the sketch of Daniel from my bag. "He kind of inadvertently did me a huge favor, and I owe him big-time." It was partially true. If it weren't for Daniel changing Bella, I never would have met Johnny. Naturally I left out the fact that Daniel was a brutal, sadistic, murdering bastard, but that was unnecessary, being that brutal, sadistic, murdering bastards were mostly whom Felix associated with.

Felix took the sketch from me and recognition immediately flashed in his eyes. "What's in it for me?"

"You know him, don't you?"

"Answer my question, Gia." His voice took on a hard edge.

I fought the terror that threatened to shatter my composure —I did *not* want him to smell fear on me—and handed him an envelope. It contained ten tickets to a concert by the Caged Animals, a very popular band headed by one of my werewolf authors. I'd called in few favors and had his assistant messenger over the tickets to me earlier that afternoon. The band was playing Madison Square Garden and the show had been sold out for months. The tickets could fetch an easy twenty thousand if sold separately.

Felix looked at them. "Front row. Nice."

"So do you know this guy?" I gestured toward the sketch of Daniel.

"Yeah, but you're not telling me the whole truth, and I'm not sure I want to give you the whole story on him. He's a pretty powerful member of my community and we do business from time to time."

"What else do you want, Felix?"

He leaned in toward me. "Your boyfriend killed one of my best customers." Clearly *some* news traveled between overlapping vampire circles.

"He's not my boyfriend." I crossed my arms in front of my chest.

"That's not what I hear." He leered at me. "I hear you got Johnny-boy totally whipped. Stringing him along like a fuckin' tease." When you gonna let him get a taste of that?" He motioned toward my chest—a very classy guy. "I hear you're being downright cruel to the motherfucker."

"Well, you heard wrong." I tried to look bored. "And consider your source."

"Suit yourself." He played with one of his gaudy gold rings. "Either way, I'd say I'm short about twenty-five grand as a result of Jonathan's little jealous tantrum."

I had no doubt that Billy was a customer of his, but hardly

one of his best, and I was even more sure that his strippers didn't cost enough to rack up that kind of tab. Still, I went into my purse. I had told Bella that it would most likely come down to cold hard cash and she'd supplied it. I counted out ten thousand dollars. "This is all I have on me. I can get another ten tomorrow." He was about to argue. "Come on, Felix, we both know Billy was a cheap bastard—he never would have dropped ten grand in a whole year. And let's not forget that I give you a shitload of business."

Felix grinned. He knew I was right. "Okay." He sat back and looked again at the sketch. "He goes by Dante these days, and he's up in Federal Hill—you know, the mob up in Providence?" I nodded. "He used to come to me when he was in New York, but he's not as conscientious as you are. I never get any of my girls back when he's done with them." He folded up the paper and handed it back to me, looking serious for a change. "Gia, I like you. You shouldn't fuck with this guy. He'll eat you alive."

"Thanks for the advice. A messenger will bring by your money tomorrow." I got up and put my bag over my shoulder.

"Can I buy you a drink before you go? You can trust me not to slip you any rophies." He gave me a sleazy smile.

"Since when do you have to resort to drugs?" I gave him a wiseass grin. "You losing your touch, Felix?"

He laughed heartily and I restrained myself from visibly recoiling at the sight of that gold fang. "Damn, you're one fucked-up human. You must be driving Jonathan crazy."

Oh, I think that feeling was mutual.

9

Unless That's Another One of Your Freaky Turn-ons

The next Friday was awful. I had three awful meetings, I had to give my awful assistant her awful performance review, and I had awful early-morning media the next morning—yes, I had to work on a weekend.

Sometimes I hated my job.

The meetings were unproductive, my assistant cried when I put her on probation, and I was positive my client—a voodoo priestess who specialized in love spells—would get bumped from the morning show the second we walked into the green room. I wouldn't want to trade places with that producer after he canceled this woman's segment. Just because she specialized in love spells didn't mean she didn't know a few wicked

Santerian coconut and snakeroot curses that would cause him some serious health problems.

To top it all off, I had the start of a migraine and cramps that had to be the worst in recorded history.

Earlier that week, I'd called Bella and filled her in on what I had learned about Daniel/Dante and told her to wire me ten thousand dollars. She was very pleased to find out that I had so much information so fast, and that I'd be calling two of my New England underworld clients next week to find out more.

Unable to look at my office walls a second longer, I left at five for a change. I didn't know what I wanted more: chocolate chip mint ice cream or red wine. Maybe both. I took my call sheets with me—I'd rather work from home with a heating pad on my lap.

Bella was in Denver today and I had a good media escort in that city, so I didn't worry about her event there. Lola's new book, *Are You Howling at Me?*, wasn't coming out until January, but I just got in the advance reading copies and wanted to pitch to the long-lead magazines soon. A car service had to be arranged for tomorrow morning to pick up my voodoo author at five a.m. for her 7:15 interview on *Good Morning Saturday*—ugh, I hated the hosts of that show. All stuff I could do from home.

Stopping off on the way, I bought some wine, Tylenol, and ordered a hamburger to go from the diner (one had to replenish one's iron at this time of the month). Goth chick was at the counter again—reading a horror novel. I also accidentally ordered a giant piece of chocolate cake to go with it.

At home, I kicked off my heels and switched on my computer. My phone immediately started ringing. It was Lola, excited because she'd be spending the moonrise with Max again. I asked her to call me tomorrow when she recovered to check in, then hung up.

I was just not in the mood to talk. In fact, I wasn't in the mood to work, either. I made only the necessary phone calls and headed to the couch with my hamburger, bottle of wine, and cake.

If it weren't for my nightly calls from Johnny, I would have turned my phone off. The downside of that was that I answered it when my mother called. She lived in the Catskill Mountains, not too far from Lola. "Hi, Mom. What are you doing?"

"Just driving home from the mall; how are you, dear?"

Let's see, I have a headache, I'm hungry, my food has gotten cold, I have terrible cramps, and I'm miserably lovesick over a vampire. Of course I replied, "I'm fine." I looked at the clock; it was after seven. "Mom, you should really try to get home earlier on full-moon nights. You know, all the drunk drivers come out with the full moon." Not to mention the local pack of werewolves.

She was dismissive. "Oh, Gia, you and your crackpot theories about the moon."

"Statistics show it, Mom. There are more accidents on nights when there's a full moon." And maulings by wild, bloodthirsty lycanthropes. "Just be careful."

We talked a few minutes more when my call waiting chimed in. It had to be Johnny. "Mom, I'm getting another call; I'll call you later. Say hi to Dad. Love you." I hit the flash button. "Hello?"

"Hey baby, what are you doing?"

"Trying to eat my dinner for the last hour. Do you mind if I chew while we talk? I'm starving." I was picking at my cake.

"No, go right ahead. What are we having?"

"Oh, it's a very balanced meal." Between bites I told him what was on my menu.

"Ugh, all at once."

"This from a man who feeds on homeless people?" Silence. I guessed I went too far again. "Hey, you there?"

"Yeah." He took in a deep breath. "I just put it together and realized why you're eating all that crap. And I'm trying to restrain myself."

"Johnny, you're disgusting, and I'm way too crampy and cranky for this kind of freaky phone sex, so you'll just have to use your imagination." I just hoped his bizarre power to make me bleed uncontrollably couldn't work over the phone.

"Done and done." He didn't sound done, but to his credit, he changed the subject. "Did you get the flowers?"

"Yes, they're beautiful." Johnny had been sending me flowers at the office, sometimes twice a week. It was a nice gesture, but totally unnecessary. "But you have got to cut this out. My office is beginning to smell like a funeral parlor—unless that's another one of your freaky turn-ons."

"Leave it to you to come up with something like that. How was your day?"

I started in bitchng about my day. He, in turn, bitched about the media escort I hired for Bella in St. Louis. Apparently a group of especially obsessed fans were following her tour around the country. Although most horror fans are harmless, we always had to watch out for the potential troublemakers. This group showed up in St. Louis and the stupid media escort let them talk her into allowing them into the bookstore's back room for a little personal chat. Johnny had been outside talking to the security detail, and came back to find these four obsessed fans entering the stockroom with the escort. Upon seeing Bella, the so-called fans launched into a religious rant about how she did the work of the devil and had to be destroyed before she could poison any more of the innocent. Jonathan quickly had the store's security team throw them out, since he was afraid he might accidentally kill one of them.

It sounded like he had his hands full. "Do you need me to hire more help? If you really need it, I can fly out to your next city after my morning media tomorrow."

"No, I can handle it. We're both just going to have to make it clear to these media escorts that they have to be more careful."

"I'll take care of it."

"Thanks. Now let's concentrate on getting you out to LA. It was great seeing you last week, but it was way too short."

For my visit, Jonathan booked us a suite at West, a trendy hotel in Westwood that welcomed vampires. One of the owners was a recent vampire himself, and it was a smart business idea since most vampires were decadently big spenders. At night, the lobby turned into a nightclub. Beautiful would-be actors and actresses and other attractive people from the industry mingled with high-end prostitutes and the heroin chic there, and it was practically room service for the vampire clientele.

Even though I hadn't told him yet that I was planning to let him change me, I took it as a good sign that he was on the same wavelength, booking just one room. I told Johnny I'd be getting in next Friday at 7:18 p.m., and we ended the call on that happy note.

10

Would You Offer Your Throat to the Wolf with the Red Roses?

The week before my flight to LA dragged on endlessly. I was nervous and jumpy. I must have broken six glasses and I kept forgetting where I left things. I accidentally booked one of my vampire clients on an eight a.m. flight instead of an eight p.m., not to mention several other screwups at the office. I couldn't eat a thing, either, but at least I'd look thin when I got to LA.

The good news was that I had made more progress on Bella's project. I talked to a witch from Newport, Rhode Island, a romance author who wrote *Saucy Sorcery*. She knew all about Daniel/Dante and informed me that he was known for his work in the human trade. He dealt primarily with strip clubs, prostitutes, and porn films, but the drug trade wasn't out of the question for him, either. He was currently MIA, but she seemed to remember someone saying he was planning to relocate to South Beach, Miami, shortly, that things in Providence were drying up for him. All vampires had to change cities every few years when the locals began noticing that they never aged. I was sure there were other reasons for his relocating, too—like suspicious piles of bodies left in his wake.

I got more information that week from a werewolf client, Brian, who lived in Plymouth, Massachusetts, just outside Myles Standish State Forest. He told me that those piles of bodies that Daniel left behind were legendary and not always composed of humans. Apparently Daniel enjoyed a challenge and often hunted werewolves and other vampires for sport. They put up a better fight than humans, given their heightened senses, strength, and speed. Several members of Brian's pack had been brutally murdered by this monster, who had a voracious appetite and always fed completely. With the exception of enslaving his strippers/whores/porn stars, he always killed for his food. Dante, was a fitting pseudonym, since he was responsible for his very own circle of hell.

I knew a lot of vampires in South Beach; the undead liked places with tourists and other transients. Maybe my next career would be as an underworld private detective—I was really good at this.

My boss, Lois, came into my office and closed the door the morning I was leaving for LA. That's never a good sign. I should have expected this, given the mistakes I was making at work. I was distracted and absentminded. I was paying way too much attention to Bella's project and not spending nearly enough time on my work.

"Gia, I know you're trying to wrap things up before your flight but do you have a minute?"

"Sure, what's up?" Besides the fact that I had screwed up a major television interview, mixed up travel plans between two rival necromancer authors, and forgot to get a major review copy mailing out? I was starting to act like my dingbat assistant.

"Nice flowers." She nodded toward the Wildcat Blood Ruby orchid Johnny had sent me on Monday.

I found them a disturbing choice. Not only because of the hit-you-over-the-head symbolism in the name, he wasn't letting me live down that comment about my office smelling like a funeral home—but the orchid also reminded me of *The Big Sleep*, when Philip Marlowe visits General Sternwood. Sternwood says he never much cared for orchids because although they seem beautiful, they released a strange odor and their petals felt like human flesh. Sound like someone I know?

"Are they from Jonathan?" she asked.

I never spoke about our relationship with her, and I always kept my distance from him whenever there were Speculation people around. Still, she wasn't stupid.

"Yes, Jonathan and Bella." Okay, Bella didn't sign the card and I'm sure she didn't share the sentiment of his message: *Sorry I suck. Love, Johnny*, but in the scheme of things, this little white lie was the least of my worries. Besides, it was totally believable. Authors often sent me gifts when a tour was going well, since you catch more publicists with honey than vinegar.

"Listen, Gia, I'm not sure I should be the one talking to you about this, but . . . Don't you think you're getting a little too close with these vampires? I don't have to tell you that they have certain powers that are hard to resist."

She was right; she didn't have to tell me.

"I mean, did you see that one at the Union Square book signing, that blond guy? He looked like trouble."

Somehow, I didn't think I'd alleviate her misgivings by telling her that Billy wasn't a problem anymore since our author's manager had put a wooden stake through his heart.

"Thanks, Lois, but I'm okay. It's just the flavor of the month. When this tour is over and Lola's book comes out, I'll be all about werewolves. I'm simply immersed in my work right now, and it's wearing me out. That's why I'm taking this little getaway."

She eyed my suitcase by the door. I hadn't told her where I was going, and I certainly wasn't going to now.

"Well, I'm glad you're getting a weekend away. I think you're right; this project is getting to you." She changed the subject. "So, you put your assistant on probation. How did she take it?"

"She cried."

We both laughed. There was no crying in publicity.

I left work early to catch my plane. I had a glass of wine at the airport and another on the flight, along with some of my special herbal tea from the good witch doctor. If things went as planned I wouldn't get much sleep once I reached LA, so I wanted to relax, read a book, and try to get in a nap. Too bad I had a chatty five-year-old on one side of me and an overly curious businessman on the other side. I was interrogated by the kid about the color of my nail polish and my earrings which was preferable to the businessman who wanted to know *everything* about being a publicist. When he found out I worked for Belladonna Nightshade, he may have actually squealed with excitement. She was his favorite author. When he took out his copy of her book to prove it to me, I put away the paperback I was trying to read, resigned to the fact that I would be answering questions about Bella for the rest of the trip. *More wine, please.*

My flight was delayed and it was sunset by the time I arrived. I called Johnny the minute the cab pulled out of LAX; he sounded really excited to see me.

"Damn, I thought you'd never get here! How was your flight?"

"Terrible. I'm starving. They don't serve food on these flights anymore."

"My poor baby. Do you want me to take you to dinner?"

I was thinking more along the lines of room service, but I didn't want to come off as a total hoochie-mama. "Maybe. Where should I meet you?"

"I'll meet you at the lobby bar. I'll be the guy with the fangs. Well, one of the guys with fangs—this place is crawling with vampires."

"Great, I'll see you there. I'll be the slut in the f-me boots." As we spoke, I was changing from my flats to my very high and very sexy new black boots that I had bought just for this weekend (I was already wearing the special new leopard underwear I bought for the occasion). Then I tried to repair some of my face in the backseat of the darkened cab. Nothing like a cross-country flight to age a person ten years—not to mention that I had been up since four a.m.

By the time my cab pulled up to the hotel, the nightclub was just starting to liven up. All the bellmen were tied up, so I had to take my luggage past the velvet rope to get to the check-in desk, which was somewhat surreal. I had them send my bag to Jonathan's room and slipped into the restroom for a final touch-up to my makeup in the better light. Since I was pale and drawn, I'd fit in with the undead clientele. I put on a little blush and lipstick and attacked my hair with a brush. After traveling three thousand miles, it now looked like a stringy spider's nest, so I twisted it up into a knot on top of my head. Being a neck man, he liked me better with my hair up.

I walked into the lounge and saw him immediately, standing at the end of the bar drinking bourbon. He was wearing black leather pants, a leather jacket, and that stupid black silk shirt. What was it with vampires and silk, anyway? Very pretentious. He had good color in his face, which also meant he had fed recently, so maybe we could talk for a whole five minutes before we started chewing on each other. His hair was different, too, longer and kind of ill-kempt, but he pulled it off. He looked so damn good.

Thanks to my very high-heeled boots, I managed to walk slowly—not run—to him. I'm sure I looked very suave as I concentrated on not falling and breaking my neck. We hugged and that familiar, delicious warmth spread through me. I had missed him so much I had nearly gotten used to the hole in my chest. I was only complete when I was in his arms.

He kissed my cheek, then nuzzled my hair, not rushing anything. He whispered in my ear how good it was to see me, even if I did smell like an airplane. I felt his voice move through my stomach, like he was feeding me each word. I was so far gone—there was no way I was going to last a whole five minutes.

"You look beautiful."

I pretended to fluff my nonexistent curls. "I'll bet you say that to all the girls." And there were quite a few gorgeous ladies in the immediate vicinity. I was sure he had no trouble finding his meals in a place like this. Was I jealous already?

"Listen, I'll go get us a bed and be right back. Order yourself a drink and charge it to our room."

Don't get any ideas. Let me explain that the bar at West had these seating areas with beds and chaise-loungey things hidden behind screens and drapes, making cozy little alcoves for making out, feeding, or both. Obviously designed by the owning and operating vampire.

I stood at the bar and waited for my bartender/actress to notice me. Since I didn't look very industry, she was ignoring me. A guy who looked like Scott Weiland came up beside me and she immediately came over. He ordered a scotch and offered to buy me one. I smiled back politely but refused. "Thank you, but I'll have to pass. I'm trying to limit my dependence on foreign whiskey." I ordered a Maker's Mark.

The Scott Weiland look-alike leaned in close to my ear to speak over the noise. "Did you know your nose is bleeding?"

I reached up to touch it and my fingers came away bloody. I grabbed my cocktail napkin and held it to my face. "Thanks." No wonder the bartender was keeping her distance.

"You know, I could get you better shit that won't tear up your nose like that."

He thought I was a cokehead? Somehow the fact that this scenario was better than the truth didn't disturb me. I had clearly become jaded.

And I didn't have to turn around to know Johnny was there; how else could this have happened?

"Is everything okay?" He now stood protectively over me, hand on my shoulder. The Weiland-ish drug dealer guy was just being what he was and didn't deserve Johnny's jealousy, so I saved his life.

"Yeah, he was just helping me with this nosebleed." Johnny looked at me and got a little pale (well, paler). "Do you want to go sit down? That looks pretty bad."

It was pretty bad. I had already gone through three napkins. Remembering what the witch doctor had said, I realized that I should tend to this immediately. "Let's go up to our room. This won't stop anytime soon."

The minute we got to his suite I started rummaging through my purse, looking for the magic potion from my friendly neighborhood witch doctor. "Be a sweetheart and make me some boiling water in that coffeemaker, will you?" He quickly went to the bar and started to fill the coffeepot, looking concerned by the sight of so much blood. Then he went into the bathroom and got me the box of tissues since I was bleeding faster now. As we waited for the water to boil, he took the chair across from me, completely rigid, with clenched fists. I suppose you've reached a new level of sexy when your man is totally turned on by your nosebleed.

I looked at him across the room. It was time. "Well, I was hoping to tell you this over dinner, but I've been to my new doctor again, and you should know that this kind of thing will be happening more frequently." I gestured to my pile of bloody tissues. "It seems that your love brings out the B positive in me." I explained that it all started with the inability of my cuts and bruises to heal. "So apparently we've graduated from you not allowing my wounds to heal, to making me spontaneously bleed at the very sight of you. You must really be turning on the charm tonight. He said it would only get worse."

Johnny listened with his head in his hands, and when he looked up, he looked pained. I expected him to say something like, What do we do now? And then I'd explain that I was ready to embark on the great adventure that would become our eternal love affair—or something sappy like that.

"I'm going to miss you so much," he said.

What? I couldn't believe what I was hearing. "Just you wait a second. That's *not* the only option here," I snapped.

"Well, then, what are we supposed to do?" He got up and began pacing, running his fingers through his hair. "Change you here and now while you're hemorrhaging, and call it a day?"

"Well, that's actually what I wanted to talk to you about. I've been doing a lot of thinking, and—"

"No fucking way! Gia, do you know what you're asking for? Look at yourself. You're *so* not ready for that!" he yelled. "Think about it. It doesn't seem like a particularly good idea right now."

I yelled right back. "I've been dealing with every conceivable type of monster for ten years now. I have a Rolodex full of suppliers for meals ranging from livestock to strippers. Do you think I'm a complete idiot and have no idea how you spend your time? You must think I'm a total moron." Some of my self-righteous venom was lost through the wad of tissues, unfortunately. "Where did you think this relationship was going? Did you expect us just to flirt like this until you got tired of me or I got too old?" I stormed over to the bar. "Is that damn water hot yet?"

I hurriedly made my tea and he began to pace like a caged animal. Jeez, he was as bad as Lola when she was pissed off, and she was part wolf. I drank my tea too fast and too hot and burned my tongue, which pissed me off even more.

He fell back into his chair and looked at me while I gingerly tapped at my nose with my hand. It had stopped bleeding already. Maybe it was the tea, or maybe he wasn't turning on that charm anymore. In fact, he was giving me a dirty look.

"Well?" I asked in an almost normal voice, though I was shaking from our fight.

"Well what? You think you can just come in here, lay this shit on me about bleeding and changing, and I'm supposed to be happy about it and dive right in?"

Actually, that's exactly what I thought. I'd been dropping hints for ages hoping he'd ask me, but I guess I was a hopeless romantic—that is, if you think giving up your entire life for a guy is romantic.

"I have a rental car. I'll drive you to LAX; I'm sure there's a red-eye you can take back to New York."

"You're kicking me out?" I couldn't believe my ears.

"You can't stay here. You'll . . . you'll . . ." His normally deep voice was now a raspy whisper. "You'll bleed to death if you stay, and I think we need as much distance between us as possible now." He stood up and got his keys. "I'll drive around and meet you out front."

Just like that, he walked out. I'd flown across the country to see him and offer him my life, and this is what I got? I offered my friggin' throat to the friggin' wolf with the friggin' red roses, and this is what happens? That was *not* the way it was supposed to go. What were all those phone calls about? Just what did he think would happen if I came out here? Did he really think we could continue like this and not go on to the next level? I grabbed my suitcase and barreled out of the room.

I had to walk through the lobby nightclub to get outside. On autopilot, I didn't really take in any of the scene around me. That was a big mistake: in a room teeming with vampires, I smelled like fresh blood and I was dressed like I was asking for it. This was not the wisest thing to do.

I heard a moan before her hand shot out from behind a curtain and pulled me onto a chaise. Her grip was like iron and she was impossible to fight, but I gave it my best shot. She turned my wrist inward and sank her teeth into it.

The feeling was overwhelming and scary as hell. It was as if I soared out of my body and hovered over us. She was pulling hard on my wrist, sucking and grunting like an animal, but not getting much satisfaction. I was impressed to see myself still fighting to keep my throat away from her.

Then I saw Johnny. He must have come looking for me when I took so long to come outside. Or maybe he just now remembered that he'd sent his bloody girlfriend alone into a room full of vampires.

He grabbed her by the hair and wrenched her from my wrist, then twisted her head so that her neck broke with a sickening sound. She reached up and righted it, but there seemed to be too much skin—it was a gruesome image.

"Come on. She'll be well enough to tell her friends in a few minutes." He grabbed my unbitten arm and pulled me and my suitcase from the alcove.

He opened the car door, threw my bag into the backseat, and tucked me into the passenger's side. He ran around to get in his side and tore off toward the airport. "How do you feel?"

How did I feel? Everything had happened so fast, I didn't even have time to take stock of my feelings. I looked down at my wrist. It was still pink, but there wasn't a mark on it. I felt dizzy and a little sick. "I feel like I've got a hangover."

"That's good. If you felt good, it may have been too late. It was lucky she only got your wrist."

He kept his eyes on the road, his jaw set in a hard line. Was this how he looked when he killed Billy? I had just seen him break a woman's neck and calmly walk away. I realized then that I hardly knew this side of him, that I had never seen him angry.

"I can't believe how hard you fought her. You're stronger than I thought," he said.

Okay, I know he was talking about little ol' human me versus the superhuman undead bitch from hell, but I was still kind of offended by that. "Luckily I had plenty of adrenaline from being totally pissed at you. Unlike you, the world's biggest tease, I knew what I wanted, and I wanted it tonight. And I didn't want to let *her* take it from me."

Now that the initial shock of being attacked was over, I a) realized just how close I could have come to dying, b) realized just how close I could have come to being changed by a complete stranger, and c) remembered that I had just received the ultimate rejection from the man who was supposed to love me.

"Just what is that supposed to mean? Listen, Gia, I don't know where you're going with this, but . . ."

That was it; we were almost at the airport and I was not going to let him drop me off like this and not know how much of an asshole he was. "No, *you* listen. You don't know where I'm going with this? What are you, fucking clueless? Just what did you think I came out here for? We can't keep sucking on each other's fingers forever. Eventually I would like to tongue-kiss you, you know. Not to mention that if you don't do something about committing to a more permanent relationship with me, I'm going to bleed to death. How's that? Did I miss anything?"

He had pulled up to the unloading zone and was staring at me with an indiscernible look on his face. He opened his mouth to say something, but I was worked up into way too much of a lather to back down now.

"You know, I was prepared to give up everything for you. *Everything!* And you get cold feet over a freakin' nosebleed? I managed to find the only vampire in the world who gets squeamish at the sight of blood." I met his eyes one last time. "I thought you loved me enough."

I got out of the car and angrily wrenched my suitcase from the backseat, managing to slam it against my leg, bruising the hell out of it. "Fuck!" I wasn't good at dramatic exits.

I threw a parting remark over my shoulder, so he couldn't see the look of frustration and sadness on my face. "It was nice knowing you."

I slammed the door and didn't look back.

11

I've Used Up All My Sick Days,
So I'm Calling In Dead

The airport personnel didn't even bat an eye when I limped up to the counter and asked to buy a last-minute ticket for the 11:20 red-eye to New York. I cried and ground my teeth all the way home.

This was so f-ed up! Not only was I just bitten by a complete stranger after ten years of avoiding that danger, but I was also just dumped—and not only by the love of my life, but the man I still had to work with. I had a conference call on Monday with Jonathan, Bella, her agent, and the publisher of Speculation, so I'd be talking with him again—like it or not—within seventy-two hours. This really sucked.

I needed to talk to Lola. I called her when I landed, and

told her to stop having sex for a few hours and meet me at my apartment.

I then drank martinis and yelled things at Lola. She did the good girlfriend thing and nodded noncommittally to everything I said. She asked if I wanted to see Dr. Laktarnik about the bite, but I said I was fine, though I promised to call him if I felt any effects. She left Sunday morning. I couldn't expect even my best friend in the whole world to put up with my psychotic ratings forever.

I'm not sure if it was the martinis or sheer adrenaline that kept me from feeling sick, but by Sunday night I was in bad shape. I knew from my vampire friends that most people's reactions to a bite only lasted twelve to twenty-four hours. Something was wrong. I had all the symptoms of a stomach flu, but they didn't hit me until that night. I called Dr. Laktarnik.

He asked a few questions: where the bite was, how quickly it healed, etc. He told me to treat it like a flu, that the toxins should work their way out of my system by the end of the week. He said that the herbs I took to stop the bleeding had prevented her from getting too much of my blood, but also made my reaction a little more intense. He also told me I did a good thing by abandoning my plans to change. Like that was my idea. So on top of feeling incredibly sorry for myself, I was going to be sick for a week, but at least a crazy old warlock/vampire killer from Brooklyn thought I was being a good girl.

I made myself some dry toast. How could things possibly get any worse?

I didn't have to wait long: I woke up Monday morning feeling like someone had run over my head with a truck. I had the vampire flu *and* a hangover. I threw up, showered, dressed, and dragged my sorry ass to work.

I considered calling in to my boss and saying "I've used up

all my sick days, so I'm calling in dead," since I was sure death couldn't hurt this much.

On top of all my other symptoms, the sunlight hurt my skin and burned my eyes. The good doctor had neglected to fill me in on that little side effect. I put on my sunglasses and hailed a cab; there was no way in hell I was getting on a subway in this condition.

I showed up late and skulked past the editorial assistants. They all giggled behind their cubicles—guess who's got a hangover? My assistant, of course, wasn't at her desk. The message light on my phone was on, and I wondered if she was just late or sick. I was glad that I'd managed to come in to work after coming within an inch of my life, when my assistant couldn't manage to set her alarm clock.

My butt had barely hit my chair when my boss came into my office with a thick sheaf of paper in her hands. "Hungover, are we?"

I groaned. "You don't want to know."

"Well, at least you let off some steam this weekend." I let her think I had had too much fun with the girls. "You look like death warmed over, but I'm glad you let loose. I'm sure that when you sober up, you'll feel like a new woman."

Death warmed over, eh? Now where had I heard that before?

She dropped the papers on my desk. "I'll need you to attend this proposal meeting this afternoon after our conference call. It's about giant spiders from outer space who make crop circles in Nebraska."

"Spiders from Mars? It sounds like somebody listened to too much David Bowie in his formative years."

She left and I looked at the proposal. I'd been thinking of going home after the conference call this afternoon, but I wasn't going to be cut any slack. No rest for the wicked, I suppose.

The first of my five messages was my assistant calling in sick—big surprise. Then Lola checking in on me; a horror magazine that wanted to do a Q and A with Lola for *Are You Howling at Me?*; a reporter at the *Oregonian* requesting an interview with Bella when she was in town later this week; and Brian, my Massachusetts werewolf contact, left word that Dante/Daniel had struck his den and now there were only two left in his pack. This vampire was more of an animal than the werewolves he hunted. How the hell had Bella escaped him the first time, and why in heaven's name did she want to find him again?

There was not a word from Jonathan. I had thought, well, hoped, that maybe he hadn't called my cell or home phone because he was too embarrassed and ashamed to talk to me live, but that he'd surely leave me a message at work telling me how right I was, and how wrong and sorry he was. And then maybe he'd pass me a note in gym class: *If you like me, check this box.* I think I may have completely regressed to thirteen years old. It was time for some coffee—strong and bitter, like me.

Lois and I went into the publisher's office after lunch for our conference call. I couldn't find an excuse to keep wearing my sunglasses, so I took out my contacts and put on my regular glasses. I hoped the reflective glare from the overhead lights would disguise my red-rimmed eyes and draw attention away from my sallow cheeks.

I needn't have worried. Lois assumed I was still hungover, and George, the publisher, who resembled an older version of Jeff Goldblum's character from *Jurassic Park*, was busy walking around the room gesticulating and talking excitedly about the *Honor of Lady Von Rastenbourg* being number one on the *Wall Street Journal* bestseller list and dropping down to number three on the *New York Times* bestseller list this week.

I just kept agreeing with him. Yes, it was an absolute travesty. Now if only he'd stop ranting so loudly.

The call came through the speakerphone right on time, and lucky me, everyone but the vampires was overcompensating for technology and yelling into the phone. For crying out loud, people, it's not two cans and a string! Lois, the loudest of the group, ran the meeting.

The call was unbearable. It was an ass-kissing festival and nothing was getting accomplished. Or maybe I was just bitter because Jonathan addressed everyone on the call except me. Oh, he referred to me from time to time. "Giovanna has done a good job at getting Bella on the radio as a vampire expert, so I was thinking about branding her and pitching her for a program on satellite radio. Sort of an Art Bell kind of program."

I chimed in. "That's a great idea, Jonathan, but we have to be sure she can broadcast from any location, since Bella likes to travel and there are her book tours to think of, too. Perhaps we can try it as a once-a-week program to start with. Bella? I think it would work really well if you were able to have guests call in. I could supply you with tons of other authors, as well as other experts in the field, and maybe some controversial people with opposing views. Jonathan, why don't you call me later and we'll come up with a treatment."

There, I gave him a legitimate reason to call me later and forced him to address me here and now.

He said, "Bella, let's flesh this out a little more before Giovanna gets working on a pitch."

Son of a bitch! What a weasel. Okay, I could handle this.

"Yes, call me when you two have it worked out." Even to my own supercritical ears, I sounded incredibly professional. I was über-publicist in spite of him . . . he just better watch out when I became über-bitch.

Bella kept quiet the whole time. I'm sure she knew something was going on between us, but kept out of it.

The call wrapped up ten minutes later, and I had to run to the *Spiders from Mars* proposal meeting. At least this guy was just full of crap and not an actual alien. I was getting really tired of my clients writing from experience.

And speaking of writing from experience, I had to call Brian back and find out the details about what Daniel had done.

He didn't pick up until the fourth ring.

"Hey, it's Gia, how're you feeling?"

"Hey, Gia, thanks for calling."

"You sound like shit."

"Thanks, I feel that way, too." He drew in a ragged breath, audibly shaken. "Listen, maybe it was your call about this bastard, but something told me to sleep with one eye open. It's the only reason I got out of there. I'm just pissed I could only get one of the others out with me."

He sounded on the verge of tears—not typical for this guy. "What happened?"

"We had just come back from a run. It was maybe minutes before dawn and you know that we sleep hard when we're changing back. But I was thinking about our conversation and I just couldn't sleep. I was anxious and I couldn't find a comfortable position. Eventually the others got pissed and started biting me to tell me the get the fuck off of the pile." Werewolves often slept in great heaps in their den after a hard run. Apparently the warmth helped their muscles in the transition back to their human form. "I moved over to a corner and Emma, my female, came with me. I may be crazy, but Gia, I can swear the sun had already risen when I heard the cries. He came in and took on five of them at once. Granted, we were sleeping, but five of them? It was vicious. I wasn't even fully back to human form, but I grabbed Emma and hightailed it out of there during the chaos. If it was possible, I heard him shudder over the phone. "Gia, he's the f-ing strongest thing I've ever seen."

I couldn't help but wonder, if my poking around have triggered this attack? It didn't make sense, but somehow I felt responsible. I told Brian that I'd work on getting him and Emma a safe place in New York. I'd have to call Lola and ask for her advice, which would be tricky, since I hadn't told Lola anything about this project. Note to self: get the hell off this project. But there was one more thing I could check before quitting, and as dangerous as this was, I hated to leave anything unfinished. I made a little deal with myself: after I called this one last lead, I'd drop the whole thing. Though I knew that dropping it wouldn't stop someone like Daniel if he had any idea I was behind this investigation.

12

Dignity Was Overrated

Okay, so I know I seem bitter and vindictive lately, but if I were morose and mopey, I'd be eating way too much dark chocolate and drinking way too much vodka. This way I went running every day, threw myself into my work, dated a lot, *and* ate way too much dark chocolate and drank way too much vodka. I was getting out more, kicking some major butt at the office, and getting some exercise to boot, so bitter and vindictive seemed like a better plan to me.

My mom was thrilled that I was dating again. I'd never told her about Jonathan, but she figured I was in some relationship with a guy I didn't want to her to meet—I mean, come on, moms know these things.

Most of the guys I met were total losers. Lois set me up on a date with a guy she had met at an awards banquet, some trust-fund baby who said he loved music, books, and the theater. I asked if he liked Audioslave and he told me that he had never read it. So, no, it wasn't kismet.

I also double-dated with Lola and Max from time to time. Nothing like having built-in security if my date went badly.

Like a good friend, Lola never said anything stupid like "stop comparing every guy to Jonathan," even though it was clear that this was exactly what I was doing. But I was such a delightful human being these days, these guys rarely called me for a second date anyway. If they did, I just pretended that I'd had a wonderful time and suggested a more serious relationship. You know that joke: How does a single woman in New York get rid of cockroaches? She asks them for a commitment. Worked like a charm.

This year Halloween fell on a Thursday. As you can well imagine, Halloween was a big deal at Speculation. Our parties were legendary and costumes in the office were mandatory. Authors and agents were invited and the shindig became a bigger deal every year. Even my new assistant Ian (luckily, my lame-ass assistant wound up quitting before I had to fire her) was dressed up. I made the mistake of commenting on his Obi-Wan costume.

"I'm not Obi-Wan," he said indignantly. "I'm Anakin Skywalker." He rolled his eyes. "There's nothing scary about Obi-Wan." He had a good point there. He'd fit in just fine here at Speculation.

Since I was acting like a total slut lately, I let my costume reflect it. And I have to say, I really outdid myself this year. I wore those very hot black f-me boots that I had bought for my trip to LA (and they must have worked, since I totally got f-ed on that trip), white fishnets, a white gauzy short skirt, a white bustier, a black leather jacket, and fairy wings. I topped it off with all my heavy-metal jewelry from my high school days—I got a little nostalgic for my friend Billy—and I fashioned a wand with a partially blackened tooth at the end. I was the rotten tooth fairy. Cool, right?

Our publisher tended to put a lot of pressure on the publicity department at parties. After all, it was our job to be charming and witty and outgoing. Bella and Jonathan were, thankfully, not in attendance. I moved through the crowd for a good half hour, then slipped off to the bar to drink beer with Lola, who was dressed up as a sheep (very cute). I had a good time in spite of myself, and a few beers later, Lola and I were dancing with Kenny and Larry from the ad/promo department.

After the party wrapped up, Lola and I met up with two of our human friends, Karen and Elena, and headed out to karaoke. I got very drunk and by the end of the night did a rousing rendition of "Jambalaya" by Hank Williams and fell off the stage. Soon after which, Lola put me into a cab.

I got home about four a.m. and headed for the shower. I stripped, checked out the new bruises on my knees from the fall, and washed the cigarette smoke out of my hair. Yes, I had started smoking again, too, but I figured the running every morning canceled that out. As I was soaping up, trying to stand upright, and singing to myself, I had a weird feeling I was being watched.

I grabbed a towel and jerked open my shower curtain, but no one was there. Spooky.

I called out. No response.

My first thought was that it was Johnny, but even in my inebriated state, I realized it couldn't have been him. For one thing, he wasn't in town and I would have heard about it if he was; two, I wasn't uncontrollably bleeding anywhere; and three, believe it or not, that thing about vampires entering a person's home only when invited was true. So I was most likely just having a booze-induced panic attack brought on my wishful thinking—I still missed him all the time, especially when I was drunk. Regardless, I was freaked out.

My next thought was of Daniel. Could he have learned that I was looking for him? The same invitation-only rule would have applied to Daniel, but Brian had told me that the sun was up when Daniel attacked his den. Could other rules be broken, too?

I put the chain on my door and then felt rather silly. Like a chain would keep out monsters? Immediately sober, I went into the bedroom, but had a feeling I'd get no sleep.

I lay there and thought about what I was up to while I was trying to control my terrible case of the bed-spins. My search for Daniel was just as destructive as my amoral behavior. I knew that neither could go on much longer. I was searching for something that would distract me from the pain, and as a result, I self-inflicted different painful situations.

But it wasn't working. I thought about Johnny all the time.

The first time we met was at a meeting about the first installment of the Von Rastenbourg series. It was fall and I had just come back from working so many trade shows that I had very few clothes back from the dry cleaners. I was wearing my most uncomfortable, itchy, gray wool suit and I was feeling grumpy and schlumpy. I went to the restroom to see what I could do about my appearance before the meeting started, and on my way back to my desk I saw Jonathan and Bella in the reception area.

She was incredibly beautiful, and he was—well, beautiful didn't even begin to describe him. He was stunning. I was positively shaken by him. I pretended to check with the receptionist on the arrival of a package just to get a better look at him. In retrospect, I must have seemed painfully obvious.

When I got back to my desk, my boss was waiting for me.

I said, "I know, the meeting starts in five minutes. I'll be right there." I was hoping I had some better, sexier shoes under my desk that I could change into and wishing that I had worn a lower-cut shirt, too.

She closed the door. "Don't worry, you're not late. There's just something I have to tell you before the meeting starts. You've probably already guessed that she's really a vampire, and so is her manager."

"I figured as much. Mortals usually aren't that spectacular."

She raised an eyebrow at me and shot me a conspiring grin. "Yeah, he is easy on the eyes, isn't he?" I was spraying perfume on my neck and she asked for some, too. "Hell, I'm married, I'm not dead." We both laughed at her choice of words.

Jonathan and Bella were escorted to the conference room and Lois and I joined them after they'd been seated and given coffee. Bella shook my hand and I introduced myself. Then I shook Jonathan's hand and he smiled at me. His hand was cool to the touch, but I felt a gentle warmth from him, along with the strangest sensation—like I should have expected to see him before now. I started to have trouble breathing and pretended to cough.

While they sat across the table from me, all calm and impressive, I sat there nervously fidgeting in my itchy suit, trying to act professional and control my breathing and the blush that kept creeping up into my cheeks.

There was an instant attraction between the two of us, but neither of us acknowledged it at first. I thought, *So I'm attracted to a hot guy*—human or not, it was no big deal. Of course I would be into him—after all, he was a gorgeous predator, it was his job to be bedazzling. Besides, at that time I was going through an I-want-to-settle-down-with-a-husband-and-a-family stage; I even had a semi–long term boyfriend.

We were both strictly professional for at least the first six months. But slowly we began to loosen up, and began to realize how much we liked each other as friends. We traded bad jokes with each other and forwarded stupid e-mails, and before we knew it, we were hanging out and drinking together at bars whenever he was in New York or if I was in DC, where he lived. (Or should I say dwelled—vampires really don't live, do they?) It wasn't as much fun as it could have been, given that he remained sober and by the end of the night I was usually half in the bag. He would always make sure I got home all right and always call me the next day to tease me about my hangover. He was very funny, too—something I didn't expect from a vampire. And much like Jessica Rabbit, I could really fall for a guy who could make me laugh. Oh, and let's not forget how magnificent he looked all the time.

How did it ever get so out of hand? Had I fallen the day I met him? I was so totally in love with him that I couldn't think of anything else. Why wouldn't he take the next step with me? Why did it have to go so wrong? For the hundredth time that week, it seemed, I cried myself to sleep.

When I woke up three hours later, I really did feel like calling in dead. My hangover wasn't so bad (Lola had kept me hydrated), but I was totally exhausted. But how would it look if I called in sick after a major party night? It was Friday, so at least I could wear jeans. I dressed gingerly, minding my bruised knees, and once again dragged my sorry ass to work.

Thankfully, it was a slow morning. I typed up a few press releases as I nibbled on a greasy egg-and-cheese sandwich. I had thrown myself so hard into my work that I was actually caught up.

After learning about Daniel's attack on that New England pack, and given my scare last night, I decided that I was going to back off on that front. It just seemed sensible. I wasn't looking forward to telling Bella that I was going to end my investigation, but it was really creeping me out. I'd wait to talk to my witch author first—she said she knew his accountant (I don't know why, but that struck me as funny), but after that, I was going to call it quits.

Of course I kept missing that author, and it took me a week of phone tag before we connected. Daniel, as it turned out, was extremely diversified, but surprisingly legitimate. His properties and investments were all above reproach—not a strip club or dog track in the bunch. He was one of the vampires who owned West, which was not surprising. Leave it to him to create such effective bait and develop an environment to attract humans in droves, eliminating the need to hunt. As interesting as this information was, it didn't help me locate him, and I was disappointed that the lead went nowhere.

Bella called me the following week and wanted to meet me when she was back in town. I knew she wanted an update on my Daniel research, but I also knew she would want to talk to me about Jonathan. I just didn't feel up to discussing either with her. She was always so dead-on when it came to her assessment of me, and I really didn't feel like going under the microscope with her right now.

I set up a drinks date with her later in the week, hoping I would think of an excuse to cancel before the actual day.

I couldn't come up with a believable excuse, and we met after work at a hotel bar. I sat across from her at a private table. She commented on my weight loss. I told her with her tour over, I had time to run in the mornings, so I dropped that extra weight I had wanted to lose. She looked at me like she didn't believe me and said, "Well, don't lose any more weight or we'll have trouble finding you."

"Then maybe I'll start working on being too rich." The waitress came over and we both ordered red wine. It was unseasonably cold for November, and I'd been cold all day. I pulled my scarf more tightly around me and we remained silent while we waited for our drinks. There was no use starting our conversation, when the waitress would come back at any moment. The drinks came, and Bella barely waited for the waitress to be out of earshot before we began.

I told her that I had tracked down Daniel to his current address in Providence just yesterday (my witch had come through with one piece of useful information in the eleventh hour). I also told her the location of his new town house in South Beach. Then I told her that I had one more lead, but after that, I felt it was getting a little scary for me and I wanted out.

I figured she'd be pissed off that I was quitting the project, but I was wrong. Although she had originally wanted to know more, like how many vampires were in Daniel's coven, after hearing about Brian (I kept to myself about my paranoia in the shower), she wanted me to stop digging right away.

"I can take it from here. It would be too dangerous for you to continue."

I'd been tracking down this bloodthirsty, sadistic murderer for the last two months. Why was it suddenly too dangerous now? "There's one more thing I want to check before I drop this. I have a very trustworthy contact in Miami and she's willing to do the research."

My contact was a retired author. Unlike my other vampire authors, she used to write murder mysteries with no supernatural element. She had simply tired of writing and painted now. I had kept up our relationship, and she was willing to do me this favor. Most of the people I talked to about this were willing to do anything to get Daniel off the streets.

"No, Gia. I have to insist. You've done enough." She sipped

her wine. "I didn't expect you to get so much information so fast—you're very good at this." She raised her glass in a little salute. "But I can take it from here. I've already completed the next installment of the series, so I have nothing but time until I hear back from Speculation. Besides, the weather in Miami in November is simply divine."

I was worried about her. Why was it all suddenly enough? Had she heard something, or had I really gotten her enough information? And what was she going to do once she found Daniel? She couldn't possibly be planning to confront him herself. He was the most skilled killer I'd ever heard of. "Bella, what are you planning?"

"I'll be sending over your payment next week. Let's change the subject." She motioned to the waitress to bring us two more glasses of wine. "So I hear you were bitten a few weeks ago. How do you feel?"

Okay, evidently the subject was closed. "I'm fine. Nothing a few days of violent stomach cramps and sunglasses couldn't fix."

"You're lucky it was only the radial vein." I heard you put up quite a fight. That's impressive. That was no young vampire you fought off."

Vampires acquired strength with age, but they also always kept some of the strength from the vampire that changed them. It could all get very confusing, which was probably why vampire myths varied so drastically.

"Let's just say I had one of those freak adrenaline rushes brought on by . . . what shall we call it? An intense shock?" I was not in the mood to tiptoe around this. I knew that part of the reason she asked me to come out tonight was to talk about Jonathan, and didn't want to prolong the inevitable.

"You're right. I'm being insensitive." She looked sorry and reached over to pat my hand. "How are you doing otherwise?"

I rolled my eyes.

"If it makes you feel any better, he's miserable, too."

"Why would that make me feel better? He's the one who dumped me. If he's miserable, then he deserves it."

She gave me one of those it-was-probably-for-the-best looks.

That only pissed me off more. "You only feel sorry for him because you don't know the whole story." My voice cracked, and I sipped my wine to compose myself. "I flew across the country to see him, to let him know . . . and within an hour I was dumped, then I was almost killed, then I was unceremoniously packed up and put on a plane home."

"He was very worried about how you'd react to the bite. He said you'd taken some medication . . ."

"If he was so damn worried, he could have called me. Or at the very least addressed me during our conference call."

"You're right. He could have. That was uncharacteristically rude on his part." She played with her wineglass. "You know, he went back and killed her."

I shrugged. It didn't surprise me. I'm not sure if Bella thought that would make him out to be my valiant savior. But I knew what he was and I knew how he fed himself. And if he could kill Billy, his friend, he'd have no trouble taking out some random vampire bitch that had honed in on his territory. That didn't make him my hero, it just made him as savage as the rest of his kind.

"Bella, I'm not sure what you think this little chat is going to accomplish, but we're through. I won't lie to you; I'm not even remotely over him. But still, it's over between us."

"Are you sure about that?" She was looking shrewdly at me, sniffing the air to discern whether I was lying.

"Do you know why I went out there? Do you know why he dumped me?"

"No. He hasn't said a word to me about it—hasn't said much of anything, really. In fact, the reason I'm here is because I'm worried about him. I've never seen him act this way, and I thought you could shed some light on what went wrong between you two."

At least she was being up front with me. But if she thought I was going to feel sorry for him, she had another think coming. Let's see what she thought of her perfect-gentleman cousin after I told her what a total prick he'd been.

"I hate to disillusion you, but your precious Jonathan was a complete asshole." I told her about the night at Harry's, leaving out some of the details regarding my stupidity and my excessive taunting. Hey, I needed unconditional sympathy here. I explained how I learned of my uncontrollable bleeding condition and how it was getting worse each time we saw each other. I told her about Ohio, and how I had to double up my dosage just for a brief dinner where we barely touched each other. "And now, not only is he reopening preexisting wounds, but he's creating wounds. He made my nose bleed without even so much as kissing me. It was something I was willing to deal with until we got all the details of our relationship worked out. He, however, chose to simply not deal with it and sent me packing."

"He neglected to mention that part to me. I've never heard of that happening before. It must have been very scary."

I made a *hrmph* sound. I'd done some research and I couldn't find any reference to my bleeding problem in any of my books. If Bella, an older vampire, thought this condition was scary, then it must really be frightening. "In retrospect, maybe I should have seen the end coming. I mean, look at what we had become. I had to take extreme precautions to prevent myself from bleeding every time I was in the room with him, and he couldn't eat when we were in the same time zone. We were pretty self-destructive. He must have thought that if he stayed with me a moment longer, I'd start to uncontrollably hemorrhage and he'd starve to death."

She looked off to the side. "That's not a problem these days." That was a strange response.

"What do you mean?"

"He's been feeding a lot." And not just feeding, he's been killing a lot, too." She was on the verge of tears. "He's not like he used to be. He was always very respectful toward his prey; now he's become downright barbaric, worse than Billy ever was. These days, we have to be so careful—but he has no restraint. It gets harder and harder to dispose of the bodies. I've told him he has to control himself, that he can't keep killing, but he . . . he just can't stop himself." She looked so sad.

I reached over and held her hand, my annoyance with her gone. There was no use in taking my frustration out on her; this wasn't her fault. If she'd come to meddle in my relationship, that would be one thing, but she'd come to me for help in saving her cousin. She loved him and it was she who would have to live with the consequences of his actions now.

"Bella, I owe you the whole story. You should know why I went out there: I told him I wanted the relationship to be permanent, starting that night. I told him to change me." I can't say she looked surprised. I sometimes hated that supernatural sixth sense. "I was ready to make a commitment then and there, Bella." I gave her an ironic "*ha!*" "I guess all men are the same. I mention the word 'commitment' and he dumped me."

She actually laughed at that, too. "Maybe. So what now? You can't tell me you've completely given up hope."

Right again. "As far as I'm concerned, the ball was in his court for the last few weeks and he's done nothing. I know you said he's been going a little off the deep end lately, but he could have done things differently. He chose not to. It's been too long now. Though I haven't given up hope, I'm trying to. I've got to get on with my life. I'm sure he'll sober up and move on, too."

"But he still loves you."

"Don't protect him, Bella. He's been an adult for years now, more years than most. He blew it. He made his choice." I took a deep breath. "I still love him, too, but this just can't work."

This conversation had also made my next step very clear to me. "Bella, I'm sorry, but I can't work with you anymore. He's an important part of your career, and I can't do my job if he won't speak to me. He hasn't addressed me at all since LA, not even in e-mail. He's done nothing but cc me on things. I can't do my job like this. I'll tell Lois to reassign you."

She was surprised. "No, Gia. I refuse to accept that. Please give this decision more time—give *him* more time. It's not our regular Jonathan doing this. He's been in a haze since LA. A constant haze."

My patience was thinning. I felt bad that she had to suffer his behavior now, but why should he make her career suffer, too?

"I don't care, Bella. I'm not cutting him any slack just because he's drowning his sorrows in bloodlust. I've been drinking, smoking, and running like a fiend to get over him, but you don't see me slacking off on the job. I would never let your career suffer like he's been doing. And let's not forget that I was the one who got dumped, here. I'm a mere human yet I *still* manage to get in to work on time every day *and* find time to work on finding Daniel for you. You can't expect me to feel sorry for this selfish bastard." I was careful not to yell, but I was practically spitting out my words.

"Give him time? Unlike you two, I don't have the luxury of taking fifty years to think something over. I offered him every-

thing, Bella. *Everything!* I was willing to give up all the important things for him, and he took the easy way out and drove me
to the airport." I took a deep breath. "I could have died in that
hotel lobby—and he still drove me to the airport."

Bella sat there quietly. "If I may . . ." She was extremely
calm. "I'd like you to try one more time. Jonathan . . ." She
paused for a moment and gave careful consideration to her next
words. "Jonathan has always been *alone*. Both as a human and
ever since I changed him, he's been alone. He's never known
love until he met you." She smiled ruefully. "He often told me
how envious he was of me and Julius. Told me how lucky I was
to have found someone to share eternity with." Tears began to
fall from her eyes. "And after Julius's death, when I thought
that I couldn't go on anymore, Jonathan told me that if it were
him, the memory of such an intense love would be enough to
sustain him. I'm not sure he was right about that; I miss Julius
every day. But my point is, all Jonathan ever wanted was to be
loved like I was. And he's on the brink of that with you. He
loves you more than anything." She squeezed my hand. "And
more than anything, I want to see him happy."

I knew her heart was in the right place, but she didn't see
the look in his eyes when he told me I had to leave. She didn't
hear the resolution in his voice when he refused me.

"I'll tell Lois I want your books reassigned. I'm sorry,
Bella." I left the bar.

13

Bite Me

I had settled into a groove. I would wake up hungover, run off my hangover, go into work, then go on another blind date or go out with friends. Every night I would drink and smoke too much, maybe hook up with some random guy at the bar, then crash. You know that Dorothy Parker poem?

I like to have a martini,
two at the very most.
After three I'm under the table,
after four I'm under my host.

It was my anthem. My escapades on Halloween were just the beginning. I knew it was a downward spiral, but I was comfortable in it. I lived every day like it was my last, and sometimes wished it was. Carpe diem. If I was hungry, I ate. If I was thirsty, I drank. If I was horny, I had sex. I figured that as long as my lifestyle didn't affect my work, it didn't hurt anyone but me. I didn't want to feel anything other than the basest emotions. By now, I accepted that Jonathan was out of my life. I also accepted that I was going to live what remained of my life in a new way.

So it being a typical weekday morning, I was hungover. I decided to catch up on some of my writing since there wasn't a lot going on. The only thing I absolutely had to do was think of a good lie for my Detroit media escort. She would be in charge of one of my alien authors and I had to come up with a believable excuse regarding his request to have three gallons of Karo syrup sent up to his hotel room every night. Aliens ate some weird shit.

I was typing up a pitch letter when an IM name that I hadn't seen in weeks popped up on my screen. Bite me. It was Jonathan. Was this a result of that conversation with Bella? Had she found a way to get through his haze? Maybe she'd told him he was being a jerk, or maybe she'd told him how hot I looked now that I'd lost some weight, or maybe she'd told him he'd made the biggest mistake in his afterlife and he should be kissing my human ass.

BiteMe: "Hi."

PitchAndMoan: "Hi." So far, so good.

BiteMe: "What do vampires play poker for?" Was this some kind of olive branch?

PitchAndMoan: "What?"

BiteMe: "High stakes." That was just plain stupid, and I laughed in spite of myself.

PitchAndMoan: "LOL"

BiteMe: "It's nice to see you smile."

PitchAndMoan: "It's been a while. It hurt my face." That was the truth.

BiteMe: "How have you been?"

What did that mean? How have I been since he dumped me? How have I been since I was nearly eaten alive? How have I been since I started living the lifestyle of my inner id?

PitchAndMoan: "Fucked up. And you?"

BiteMe: "I guess that's my fault. Can you talk? Can I call you?" It was actually a good time to talk, but I wasn't letting him back into my life so easily. Besides, he shouldn't get everything he wants; it wasn't fair. Not to mention that it just wouldn't do to have anyone at work overhear me yell at him for *not* killing me.

PitchAndMoan: "I'm on the phone," I lied. I blocked him and told Ian not to transfer any calls to me for the rest of the day.

Less than a minute later, my cell phone vibrated with a text message. "Call me when u r off the phone." Yeah, right. Shortly after my e-mail chimed. He was persistent; I'd give him that.

Dear Gia,

I hate doing this by e-mail, but I can see you're avoiding my calls. I know I've been a real prick, but I also know how well we work together. Bella told me you asked to be taken off the Von Rastenbourg novels. Please don't do that. You're so good with her, and I'm sure we can be civil to each other. It would be in all of our best interests to continue working together on Bella's books.

I hope you'll reconsider staying on as her publicist and I hope we can continue our friendship.

Take care,
Jonathan

I couldn't believe he was sending me a "let's be friends" e-mail. I deleted it in a hot second. I had been dumped with more dignity by the losers I was dating these past few weeks—

and most of them had spent less than six hours with me. I stewed about it for the rest of the day, muttering under my breath. Just how was it in anyone's best interest for me to work side by side with a creature who couldn't be in the same room with me?

I lost track of time, and it wasn't until Ian came in to say good night that I realized it was after six. I had a couple of hours before I had to meet my blind date du jour, so I continued working on the press materials I'd started earlier.

My phone rang, and since I recognized the phone number on the caller ID as the *New York Times*, I took the call. It was a book reviewer asking me for cover art. I was taking down her e-mail address when I got that weird feeling again, like someone was watching me. I spun around in my chair and looked up to see Jonathan standing in my office doorway. He was leaning against the doorjamb: feet crossed, hands in his pockets, taking my breath away.

Somehow I kept talking on the phone while I stared at him. He looked like he'd been through hell. This man, who normally took care to dress himself in leather and silk, was now dressed in dirty, faded jeans with tears at the bottom, and a sweatshirt with a suspicious-looking red/black stain and a hole showing a dingy T-shirt underneath. His leather jacket was worn and scuffed. His hair was long and unwashed and hung limply around his face, and he had a coarse five o'clock shadow.

The rest of his face, however, was a totally different matter. He looked very filled out and rosy; his color extended all the way down to his fingertips. He would almost pass for human, if he weren't so impossibly beautiful. Bella was right. He'd been bingeing and, although I hated to admit it, he looked healthier for it.

He was wearing sunglasses, but I could see him raise his

eyebrows at me. Apparently he couldn't enter my office without an invitation, either.

I held up my finger in a "just one minute" signal. It wasn't every day I got to have the upper hand with him, and I wanted to savor it. I chatted needlessly on the phone for at least another two minutes, then took off my headset.

He cocked his head. "Can I come in?"

I had forgotten how his voice affected me. "Suit yourself."

He came in and gracefully sat in my guest chair. "You've lost weight."

"You haven't." I said it too quickly and with a little too much venom in my voice. I'm pretty sure he knew I was commenting on his well-fed flush.

I was uncomfortable with the situation. Even though he had the sunglasses on, I knew he was trying to look right into my eyes. Just to have something to do, I got up to put a book on my shelf. I heard him suck in his breath. I was wearing what Lola called my "ass pants." They were just regular black pants, but they hugged my new-and-improved runner's ass very well. Deal with that, sucker.

"I, um . . ." My ass had him speechless. "Er . . . Your plant still looks good." He nodded toward the orchid he had sent me from another lifetime.

I went back to sit in my chair and busied myself arranging things on my desk. Anything to distract myself from looking at him. "Yeah, I take good care of it. I don't get any enjoyment out of watching things wither and die."

He gave a rueful little laugh. "That was a good comeback. Did you practice?"

"Maybe." Actually, I had. I came up with it during one of my fantasy conversations in which I said all the right things. I would look smart and in control and he would look incredibly stupid. It worked out just as I had planned.

"I've been a real asshole lately," he said.

"That's the rumor."

"Did Bella tell you what I've been up to when you saw her?"

"Yep, she told me everything. But even if she hadn't, I know you've been a real asshole to me."

He looked very tired. "Don't candy-coat it, baby, tell me how you really feel."

I hated it when he called me "baby" it sounded as if he still gave a damn about me. "You don't know what you're asking for," I shot back.

He started rubbing his temples and let his chin drop to his chest in exhaustion. He looked like hell. A very sexy kind of hell, but still, not the Johnny I was used to. Regardless, I had him in my office now and wanted to let him have it. I kept my voice down, but in my anger, it sounded like I was hissing at him.

"You were a complete scumbag just for dumping me, but to drop me off at the airport after I had just been violated like that—that took real class." I could feel my chest and face getting red. "I had just taken a huge dose of my medication— you didn't know how I was going to react. I found out she was a pretty old vampire, too—she could have done some serious damage."

He lifted his head, picking up on my use of *was*.

"Yes, I know you killed her. My fucking honor has been restored. I can't wait to tell my father what a stand up-guy you are. Oh yeah, that's right, I could never tell my parents about you. No one could know I was dating a fucking monster."

"I deserve that."

My jaw was clenched. "No, you deserve worse—but I don't have the energy. Unlike you, I haven't been eating enough lately."

I thought he winced at that, but with the sunglasses, I couldn't tell for sure.

"Would it make you feel any better if I told you that I was very concerned about your bite and that I made sure you were okay?"

I must have looked at him dubiously, because he continued.

"Of course I couldn't be on the plane with you that night, but I did fly out to New York the next day on a charter. While I waited for dark, I called Lola and told her to give Dr. Laktarnik the heads-up. When I couldn't watch you myself, I had someone else do it."

Note to self: kill Lola and the witch doctor.

Wait a second. Back up. Did he just say he was—"Just how were you watching me?"

"I asked some of my friends to help out at the clubs you went to, but mostly I was keeping tabs on you from a distance, catching glimpses of you in the street, lurking around your office building, hiding in the park to watch you run if you were out before the sun came up. I didn't want to get too close, in case I made you start bleeding again."

A barely developed thought was nagging at me. "Where were you at about four a.m. on Halloween?"

He gave me his killer half smile. My God, how I missed seeing that right fang. Out of sheer habit, my body responded. I hope he didn't pick up on it. I was torn between smacking him and straddling his lap.

"So you felt that one, huh? I knew I was a little too close."

"How did you get into my apartment? I've never invited you in."

"I was in the air shaft."

I lived in a prewar building with a three-by-five-foot air-shaft on either side. My bathroom had a window in the shower that opened into it. There was nothing for him to hold on to out there—he must have been balanced on a two-inch ledge while he watched me stumble around my bathroom naked and bruised. Not my finest hour, I was sure.

But why was I worrying about what he thought of me naked? Why did I care about what he thought about anything?

"How long were you there?"

"Long enough to know you were okay, in spite of how shit-faced you were. Lola should have cut you off long before 'Jambalaya.'"

"Nobody likes a wiseass."

He laughed the way he used to, throaty and deep. It felt like old times. It was too easy to fall back into the groove.

"So why are you here?"

"I wanted to talk to you. How come you wouldn't take my calls?"

"That whole let's be friends thing? Sorry, I'm not interested. I'm off the project."

"Gia, that's not what I wanted to talk to you about. That was a stupid e-mail . . ."

Just then, Lois rounded the corner. "Gia, I have that manuscript . . ." She entered the room and he immediately stood up to greet her. "Oh, hello, Jonathan. I didn't know you were coming into the offices today."

"I was in the neighborhood and thought I'd come visit Gia. We were just catching up; would you like to join us?" He pulled out his chair.

She was blushing, clearly drawn to him and flustered. Why should she be different than any other mortal? "No, I was just leaving." It looked as if it took all her effort to wrench herself away. "Gia, here's that manuscript."

I hefted it. It was huge. "Who knew Ziggy Stardust knew so many words?"

Lois laughed unnecessarily hard at that. She couldn't stop

herself from flirting with him. She turned to Jonathan, putting her hand on his arm to explain, "It's about spiders from outer space." Jonathan smiled and nodded politely.

When she left, Jonathan closed the door and fell heavily into my guest chair again. "Really, Gia, I wanted to tell you how sorry I am about LA."

"Sorry?" I came around the desk and sat on the outside corner, then crossed my arms defensively. "Does sorry mean you've thought it over and you're willing to accommodate me, or does sorry mean you're apologizing for leading me on, or does sorry mean you regret letting me walk through a den of bloodsuckers while smelling like fucking gravy?"

"Johnny, I came to tell you that my life wasn't worth living without you. I came to tell you that it wasn't the lifestyle I was interested in, but that I didn't see any other way for us to work. I came to tell you that you were all I ever wanted. I would have given up my entire life and my entire set of moral values for you in a heartbeat. I was willing to make all the sacrifices, and you rejected me. So tell me. Just what are you sorry about today?"

He looked appropriately remorseful. "I'm sorry about all of that. I'm sorry I'm such a fuckin' loser." He took off his sunglasses and rubbed his eyes. He kept them turned from me, but I could tell that they were red and puffy. Was he tired or crying or in another haze?

With one of those lightning-fast movements, he took my wrist into his right hand. "How *was* your bite?" I tried to pull away and although he didn't squeeze or pull, I wasn't able to break contact. I didn't want to struggle too hard against him— I knew from experience that bruises he inflicted didn't heal quickly. Or maybe I just wanted him to touch me. He was looking at the place where I was bitten. He knew he wouldn't find even the hint of a mark.

I was about to tell him that, no thanks to him, I'd survived. That the nausea, vomiting, and diarrhea I suffered were nothing compared to the last few weeks. But then he started stroking my wrist with his thumb, and I forgot how to speak.

He stood up slowly and wedged himself between my legs. His other hand grabbed my waist. He let go of my wrist and moved his hand to the back of my neck. He tilted my head back and massaged the back of my head with his fingertips. He leaned in and kissed each of my eyelids softly. When he pulled back I saw that he had his eyes closed the whole time, and I wasn't sure what to make of that—was he making sure I complied without using his scary vampire powers, or was he just doing what humans did when they kissed someone?

Wait a second. He *was* going to kiss me, wasn't he?

He leaned in and brushed his lips against mine. I had thought that I remembered what it felt like to touch him. I had thought that intense burning sensation the last time our lips touched was the most wonderful feeling in the world. That was, until he kissed me like this.

I opened my mouth to him and he slid his tongue inside. His mouth was slightly metallic, coppery, salty. I had wanted this for so long, I almost couldn't believe it was actually happening. I gently stroked his razor-sharp fangs with my tongue and felt him pull back when they almost cut into it. I ran my tongue all the way around each point, then up to his gums.

He moaned and pulled me more tightly into his arms, pressing against my inner thighs. He was hard and still warm from his recent meal and I couldn't help but respond. I slid my hands up his back. He broke away from my mouth and trailed his lips down my jaw and toward my neck. He dragged his teeth along the skin. I felt his fangs scratch back and forth on my neck, but he didn't let them puncture the skin.

His hand was now moving up my thigh and toward the

waistband of my pants. He undid the zipper and slid his hand inside. I was beyond telling him to stop. His lips were pressed to the pulse point in my neck. We were both still for a full minute as we felt it throb under the pressure. He pulled away within seconds, but not before I was writhing against his hand.

"Gia, look at me."

I could barely open my eyes. I was shaking.

He moved back an inch and took my chin in his hands then tilted my head so I was looking directly into his face. "Look at me." His deep voice resonated in my head. I opened my eyes and saw that the whites of his eyes were completely red and his pupils were dilated. I knew he was struggling to control himself, on the edge of his haze, but I didn't care. "Is this what you want?" he asked.

My head lolled against his hand and I closed my eyes again. "Yes." My voice sounded unfamiliar to me.

I became cold all of a sudden, and when I opened my eyes he was gone.

I must have sat on the corner of my desk for a long time because when I stood up, my legs were stiff. I probably would have stayed there longer if my ringing phone hadn't startled me.

"Hello?"

"May I please speak to Giovanna?"

"Speaking." I was dizzy and very disoriented.

It was my date cancelling, which saved me the trouble of standing him up. I disconnected.

Did what I thought just happened really happen? I looked down. My pants were open, so I figured I wasn't fantasizing.

I zipped up and left the office.

14

God-given Ass

It had started to snow. I began to walk home in the big, fluffy wet flakes, despite my shearling coat and high-heeled suede boots. I'm sure it was freezing cold, but I felt nothing as I walked the three miles to my apartment. I wasn't thinking about—well, anything. My mind was completely blank. Every time a thought threatened to enter my head, I became overwhelmingly distracted and couldn't remember what I had been thinking about. It was like I was drunk or under the influence of something . . . like a very attractive supernatural guy named Jonathan, perhaps?

I found myself walking through Carl Schurz Park along the East River before long. The river looked cold and black, but oddly inviting. I stopped and held on to the railing as I watched the current. The park was located on a strait, near a passage called Hell Gate where several waterways, including the Harlem River, the Long Island Sound, and the East River met. The currents were notoriously wicked.

Looking at the turbulent current calmed me. It's not that I was thinking about suicide. Like I said, I wasn't thinking about anything, but I simply felt drawn to the water. Without thinking, I put my foot up on the railing and hoisted myself to the edge to get closer to that calming feeling. A strong gust of wind hit my face, knocking my hood back. The fluffy snow had changed to biting pellets of ice and it was the stinging sleet that brought me back to reality.

I looked down again at the water and was surprised to find myself leaning dangerously over the railing. *How did I get here?* I felt a hand on my arm and turned to see Johnny standing beside me.

"I can think of better ways for you to die."

I wanted to say *me, too,* but all of a sudden, I couldn't stop shaking. The spell I was under was lifted and now I was freezing.

"Hey, are you okay?" He appeared more alarmed by my uncontrollable shivering than by my nearly diving into the East River.

I nodded, but I know I looked far from okay.

"Listen, I'm really, really sorry about back there in your office." He ran his hand through his hair and shook his head. "I still can't believe I did that to you. And I *really* can't believe I did that to you in your office. I honestly just came to your office to apologize to you for LA. How can I ever get you to forgive me for kicking you out, and for letting that bitch take a bite out of you? I've been a total asshole."

He took my hands in his. "When I came to see you at Speculation I just wanted to see if you'd give me a second chance. But you looked so . . . and I got carried away . . . I mean anyone could have walked in and seen us . . . and I was in no condition . . . I mean, wasn't exactly thinking clearly enough to hear it if someone was coming . . . and then I just ran out of there . . . I'm such a scumbag . . . I'm . . ."

"Just stop." I reached up and took his face in my hands. My mind was suddenly clear. All I wanted was to be anywhere with him. I didn't need his apologies. I wasn't good at playing girlfriend games with guys; I had no patience for "the Rules." I didn't care that he ran out of my office; I was just glad to have him here now.

I looked right into his eyes. "Hey, you can't be held accountable for your reaction to me in the office." I flashed him a wink and a smile. "It was my ass, right? My ass hypnotized you, right? Vampires may have that scary eye-contact thing, but my God-given ass has brought down many a man."

His face split into a grin. "I can't lie; your God-given ass was definitely part of it." That wicked smile of his was driving me mad. "Listen, Gia." He took my hands in his again. "I don't know what came over me in LA, about the whole nose-bleed thing." I started to interrupt. "No, let me finish. When I saw how much blood you were losing just from being in the same room with me, it scared the shit out of me. And you don't even want to know the impact it had on my appetite. I was so incredibly close to biting you then, and I thought I probably would have killed you. I should have told you why I was so worried. I should have told you to go ask the witch doctor what to do. But instead, I panicked. The smell of your blood had me on the edge of a haze and I was only thinking about getting the hell out of that hotel room. I didn't even think about the danger I'd be putting you in by letting you walk through that lobby. I think you sometimes put me in kind of a spell—I can never seem to think straight around you. With or without seeing your ass." He smiled, then shook his head. "I was so pissed at myself, I proceeded to eat myself into a total depression. You'd think that by now I'd know how to act like an adult."

I found myself forgiving him instantly. "And here I thought you were just being a regular guy and you were afraid of a little commitment."

He smiled. "I'm far from a regular guy. And I always knew I wanted to spend eternity with you—from the day I met you and you were fidgeting around in that godawful gray suit." We both smiled at that. "It's not like I didn't get all your little hints—I've known for a long time that eventually you were going to ask me to change you, and I was planning to broach the subject in LA. You know, make sure you really knew what you were asking for." He held up a finger to stop me from interrupting. "Which I know you do, but I thought we'd also talk about where and when, too. But when you started bleeding . . . like I said, I panicked."

"And as long as I'm apologizing, I really am sorry about what happened in your office. I really did want to talk to you. I wasn't intending on lunging at you like that, but I could smell your neck from across the room and I was still kind of, you know . . ."

"Yeah, hazing. You'll have to get over this vampire guilt thing with me; it's boring. I'm the mortal who gets it, remember? Now shut up, I'm just so happy to have you back."

"But I'm still a little confused about how I'm supposed to feel. I mean, how do I know you're not going to run off again the second I start bleeding? And that should be happening soon."

He took me into his arms. "I can't promise I won't have to run away from time to time, but I can promise you I'll come back every time."

All that bingeing had made him warmer than he'd ever been. It felt weird, but I liked it and I let him hold me.

I finally stopped my teeth from chattering long enough to say, "By the way: yes."

He raised his eyebrows at me questioningly.

"Yes, this is really what I want. I'm answering your question from before."

He opened his jacket and let me climb inside. I couldn't get over how strange it was to feel warmth coming from him, and watched the snow melt as it hit his face. If he was hungrier, would it have stuck?

"I don't trust myself to take you anywhere warm. Hell, I thought your office would be a safe place to talk and I nearly lost it there," he said.

"You're nice and toasty for a change, so I'll be just fine here." I snuggled deeper into his jacket. "Now, what else do you want to talk about? Make it quick before I start bleeding on you."

Great, no response. Again I had taken it too far, but I did feel like a ticking time bomb.

"Okay, I'll be quick." I sensed the anxiety in him as well. "Really, I wanted to tell you that I worked out a few things. Do you still want me to change you?"

"I never stopped wanting you and I never will, and if that's the only way I can have you, then that's what I want."

"Never is a long time—trust me on this."

"I know. This is really what I want."

"Promise?"

I nodded.

"Cross your heart and hope to die?"

I nodded again. That was a really great line, but I was too speechless to acknowledge it.

He swallowed hard and took my left hand in his, then slowly slid a ring onto my finger. A totally appropriate and spectacularly beautiful onyx ring set in diamonds. It was perfect.

"Are you ready now?" he asked.

Now? As in right here? In the snowy park? Hell, why not? "Now works for me."

The smile on his face was totally worth my life.

"Okay," He got very serious. "But we have to be really careful. I've done some research and since you've got this whole bleeding thing going on, I have to take it very slowly. It's going to take longer than usual."

It felt like this pep talk was more for his benefit than mine. "You're the expert."

"So this will only take a few seconds."

"Got it. Small bites."

"No, really. Your little clotting problem isn't that common, and I'll have to really restrain myself here."

"Hey, I think this is *our* little clotting problem. I don't seem to have this trouble around other vampires, and I hang out with a hell of a lot of them."

"You're always a friggin' wiseass, aren't you?"

"You know you love it." I winked at him.

"Okay, give me a second." He ran his hands down my arms. "I wish this could be easier for you. Better for you."

Then he held me by the shoulders and leaned into my neck. He kissed me at my pulse point again, and this time I knew it was going to happen. I braced myself.

I felt his fangs sink into my flesh and was overcome by the most exquisite pleasure I had ever experienced. He drank for less than thirty seconds, then wrenched himself away with great effort.

He staggered back a few feet. He was breathing hard and shaking worse than me. He had a shocked look on his face. "Holy shit!"

"Yeah." I was out and out panting, leaning on the railing behind me for support.

We both just stood there staring at each other, open-mouthed, each of us totally surprised at our reactions. "I didn't expect it to be *that* good."

I was still grinning stupidly. "Thanks a lot."

"You know what I mean." He ran his hands through his damp hair. "I knew it would be special with you, but . . . Holy shit." He was shaking his head as though he couldn't believe what just happened. "Okay, your turn. But you only get a drop, okay?"

I nodded. He took me back into his arms and put his index finger in his mouth. A bead of his blood stood on the fingertip.

"Come closer to me." He brought his finger to my lips and allowed me to lick the tiny drop from it. I barely tasted him at all, but the feeling of closeness was overwhelming. He pulled his finger away, backed up, and jammed his hands quickly into his pockets. He was trembling.

"That's all I'm allowed to do right now. You really have to go home. I can't be near you for much longer."

I didn't understand it, but I was too overcome with emotion to argue. Out of habit, he started to put his arm around me, then abruptly pulled it away. "Sorry. I've got to keep some space between us." We started walking the few blocks to my apartment, keeping at least two feet between us.

By the time I reached the steps of my building, I had recovered enough to speak coherently. I turned toward him. "Johnny, at least come upstairs to talk . . ."

"Shhh. Please don't ask me in. I couldn't stand it. I'm way too aroused to keep my distance." I tried to appear understanding, but I could feel the disappointed look on my face. "I'll explain everything tomorrow night, okay?" I shrugged. What choice did I have? "Don't worry, after that you won't have your bleeding problem around me anymore. Oh, and when you see your neck, don't panic." The wind started blowing again from behind me. He breathed in my scent. "I promise, I'll explain everything tomorrow." He shook his head and ran down the street with inhuman speed.

When I got to my apartment I felt a little more like myself, grounded by the familiar surroundings. I looked at myself in the hallway mirror. I was very pale and my lips had a blue tinge. I didn't know if that was from Jonathan or my three-mile walk in the cold.

I could still feel his lips on my skin and pulled down the neck of my coat to look at my throat. I was surprised to see two puncture marks and a growing bruise. What the . . . ? Is that what he meant by *when you see your neck, don't panic*? Did he know this was going to happen? Vampire bites always healed within seconds; I'd seen it happen to others countless times and I had experienced it myself in LA.

I pressed on the bruise. Such an intense wave of pleasure rolled through me that I nearly collapsed. I grabbed the wall to steady myself and tried to catch my breath.

Well, there's something I didn't expect. I unsteadily made my way to the couch. Bone tired, I fell asleep within seconds.

I woke up confused. I wasn't in my bed. I looked around. Okay, I was in my living room, completely clothed—that was good. Then the memory came rushing back to me. Johnny bit me last night! I looked down at the ring on my finger. It was real. It all really happened. I was being changed.

Okay, Gia, calm down and take it slow. I lay completely still, waiting for nausea or other symptoms to kick in. But I felt great. Of course, that could have been because it was the first time in weeks that I hadn't had a drink in twenty-four hours. But I felt way too good for that to be the case. I felt like running a marathon. Where were my sneakers?

I got up and dressed. Over the past few weeks I had been

running to dull my pain, pounding my feet into the pavement with a ferocity born of frustration. Now my feet barely touched the sidewalk. Before I knew it, I had run eight miles and I would have done more, but I had to meet Lola at Macy's. We were going to our friend Elena's Christmas party, and although it was pretty casual, we were still using it as an excuse to go dress shopping.

I went home to shower and looked at my wound again. I still had the holes, and the bruise was even more pronounced. I couldn't resist. I touched it again and actually moaned out loud.

I was thinking of calling the witch doctor later to ask him about the bruise, but I figured my body was simply confused by the two supernatural forces at work: the natural tendency for bites to heal immediately and my inability to heal when Johnny turned on the charm. That explained the bruising and the scabs, but it didn't explain my other reaction. Either way, I wasn't complaining.

As I dressed, I decided not to tell Lola yet. I was enjoying my little secret too much. I covered my mark with a scarf, but not before touching it several more times, reveling in the memory of the moment he penetrated me. I was beginning to become addicted to the sensation. I took the ring off my finger and stuck it in my pocket. I wasn't sure which would draw more questions from Lola, the ring or the bite.

It was only 11:30 a.m. so he was probably sound asleep, but I called to leave a message on his cell phone anyway. "Hey, it's me. Just calling to say hi. Thanks for telling me not to panic. The mark is . . . unsettling. I love you. Call me." It was lame, but I didn't know what else to say.

I met Lola at Macy's and even though it was still a week before Thanksgiving, the Christmas decorations were in full swing, as were the Christmas shoppers. It was as hot as blazes in there and we were sweating before we made it to the dress floor.

Lola was panting. "One good thing about it being so damn hot in here, I want to rip off these clothes and try on stuff." I hadn't thought about it until she said that, but trying on dresses was going to be somewhat of a problem. Even if I could talk Lola into separate dressing rooms, she'd want to see what I was trying on, and unless I was trying on a parka, she'd see my neck. Why didn't I cover up my mark with makeup? I was just going to have to pretend nothing fit me.

"How's it going in there?" Lola called over the partition in the dressing room.

"Not good, this dress gives me uniboob." I called back.

"Let me see."

"I already took it off," I lied. The dress was fantastic. I was thinking of coming back on Monday to buy it. I was worried that she could hear the deception in my voice.

This went on for about fifteen minutes, when I heard a strange thunk above my head. I looked up to see Lola leaning over the partition, looking down at me. Werewolves were incredibly agile, and she balanced atop the dressing room wall with no trouble. "Let's see the next dress." Then she saw it. "Gia, what's that?"

I wondered if I should play it stupid or maybe pretend it was a hickey. "What's what?" was the best I could come up with.

She scaled the wall in the next second, landing lightly on her feet. She turned my head and looked at my neck. She made as if to touch it, but I pulled away.

"Leave it!"

"Get dressed. We're getting out of here." She stormed off through the door and went back to her own cubicle. I barely had my jeans on when she pulled my arm out of the dressing room. "How long were you going to sit on this one?"

"Oh, Lola, lighten up! I just wanted to digest it for a while."
We were outside the dressing room and heading for the escala-
tor. "Johnny stopped by to see me last night."

"Well, duh . . ."

I thought about how good he looked standing across from
me in my office. I remembered his words. *Is this what you want?*
Oh yeah. He didn't know the half of it. I was lost in thought
when Lola broke in. "Come on, spill it."

"I guess I can't have any private moments?"

"I guess you can't," she shot back.

I told her most of it. She was curious about the fact that I
didn't heal right away and I told her my theory.

"How did it feel?" she asked.

"Better than I could have ever imagined." I told her about
the bruise's side effect and sighed. I actually sighed, then
grinned wickedly. "And I can't wait for more."

"Slut." She was smiling.

"Bitch." Good, she was okay with it. Now I wouldn't have
to defend him to her. After seeing me suffer through my self-
abusive behavior for the last few weeks, she was happy to see
the change. Another thing I liked about Lola was that she was
quick to understand a situation, and once she did, she was very
accepting.

"So do you want to go back and buy a dress?" Lola was
already turning around.

"Sure. Should I get black to go with my ring?" I slipped it
back on my finger.

Lola snorted at the black stone. "Fitting. And very pretty.
Let's get burgers before we go back. I want details, Chickpea."

I sang her a little, "What ever Lola wants, Lola gets."

I took the subway home, my arms burdened with packages.
Lola and I got sucked into the frenzy and in addition to pick-

ing out two killer dresses, we couldn't stop ourselves from doing some Christmas shopping.

I looked at my reflection in the train window. I was pale and my breathing was labored, but overall I still felt incredible. I hadn't heard from him all day, but it was only 5:30; he was probably just waking up. I was jumpy and anxious. I felt the eyes of several passengers on me—I was sure I was a sight.

The moment I got out of the subway, I checked my cell. Nothing. I walked home quickly, thinking that maybe he had left a voice mail for me there. Then I rounded the corner and saw him sitting on my front stoop.

My heart started pounding and I ran the rest of the way to him. He grabbed me and kissed me hard on the lips. It was closed-lipped, but I felt like he was embracing me from my lips down.

He set me down—had he lifted me up? I hadn't noticed. "I was hoping you'd be here." I smiled.

"I was hoping you didn't hate me for not calling." He was the Johnny I knew again. Clean, shaven, and for crying out loud, in a silk shirt under a new leather jacket.

"It was killing me all day that you hadn't called."

"Yeah, I crashed hard after I left you—I haven't really been sleeping since LA—and only woke up about an hour ago. It won't happen again. Promise."

"See that it doesn't." I couldn't stop smiling.

He kissed me again, then saw that I was shivering. "We should get you inside. You're freezing."

"No, I'm not. I'm just shaking." Surprisingly enough, it was true. Normally I was unbearably cold from September to June. But I didn't feel the cold at all. I was shaking at the sight of him. "I'd rather take a walk." This too was true. "I've got energy to burn today." He took my packages from me and handed me a bouquet of roses. I guess romance *is* dead. Well *un*dead, anyway.

"So other than having energy to burn, how do you feel?" He held my hand in his, his thumb stroking my ring. He kept looking down into my eyes as if he were looking for something specific.

I inhaled deeply and took my head out of my roses. "I feel great."

"No nausea?"

I told him that no, there were no side effects like that, just my endless energy today, and that I had actually run eight miles when I woke up.

"So no side effects at all?"

"I didn't say that." I grinned up at him. "You left me with a very naughty souvenir."

"Yeah, there's a mark, right?"

"Something like that." I led him to a darkened doorway and pulled him close. "Watch this." I opened my scarf. Before he could say anything, I took his hand and made him press on it. My eyes rolled back into my head. It was even better when he touched it. I grabbed at his arm and squirmed against the brick wall until he let go.

I was breathing hard and still kind of dizzy when I realized he was talking to me.

". . . and it's been like that since?"

"Oh yeah, baby!" I grinned lasciviously. "This has been like a built-in vibrator since I got home last night. You don't know how much trouble I had in Macy's trying to keep myself from running into the ladies' room and pressing on my neck." He gave me his crooked little half smile. How did I live without that for the last few weeks? "You know, that smile of yours will be the death of me." I dove into his jacket to nuzzle his neck. I couldn't get close enough. "So, what's next?"

"I think I'll let you take me home tonight."

15

Actually, That Did Suck

We walked back to my building, where he stopped on the top step and turned to me. "You'll ask me in, right?"

"Duh." I couldn't believe he was still so insecure. Taking full advantage of the situation and the opportunity to have a little power trip, I asked, "So I have to literally invite you into my home?" He nodded. "So you're like a Jehovah's Witness of the night. Okay, then, won't you please come in?"

He smiled. "Thank you. That will make things easier. And I'll make sure you know all our rules, what's fiction and what's fact. We'll have plenty of time. If I do this right, it's going to take a few days."

I was surprised and disappointed; Bella had told me she'd changed him in a matter of minutes.

We sat at my kitchen table. He got me a big glass of water and insisted I drink it. "We've got to talk."

"Okay, but first, I need to know what the hell is going on with my bite. That's just weird." Weird being very relative here, of course.

"Okay, but you have to promise not to get mad."

"No."

He gave an exasperated sigh. "Fine. While I was in town spying on you and hazing pretty hard, I went to see your friend Dr. Laktarnik."

I started to get up. "What are you, fucking crazy? You know he's a—"

"Relax." He gently pushed me back into my seat. "He's semiretired from his days as a slayer, although he still has some pretty scary connections. He's a *dhampir;* they're the best of the best. I had Lola call ahead to vouch for my character, so he agreed to see me."

First of all: since when did Lola start keeping things from me, and second: I knew exactly what a *dhampir* was—being that monster promotion was my business. They were the original slayers from the old country. They were usually half vampire/half human and part of a very powerful society with lots of vampire extermination methods up their sleeves. I wasn't so sure I liked the idea of Johnny visiting such an old and wise warlock/slayer. Retired or not, it wouldn't take a lot for the witch doctor to call in the reserves.

"Anyway, I went to him about the bleeding thing. I'd never heard of anyone bleeding just from being around a vampire. I looked it up, asked around. No one knew anything about it—other than your witch doctor."

"What did he say?"

"He said that I loved you." I restrained myself from saying "duh." He must have seen that impulse on my face, so he qualified that. "Okay, I knew I loved you, but I didn't realize how powerful it was. Dr. Laktarnik said that to his knowledge, this hasn't happened for a century."

"Has he been around that long?" Nothing would surprise me anymore.

"No, but he's got records going back to Vlad III. It seems my attraction to you rivals only a handful of others."

I shook my head. "I knew we were good together, but . . ."

"It gets better. It seems he's somewhat of a romantic. He's the one who actually told me what it would take to change you. Basically, I have to restrain myself and take lots of small tastes to allow your blood to acclimate to me. You'll eventually begin healing better and better with each bite. Once that happens, I can taste you properly and not worry about you dying on me." A look of deep hunger flashed in his eyes, but he quickly composed himself and grinned lasciviously. "The good doctor also told me how to handle a few more, um . . . intimate details."

I raised my eyebrows at that. "Is he the Dr. Ruth of the supernatural?"

"I guess you can add that to his list of skills. You know I was very concerned about it. I don't think he knew you'd bruise in quite this way," he reached over and lightly traced the puncture marks on my neck and I held my breath until he stopped.

"A romantic, retired vampire-slayer-warlock who also gives out relationship advice. This shit just keeps getting weirder. I wonder if he has a literary agent."

Johnny laughed at that. "Maybe you should ask him. Anyway, he's fascinated with us. He's gonna flip when I tell him about your little orgasm wounds."

He went to touch my neck again, but I waved him away. A

girl needs to think clearly sometimes, and I wanted to hear the rest of what he had to say.

"He likes you a lot, you know, and he wants to see us to-gether afterward for his records. He said you were pretty sad, and he'd like to see you happy."

"Yeah, I was pretty sad the few times I saw him."

"I'm sure going through Jonathan-withdrawal must have been hell for you."

"You're so very humble. Now aren't we supposed to be talking about our future?" I chided.

Almost immediately, I was sorry. He began talking about getting my affairs in order. I didn't even think about all the details when I went to LA, but there were tons of loose ends to consider when planning to "die." He explained that these days, a vampire had to be extremely careful about changing somebody. That modern science and advanced police inves-tigation methods took a lot of the spontaneity out of it. So I couldn't make it obvious that I was leaving the world of the liv-ing, but I could make some preparations to make things easier on my loved ones. "I have a lawyer friend who can predate a will for you so it doesn't look conspicuous—otherwise people think it's suicide."

"You have a bloodsucking lawyer?"

"Ha ha, and I've never heard that joke before." He was gently stroking my fingers when he talked, lingering on my ring finger. I reluctantly pulled away. It was all I could do to concentrate. "You have a good situation with Lola, so at least you won't have to abandon all your friends. How do you feel about your parents?"

"Not good." This had been weighing heavily on me. "I don't know how they'll react. What, I mean how . . . ?"

"We'll give you a believable death, but nothing suspi-cious. It will have to be something that can't be blamed on anyone. No getting hit by a bus or anything; that way there's no legal repercussions. The more mangled your body is reported to be, the less chance you have of them demanding to see it." Damn, he thought of everything. "Maybe a shark attack." Yuck.

A really morbid question came to mind. "What will you do for a body?"

He gave me a rather grim look. "There's usually not a shortage of those around our kind."

I felt sick. "Johnny, I don't think I can be responsible for someone's death."

He took my hand. "We'll have to take you someplace warm for this to work. If we go to a resort town, there will be lots of drifters, prostitutes. We may be able to find someone already dead or at least on death's door—at least I'll try, okay? You'll soon realize that there are a lot of people in this world who will never be missed."

What an awful thought.

"Great, well at least my last days as a human will be in the sun."

"Speaking of, how did the sun feel today?"

I hadn't thought about it. "It was overcast."

"You're taking this really well."

"As dark as this conversation may be, I made up my mind a long time ago. It's been you who's been hesitant. You've been no fun."

"I'm so much fun." He kissed me then, like last night. Gentle, but open-mouthed. His mouth didn't have the same warmth of the night before. The sensation of his cool tongue stroking mine gave me chills.

I was breathless. "You're really going to drag this out for a few days?"

"Yep. My turn to be a tease." He took my hand and led me

to the bedroom. "Trust me, I have a feeling we'll both like this."

There wasn't a doubt in my mind.

I've said before that a vampire's mouth contact can be a very special gift, but that gift comes nowhere near what actual penetration can mean. His mouth was all over my body, paying special attention to my wrists and ankles. He dragged his fangs along my pulse points and gently punctured my skin, but didn't drink a drop. It was maddening. I took his lead. He liked my little human bites that couldn't break his skin, saying they were like foreplay.

"This time, ladies first." He bit into his finger again and allowed three small drops to fall into my open mouth. I reached up to suck more, but he pulled away and continued to nibble on me, teasing me into a frenzy. He held off on actually drinking from me until we were well into the act.

Yeah, that surprised me, too. Here was one little mystery solved: vampires were physically capable of having sex—very hot and very satisfying sex. He took my neck at a very pivotal moment and I screamed. When he broke away from me, he let out a similar cry of relief. I knew my upstairs neighbors would be happy to see me go.

We were lying in bed like regular lovers. Well, regular lovers where one didn't have a pulse and the other was half a pint low on B positive. I had my head on his chest and he absentmindedly stroked my shoulder with his fingertips.

"Oh, we're doing that again," I said.

He looked down at me. "Don't be greedy, you'll have to pace yourself."

"But—"

He cut me off. "And you have to give me some time, too.

It's not exactly easy for me to stop after just that tiny little sip of you."

"But—"

"No buts, you slut. I'm not like all those other guys you've been sleeping around with."

"Oh, yeah, I guess you know about that, too." I muttered, "Stupid spying vampires."

"I was just as much of a whore while we were apart. We'll both have plenty of time together to get over it." He was right. Except for him, whoring around meant something completely different. He seduced and drank his women, whereas I only drank too much and slept around. I wanted to say *it's you who had the real drinking problem*, but for once in my life, I restrained myself.

"You know, I didn't know vampires could have sex," I said.

"And you were obviously very wrong, weren't you?" I rolled my eyes at him and he pulled me in closer. "Seriously, we can have sex, but feeding can be so incredibly pleasurable, we don't normally really want to."

Was I abnormal? "What do you mean by *normally*?"

"You'll see soon enough." He gave me a little knowing smile. "But as you just found out, we're fully functional. Don't worry, I'm glad you're not normal." He rolled over and started to trace my collarbone. "With you, I wanted to have my cake and eat it, too—so to speak."

"Cute. So how long has it been for you since . . . ?"

"Since I've had actual sex?" He was very nonchalant. "Oh, about two hundred and eighty-eight years."

What? I mean I knew he was old, but I didn't know he was that old. I was in a bit of shock. "You are one old fart! Two hundred and eighty-eight years? Now I know why you never told me anything about your past—because it'd take too long."

He laughed. "Guilty."

I got up on my elbow so I could look into his eyes. I no longer worried about his eye contact. I didn't care what happened. He, however, still wanted to take it slow, so he turned away.

I let my eyes drink him in. His body was toned, hard, and scarred from another lifetime, but Bella was right, that only made him more perfect. He was exactly as I thought he would be and I couldn't stop looking at him or touching him.

I caressed his stomach and felt it rumble beneath my fingers. "Hungry?"

"You really are a terrible tease." He picked up my hand from his stomach and placed it on my own hip.

"Am not. A tease is someone who won't give it up, and I'm giving up a hell of a lot."

That may have been the wrong thing to say. He looked sad and worried, as if he had major misgivings about his part in this decision. "You know, Gia, it's not too late to back out."

"Are we really going to start this again? Keep your dramatic vampire guilt to yourself. I'm the one human in the world who fully understands the consequences of her actions." I defiantly went back to stroking his stomach. "I've been voted least likely to regret her decision by several covens."

He smiled at that.

"You know, if anyone has to be worried about regretting his decision here, it's you." He raised his eyebrows. "I know I'm one tasty little human girl, but what if I make a crappy vampire? But even if you don't like the end product, I'm not letting you go. Ever." I phrased it like a joke, but I knew he could see the very real worry behind my eyes.

He pulled me close again. "I won't lie, your humanity is very sexy; but you've got nothing to worry about. I think the last hour speaks for itself. Other than you, I haven't been turned on by anyone, human or vampire, in the last two hundred and eighty-eight years. I don't think that's going away anytime soon." He kissed the top of my head. "I just hope forever is long enough for me."

I kissed his forehead as he usually kissed mine. "I love you, too. I'm the first lay you've had in two hundred and eighty-eight years. How was it for you?"

"It didn't suck. And how about you?" Before I could respond, he refreshed my memory. He reached down to touch the two new puncture marks on my neck. I moaned and gripped his arm as I instantly went into convulsive pleasure. In the throes of passion, he had tasted me from quite a few locations. I had four holes in my neck now. He let his fingers linger on all of them and waited until I could focus before he continued. "It's not every day you get a pair of fangs in your jugular. How was it for you?"

I had barely recovered enough to speak. "Actually, that did suck."

"Wiseass."

"Stop changing the subject and let's get back to why it has been two hundred and eighty-eight years since you've gotten any action."

"You have such a way with words. Let's see, I didn't get any *action* because the last time I wanted any was way back when I was human. I didn't really have the desire until I met you. Do I need to count off the reasons? Giovanna Felice is fabulous for the following reasons, a) . . ."

"Oh, do go on. Tell me more about my eyes." I batted my eyelashes.

He laughed and kissed me. Just lips, no fangs. He was still smiling when he said, "Okay, you want to know more? I'll give it to you. But you're going to have to back off a little bit. You're driving me crazy, and I don't want to have to literally run away from you like I did last night."

I complied and gave him some space. I didn't want him to leave.

"I always knew there was something special about you—I couldn't stop thinking about you and what it would be like to have you this way, since the first time we met. I kept trying to change that. I knew it was a bad idea to start something I couldn't finish." A little chuckle rumbled through his chest. "And you can see how well I stuck to that plan. But I recently found out just how special you were." He reached over to my side of the bed and began running his fingertips along the set of puncture marks on my wrist, driving me mad.

"Hey, mister, *I don't want to have to run away*." I was beginning to get very worked up over his touch. "When can we do this again?"

"Let's get you in to see my bloodsucking lawyer tonight and we'll see how long it will take for him to get things done. I have to go back to DC for a few days, and that should be enough time. It was a hell of a lot easier in the past to fake a death."

"Are you ever going to tell me about your past? All I know about you is that you're roughly three hundred twenty–something years old and you don't get laid very often."

"Sure." He let go of my wrist and rolled onto his back.

"My family was originally from New York. You know Bella is my cousin—our mothers were sisters and our fathers were the best of friends. My father and Bella's father were in the shipping business, but wanted to branch out into tobacco farming, so they moved both families to Virginia. I was about fourteen at the time and I had already gotten a taste of my father's shipping business, and loved it. The sea was exciting and I wasn't about to turn into a boring farmer with him.

"I was young but strong and went to work on the docks. I made some disreputable friends, and by the time I was eighteen, I was running back and forth from the Caribbean with some very shady characters."

I couldn't believe this: he really *was* a pirate! That certainly explained the silk shirts.

"I got the shit beaten out of me a lot and I beat the shit out of a lot of people. My family wasn't thrilled with my lifestyle and except for Bella, I had lost all contact with them. She and I wrote letters and I visited her every time I was back in Virginia. She eventually married, and although we led two completely different lives, we stayed close.

"When I learned of Bella's death, I was destroyed with grief—she was like my sister and my best friend. I left the life and started over. Using my talent legitimately, I started shipping tobacco for my father and my uncle, among others. Ironically, in all my years of fighting I had never got seriously hurt, but in less than two years into my new business, I got hurt so badly that I was going to lose my leg.

"It was stupid: there was a storm, the deck was wet, I got thrown under some equipment, and my leg got crushed. By the time I got back to shore, I knew it was bad. Not only was the pain excruciating, but it was discolored and gave off an awful smell. I knew it was gangrene.

"On the night I was to have it amputated. I got a visit from Bella. I was pretty drunk and in a lot of pain. I thought I was hallucinating—she had been dead for years and she looked different. Sort of otherworldly and prettier than I remembered. She told me what she was, and asked me to join her. I had nothing to lose—no wife, no kids, and since leaving the business, no friends. I would have been useless without my leg. I let her change me.

"For a while, I lived with her and her lover, Julius. They introduced me to others of our kind and taught me their ways. I took on projects and learned trades, kept busy, but mostly I felt like I was just waiting these last two hundred and eighty-eight years. I didn't know what I was waiting for, but I have a pretty good idea now."

Okay, that was easily the most romantic thing I've ever heard, and I told him so.

"Yeah, I do that lovey-dovey stuff pretty good, don't I?" He sat up and looked at the clock. It wasn't even midnight yet. "We've got some time before meeting my lawyer. Want to go dancing?"

16

Closer

The club seemed overly noisy and bright to me. Johnny assured me I would get used to it. When we met up with his group of friends I got some questioning looks. I had worn a sleeveless turtleneck and bracelets to hide the bite marks on my wrists, but when my bracelet moved as I reached for my drink, I turned quite a lot of heads. They had never seen a reaction like mine.

There was something else, too. I think I must have smelled different. Those damn vampires were always casually smelling me, but tonight many of them found excuses to be near me and I caught a few actually inhaling deeply when they were in my vicinity.

One, a blonde female that looked to be about twenty-five when she was changed, was especially curious. I had never seen her before and she kept popping up whenever I was away from Johnny's side. When I excused myself to the ladies' room, she followed me. I didn't know if vampires peed, but figured I'd find out soon enough.

"You're Gia, right? I'm Jillian," she said.

"Hi, Jillian." I held out my hand for her to shake.

She grabbed it in one of those blindingly fast vampire moves and turned my wrist toward her. She pushed up my bracelets. "What the hell is that?" She was curling her lip in disgust at my marks. "Do you have them on your neck, too?" She reached up with that same speed and tugged down my turtleneck. "Are those fake? Why won't you heal? Are you sick or something?"

"It's complicated." I pried her hand off my collar. "Who are you again?"

She ignored me and sniffed at me. "You smell weird, too. Not like a slave, and not like us, either, and kind of like sex, too, but not really."

I'd stumped her with that. I'll bet it wasn't every day she smelled undead sex. "Yeah, I'm a giant whore. Now who are you again?"

"I'm an old friend of Jonathan's—hasn't he ever mentioned me to you?"

No, he'd neglected to mention that he knew an annoyingly nosy, psychotic bitch. I kept my mouth shut. I wanted to see where she was going with this.

She was looking at her reflection now and adjusting her hair. It seemed as if she enjoyed looking at her reflection— I'll bet she was really relieved to learn that vampires actually see themselves in mirrors. She was tall and blonde, the *body by Mattel, brain by Playskool* type.

"I'm kind of surprised, really," she said. "He and I go way back, and I had heard that you two were close."

Okay, maybe I couldn't take her on physically—that superhuman strength thing was a pain in the ass—but a bitch is a bitch, and I knew how to deal with her type. "No, I'm sorry, he hasn't told me anything about you. He *does* talk about his friends quite a lot, but your name never came up. Let's see, maybe we know the same people?"

She stiffened. "You're quick." She shot me a dirty look in the mirror, then turned her eyes back to her reflection to apply lipstick. "It'll take him years to tire of you."

Such a bitch. She couldn't be bitchier on the bitchiest day of the year with an electrified bitchifying machine. I was about to say something much more sophisticated, but she continued as she posed in front of the mirror, obnoxiously admiring herself. "And I do believe we have a few acquaintances in common. You're tight with Felix, aren't you?"

How would she know that? "You have very classy taste in friends. Or is he your employer?" I saw the wheels turn as she processed the fact I was calling her a whore.

"Let's just say I do some freelance work out of his club. What's your excuse?"

Shit, she'd seen me there.

Before I could find out what she knew, Bella walked in.

"Oh, hello, Jillian. I didn't know you were in New York." Bella looked down her nose at Jillian, who appeared to shrink a little—I supposed Bella was higher ranking.

"Oh, you know me, I get around." She winked. I guess she got off on being a total slut.

"Well, if you'll excuse us." Bella put her hand on my arm and Jillian got the message. She left the room without a backward glance. "How are you feeling, Gia?"

"Okay, I guess." I looked at the door where Jillian had just passed. Why did she care about me and Felix? What was it to her?

"Don't mind Jillian; that's just a bit of jealousy. She thinks that just because she was the last person Jonathan changed, she has some kind of claim on him. She hasn't been in his life for years, but as you can see, the minute he showed interest in changing you, she was instantly at his side. That's what happens sometimes. The changed vampire can become possessive or resentful of her maker."

Hmmm, interesting. I knew Johnny must have had relationships before, and it made sense that he had changed people before, but I hadn't thought one of them would follow me to the bathroom and hit me with some Jerry Springer trash talk.

I wasn't jealous. Hey, I got sex out of the deal, and I knew she didn't. But I was still a little scared of her. I had no idea what she intended by telling me she knew I had spoken to Felix, and one could never underestimate irrational jealousy. That little Jonathan connection nagged at me. "How long ago?"

"Oh, he changed her before you were even born—about forty years ago." She wrinkled her nose. "She wasn't exactly one of his better choices. He found that out soon enough and got tired of her very quickly. She left our group after about a year. I wasn't sorry to see her go. That's one of the things Jonathan and I have in common: we've never had any patience for pettiness."

"She's afraid of you. Are you the head honcho here? Is there something I should be doing now, like kissing your ring?"

She laughed. "I am pretty old, but I'm not the oldest member of our group." I raised my eyebrows questioningly. "Michael has been around since the Middle Ages."

Michael was the slight, fair vampire who looked like he was changed when he was barely twenty years old. He had fine blond hair that was always tousled, giant blue eyes, and full sculpted lips. The name Michael fit him—he looked like an angel. He was always very quiet, but exuded a subtle strength. Now that I knew his age, that made sense.

"If you're going to start kissing rings, you'll have to start with him. And you're in luck there. Jonathan has always been one of Michael's favorites, and he seems to like you, as well."

I was surprised Michael even knew I existed. He had never said a word to me. I was also relieved to learn that Jillian was relatively young and therefore weaker than most of my vampire friends. It was a plus for me that she was not well liked. "So, should I be worried about Jillian? She seems like a total cu—"

The door opened and a human walked into the restroom. I breathed in and smelled her humanness and I think I even heard her pulse. It was weird.

Bella saw my reaction and smiled. "Ah, I remember that feeling. That will take some getting used to." She turned back to the mirror and spoke very softly so the human couldn't hear her, but now I could. "Don't worry about Jillian; she'll get over this—she has no choice in the matter. She wouldn't dare start something over some petty jealous snit—she knows she's no match for any of us." I knew Bella meant that she, Johnny, and Michael would have my back, which made me feel more at ease. But that's not what I was worried about.

The human left.

"Bella, Jillian might know I've been asking about Daniel. I think she overheard me when I was talking to my contact in Queens."

Bella considered this. "Did you say anything that could—"

"No, no, nothing damning. Just that I was looking for him. I didn't mention your name at all, but my contact knew I was dating Johnny—he was busting my chops about it pretty bad, and trying to up his fee by saying Johnny cost him a customer when he killed Billy."

"It seems to me like she was only interested in the Jonathan part of that conversation." Bella put her hand on my arm reassuringly. "Jillian is an opportunist. She knew you were vulnerable from blood loss, saw you walk away from the group, and wanted to take advantage while she could. If I know her, she's already left the club in a huff, angry that she missed her one chance to frighten you." She looked at my wrists. "How are you feeling otherwise? Jonathan tells me you're having some unusual side effects."

"Do you want to see?" She nodded and I moved my bracelets aside, then held my wrist close to me. "I'd prefer it if you didn't touch. They're kind of special." She gave me a suspicious look that reminded me so much of Jonathan, it made me smile. "They're sensitive to pressure." Let her cousin fill her in on all the gory details.

Bella nodded, then turned and left.

I took another moment to process what I had just found out. I wasn't thrilled that I had a jealous vampire who wanted to pounce on me before I was completely changed. I'd just have to stick close to Johnny while I was in this in-between stage—no great hardship there. I looked at myself in the mirror. I looked pale and peaked, but I felt great.

I wasn't so sure Bella was completely right about Jillian. She seemed too unbalanced to just let this go. But Bella understood this world better than I did, so I was going to have to trust her.

Jonathan was waiting just outside the ladies' room. "I was starting to get worried about you."

"I was just getting caught up on your delightful friend Jillian."

He had the decency to look uncomfortable. "Yeah. That was a mistake."

"Yeah, you'll tell me all about it later. They're playing our song." The DJ was playing a mixed version of Nine Inch

Nails's "Closer," and I found every word irresistibly appropriate. I dragged him to the dance floor.

This time there was no more mere flirting. We were shameless, out-and-out taunting each other. We couldn't keep our hands off each other. As we danced he would grab my hip or my wrist and brush my wounds—it was exhilarating. I thought I might be experiencing my first bloodlust, or maybe it was just lust. I couldn't tell. He was pretty worked up, too, and I wasn't sure we'd be able to remain on the dance floor for long.

He moved me into a corner and slammed me up against the wall. We were kissing hard and his fangs tore at my tongue. I bit him back with my dull human teeth and I tasted his blood as it mixed my own. It excited me in a way I had never known before. In the back of my mind, I was thinking about how wonderful it was going to feel to have those special unhealable wounds in my mouth.

With a great deal of effort, he pulled away from me. "I've got to stop." He was breathing hard. "I wasn't supposed to taste you more than once tonight. We should go." He took my hand and led me out of the club. Even in this dark corner, I could see his profile so clearly. He cleaned my blood from his teeth and savored it. "We have an appointment with my lawyer and I can't put this off another day."

I looked at my watch: 3:30 in the morning. I guess I was going to have to get used to doing business at these hours.

As we left the club I felt an uncomfortable sensation, like some very unfriendly eyes were following us, and suspected Jillian was watching us leave together. I was really beginning to hate her.

We took a cab to the lawyer's home office in Tribeca. He looked like you'd expect: balding, older, fanged. He reminded me of an undead Tom Wolfe. He welcomed us into his living room and offered me some water. I was somewhat repelled by the suggestion, but Jonathan nodded at me and I realized he wanted me to drink it, so I did. I figured it had something to do with my blood loss.

We got right down to business and created a will for me dated three years prior. It wasn't hard since I didn't have a lot of assets. My parents would get my co-op, my meager savings, and my 401(k). He threw in some living-will items for authenticity and put in a stipulation that I wished to be cremated, which made sense. Apparently he specialized in faking deaths.

We talked about the time frame. I had the week off between Christmas and New Year's. I didn't want to wait that long, but we all agreed that would be the most logical time for me to take vacation down in the Caribbean, where I'd be killed. Well, that was a sobering thought. By the time we left, I was in a major state of depression.

For once in my life, I was quiet. I had nothing to say.

"You going to be okay?" Johnny took my hand in the cab as we rode back to my apartment.

"Yeah." I wiped at my eyes, crying again. "It's not like I'm regretting my decision or anything. It's just a sad choice to make. I mean, what if my parents don't recover? I'm an only child." I started to get choked up again.

"I know." He put his arm around me and held me close. "It was easier for me. I didn't have time to think about the consequences of my actions, and to be honest, there weren't many of them. As you can well imagine, I'd made quite a few enemies."

I hadn't thought of that, but I guessed an ex-pirate wouldn't be the most popular member of his community.

When we got back to my apartment, he suggested a hot bath. It seemed like a good idea. I was tired and tense and it had been a long and bipolar kind of day. I undressed and looked at myself in the mirror behind the bathroom door. I looked different. Aside from the multiple wounds, my skin looked waxy. I leaned in and looked at my eyes. Other than being a little bloodshot, they still looked normal.

Jonathan opened the door and interrupted my examination, carrying a big glass of water. "I know it will taste weird to you, but if you're going to last until the end of December, you'll have to keep your fluid intake up."

"I wish you cold just change me now, and I'd just fake being human until my death in December."

He sat on the closed toilet seat while I got into the tub with my glass of water. "First of all, we have to take it slow. Doctor's orders." He reached over and tilted the glass until I began drinking. "And then, how could you avoid the daylight? How could you go to work? Granted, your job would understand more than most, but still, you'll have to keep up appearances."

I pouted a bit. Our meeting with the lawyer had made me heartsick and the idea of what lay ahead of me was unbearable. I wanted to do it all at once. Rip it off like a Band-Aid.

It took me a second to realize that he was undressing and climbing into the tub behind me. My apartment had the original prewar giant tub, and we fit in it together very well. He started washing my back in a massaging motion, trying to comfort me. "I'll try to make this as easy as I can for you." His massage was working; my head fell back against his chest and I started to doze off.

We spent all day Sunday in each other's arms in my bed. Shades drawn. It was a good indication of what was to come. I was so tired from the previous day and night that I didn't wake up until I heard Johnny moving around the apartment at about 5:30. It was already dark and he looked as if he was about to leave.

He saw I was up and sat on the edge of the bed. "Hey, sleeping beauty." He brushed my hair from my face. "How did you sleep?"

I groaned, still groggy. "Like the dead."

"Very funny."

"Just where do you think you're going?"

"I've got to get back to DC for one day, two at the most. Remember? How are you feeling?"

Good question. I took another little survey of my limbs and told him I was a little weak, but fine. I didn't want him to leave, but I'd have eternity with him, so I had to stop being greedy.

He kissed me good-bye and found my semihealed tongue— I was still panting when he was putting on his jacket.

"Remember, you have to eat. You won't want to, but just do it. You've got to stay healthy until our vacation. And you may want to talk to Lola about going with you again. If she's up to the responsibility, it will make things a lot easier all around."

He was right, and after he left I called Lola. Max answered her cell phone. They were out at dinner and asked me to join them. I wasn't hungry, but realized I hadn't eaten since Friday afternoon. No wonder I was weak.

I met them at a Greek restaurant in Hell's Kitchen. They were already well into their lamb kabobs—yes, werewolves really did eat quite a bit of lamb. I asked the waiter for whatever red meat they had, very rare.

I caught them both up on what was going on between Johnny and me. His visit to Dr. Laktarnik—I kicked Lola under the table to let her know that I would talk to her later about her talking to Johnny behind my back—my ongoing transformation, and my visit to the bloodsucking lawyer.

"So how's the sex?" Lola was talking with her mouth full.

I looked over at Max and admonished her. "Lola!"

"Oh come on, you can talk about sex in front of Max." She licked the *tzatziki* sauce off her fingers. "He's three times as old as you are and besides, we can smell it on you. Right, Max?" She took another bite of her food. "And it smells freaky."

Thankfully, my rare steak arrived. "We'll discuss it another time." I dug in and I have to say my manners were as bad as Lola's and Max's. Between bites, I asked them for their help in faking my death. I told them that I would pay for them to come to Jamaica with me over the holidays, but tragically, they'd have to cut their trip short when I was attacked and killed by a shark.

"Wow, Gia, that's not an easy favor you're asking for. Your mom is gonna freak."

"I know, Lo, but I don't want her to find out from a stranger."

"I don't know." She looked over at Max. "I'll have to check my calendar. Can I sleep on it?"

I reached across the table and took her hand. "Of course." I knew she'd say yes, but it *was* a lot to ask, and I wanted to give her time to get used to the idea. I also knew the calendar thing was just an excuse to buy time. Everyone at our table knew the phases of the moon for the next year like the backs of our hands.

I moved the rice around on my plate. I was really only interested in the steak, and I had already completely devoured that. The table was silent. I'd ruined everyone's evening. I took a stab at easing the tension. "You know, if it will make you feel any better, I could tell your mom your secret—then we'd be even."

Max's head whipped up. "Your mom still doesn't know?"

Well, that backfired. "I'm kidding, Max," I lied. Lola kicked me under the table. Lola had very little family and her only close relative was her mom, whom she had never told about her lycanthropy. Her mother was very old and in a nursing home. Her vision was so bad that she never noticed that Lola was aging so slowly that she looked to be in her late twenties, early thirties at most, when she was really closer to forty-five. Lola knew her mother was dying and didn't want to give her such a shock. Apparently that was an issue between her and Max, and I had just stuck my foot in it. I tried again. "Hey, guys, what has four legs and one arm?"

No answer.

"A happy werewolf." I gave them a lame smile.

"Very cute." Lola was now eating my pita bread, having finished her own. "Max, why don't you excuse yourself to the men's room so Gia here can tell me what it's like to be a necrophiliac."

"Ewww, I hadn't thought of it like that. Lola, you are gross."

"Me? At least my guy has a pulse." She was getting way too much enjoyment out of this.

"Leg-humper."

"Corpse-fucker."

I got home fairly early—after all, it was Sunday night and I had work the next day. I knew I wouldn't be sleeping anytime soon, though I had way too much to think about.

I took a long run along the river, and again, I felt a set of eyes on me. I turned around and was relieved to see that my admirer wasn't Jillian, it was just some dirty old man sitting on a park bench checking out my ass. Either way, it freaked me out, so I turned around and went home to clean my apartment. I was restless and I missed Johnny.

He called at about three a.m. to check in. He made sure I was still feeling okay and that I was eating. He was having some issues and wouldn't be back in New York until Saturday, and I told him it was probably for the best—I was a basket case when he was around anyway.

17

Supernatural Sleepover at My Place

Monday was an absolute bear. It was one of those bright
sunny winter days and Johnny was right, I was extremely sensitive to it. I looked like hell, my skin was the color
of skim milk, and I was sweating even though it was only 30
degrees. I did what I could with makeup, tied a scarf around
my neck, and went in to work with my sunglasses. As usual,
the editorial assistants thought I was hungover but I really
didn't care. I was preoccupied with my impending death. That
sounded so surreal.

I worked hard, knowing these were my last few weeks—
made tons of follow-up calls, wrote lots of great pitches. I
didn't want to leave any loose ends, and I didn't want to leave
Lois in a big hole when I left. Between pitches, I worked on
the homework Jonathan's bloodsucking lawyer gave me—buy

my plane tickets, make my hotel reservations, et cetera. It took up a fair amount of my time and a huge chunk of my concentration. I was so preoccupied with thoughts of my "departure" that I prayed to Saint Bernardino of Siena (the patron saint of public relations) that I didn't forget to do anything major regarding my clients. On the upside, I would be able to come clean to my supernatural authors come January.

At about 4:30, Ian knocked on my door. "There's someone here to see you. A guy named Felix."

Here? Felix came to Speculation? That made me more than a little nervous. "Tell security to send him up."

"He's already passed security. He's at our reception desk now."

That didn't surprise me. "Okay, can you go get him? I just want to finish this e-mail." I turned back to my computer to finish composing a memo.

"Uh, Gia . . ." Ian looked very pale and nervous. "I think there's something you should know about this guy. He's really scary-looking." He stepped close to my desk and whispered, "Don't think I'm crazy, but I think he really *is* a vampire."

Ian was pretty sharp. We'd have to talk later.

"Don't sweat it, kid. I know Felix and he just gets off on being as scary as he can be. He's cool." Ian left reluctantly.

I finished my e-mail and looked up when I heard Ian tell Felix, "She's right in here."

Felix stood at my doorway. No wonder he scared the shit out of Ian. He looked like a biker today, all leather, chains, and sunglasses. He had a broad grin on his face and I figured he was getting a kick out of showing off his gold fang to my assistant.

"May I come in?" he asked.

Ian's eyes widened at that question.

"Of course, Felix, you're welcome to come in." I stood up

and came around the desk. He hugged me to him and smelled my hair.

I knew he would know that I'd been bitten. He could smell the change in me. "Ah Gia, I knew it was just a matter of time before you joined us. Welcome to the famil—"

I shushed him. "Felix, I work here."

But he wasn't listening, he was still sniffing at me. Even though I'd showered since, he smelled the sex on me. "What the . . . ?" He pulled back and looked at my eyes and his face split into a sinister grin. "Damn, Gia, you really did drive him crazy, didn't you?"

I smiled in spite of myself. "Sit down, Felix." Ian was hovering around the doorway waiting to see if I needed anything for my guest: coffee, water, garlic, maybe. "Can I get you anything? Coffee, water?"

"Coffee, black."

"Like your soul?" I winked at him. "Ian, please get us two black coffees."

Ian left, looking puzzled. I guess he thought vampires didn't drink coffee. When he returned, I said, "Thanks, Ian, please close the door on your way out."

He clearly thought better of that and didn't close it all the way.

"So what brings you to the legitimate side of town?" I asked Felix.

He leaned in and said in a barely audible whisper, "Can you hear me when I talk this low?" He realized I was still in the halfway stage and wasn't sure about my abilities.

"Loud and clear."

"Good." He looked deadly serious, which was making me a little more uneasy. "Gia, I had business in this part of town, so I thought I'd warn you in person." Okay, now I was terrified. "You've got problems. First, Daniel knows about you. That's my fault. When you asked about him in my office, I should have known better than to answer you there. There were other vampires on the premises and one of them overheard us. One of them went to him and told him you were looking for him."

I knew it. "Thanks, Felix, I've already had the pleasure of meeting the charming Jillian, and it makes sense that she told Daniel I was asking about him."

He looked surprised. "So you know she has this thing for your guy, too? That Jonathan was the one who changed her, and she kind of went off the deep end when he broke up with her?"

I can't say I knew all those details, but I nodded regardless.

Felix sat back. "She's total trash." This, coming from a strip-club owner, had to be a huge insult. "She's been working in the industry for about forty years and she's got quite an appetite." I knew by industry, he meant the stripper/porn business. That was a good place for her to work if she was hungry—she could feed on any guy who bought a lap dance. "She's been working my club for the last two years, and she's a typical mercenary. She went straight to Daniel and told him you were asking around. I'll bet she thought she'd get some kind of fat reward for that. And you don't want to be on this guy's radar. He's the type who—"

"Hunts werewolves and other vampires for sport and eats babies for a snack?" I finished for him.

"Aw shit, Gia, don't tell me you already tried to find him." But he knew by my reply that I had. "Well, it was nice knowing you. He's the kind who'll get a thrill out of having the underworld's publicist on his tail. He'll be on your ass any day now."

You know, I hadn't thought about that. My wide contacts in the underworld would be a gold mine for someone like Daniel. If I were his slave, I could put him in contact with several covens of vampires, a few packs of werewolves, entire societies of practicing witches. I could potentially provide him with a regular smorgasbord.

"I'll be careful, Felix. Thanks for the heads-up."

He shook his head. "I know it's none of my business, but why do you want to find him?"

My heartbeat and breathing had been so off since my last bite that I was reasonably sure I could lie to him. "Felix, look around." I gestured to the shelves of books around me. "What do you think we do here, make pot holders?"

He shook his head again, but seemed to be satisfied with the answer. Good, let him think I was after a book deal with the evil Daniel. Greed was something he understood.

He stood up to leave and when he hugged me good-bye, he inhaled deeply again. "Call me when you're *finished*. We'll go to dinner." He gave me a crooked grin that showed his gold fang. Yeah right, like I was going to let that happen. As an afterthought, he picked up his coffee and downed it. "That will throw off your assistant."

I gave him a little smile. "You know, we get your kind here all the time. Funny how you're the first one he's suspected."

"Yeah, I wonder why that is." He flashed his gold fang again, then left. I heard him stop Ian in the hallway. "Hey, it was nice meeting you, dude."

I heard Ian mutter, "Yeah, nice meeting you, too." And I knew he was being freaked out by Felix's ice-cold handshake.

I sat back down at my desk and saw an instant message invitation on my screen.

Ravenous: "Congratulations. You found me. I'm impressed. It seems you really are as connected as they say."

Holy shit. It had to be Daniel. How should I play this? I had a reputation for being flip and blasé about the supernatural, so I'd stay in that role.

PitchAndMoan: "Why, Daniel, is that you? Or is it Dante these days? I'm honored. You're not an easy man to track down."

Ravenous: "Are we going to kiss each other's asses all day, or are you going to tell me what you want from me?"

I decided to stick with the book deal line.

PitchAndMoan: "Surely your sources told you what I do for a living. I figure you have one hell of a story in you and I should be the one to exploit the hell out of it—as a fictional account, of course."

Ravenous: "You know, I like you better with your hair down. Take that pen out of your hair and let down that pony-tail for me."

Could he see me, or was he just trying to freak me out? Did I dare call him on it? I was sweating profusely.

PitchAndMoan: "Gee, I'd think you'd prefer it up. I was sure you were a man who appreciated a girl's neck." Even if it was covered by a scarf today.

Ravenous: "Take your hair down, Gia."

Okay, so he was a power-tripping-bloodsucking savage.

PitchAndMoan: "You're the boss." I slipped the pen out and took the rubber band from my hair and shook my head.

Ravenous: "That's better."

He had to be in the office building across the street. They had a clear view into my window.

Ravenous: "Will you meet me for dinner?"

Riiight. So he could eat me alive for the main course? I didn't think so.

PitchAndMoan: "I have plans."

It was true; I was meeting Lola. Though maybe I shouldn't, since Daniel had a taste for her kind. I needed to talk to Bella right away.

Ravenous: "I know, with your friend Lola. I can read your calendar from here. I don't suppose you'd let me join you?"

PitchAndMoan: "You underestimate me, Daniel. I've done my homework and I know your tastes. Do you really think I would invite you along?"

Ravenous: "You're good at your job. It will be a pleasure doing business with you."

PitchAndMoan: "So is that a Yes?"

Ravenous: "It's a Maybe. You'll be hearing from me."

My screen flashed, "Ravenous signed off at 5:23 PM."

My mind was reeling. I had a feeling Daniel was watching me to see whom I'd call after this, so I buzzed Ian on my intercom and asked him to get Bella on the phone for me, so Daniel wouldn't see me dial. He got her right away and put the call through to my line.

"Bella, I'm done with your project." I was speaking very softly, so my very curious assistant couldn't overhear. "Daniel's on to me—he just contacted me."

"Gia, that wasn't supposed to happen."

"Yeah, well, you can't say I wasn't warned."

"You're in incredible danger."

"I know, Bella, but what the hell do you want me to do?"

"Meet me at—"

"He's watching me now, Bella. That's why I had Ian dial from the other room. He knows I'd call whoever I'm working for, even though I told him I was working solo—trying to get a book deal out of him."

"He believed you?"

I smiled. "I can lie to you guys now."

"Oh."

"Besides, I've got something he wants. I have connections to beings that can satisfy his rather exotic tastes." I shuddered.

"I never thought of that."

"Yeah, neither did I, but I'm kind of a power mogul in his eyes. Which means I'm a pretty attractive candidate for his next slave." I ran my hand through my hair, which was still down. "Bella, I don't know what you wanted to find him for, but now my ass is on the line, and if he does get his hands on my Rolodex, so is the ass of everyone I know—including you. I'm calling in the big guns now and ending this shit." My next call was going to be to Dr. Laktarnik.

"No!" she yelped. "No, Gia, I need to talk to him first."

"Bella, I'm not risking my neck for this anymore. I'm in a bit of a transitional stage in my life here, in case you hadn't noticed, and I don't need Daniel fucking it up for me. I love you, Bella, but I'm not going to screw up what I've got with Johnny."

"You're not going to tell *him*—"

"Of course not. I made you a promise. It was stupid of me, but I won't tell him. Now I have to call a man about a stake."

"Please Gia, give me some time."

I thought about it. "We'll talk about that later, but I'm going to be working on plan B. Johnny gets back on Friday, and until then, I want security. Call your friends. I want the oldest, biggest, and strongest of your group on my ass at all times—I don't care what you tell them, but I want them here within the hour. And I want you to come clean with me."

"Fine. I'll come by tonight."

I left a voice mail for Lola canceling dinner. I was killing time and deleting emails with client contact information until seven o'clock when the downstairs security told me that two gentlemen were waiting for me. My bodyguards. I grabbed my coat and, more important, my Rolodex, and went down to meet them. Michael and the tall, black, tattooed vampire were waiting for me. I shook Michael's hand and he just nodded.

I turned to the other. "I'm Gia. I don't think we've ever been properly introduced."

He gave me a big, warm smile—well, as warm as a fanged smile could be. "I'm Orlando, and I don't blame Jonathan for keeping you to himself all this time."

I smiled back; he was very charming. "Thank you both for coming. Shall we go back to my apartment? I think Bella will be meeting us there, and you're both more than welcome." They got my meaning and we stepped out of the lobby and into the freezing December evening to a town car. The British vampire was behind the wheel. He introduced himself to me as Nelson and began driving way too fast up Sixth Avenue. I felt very safe sitting between Michael and Orlando in the backseat, and for the first time since my IM exchange with Daniel, I breathed easier while they breathed in my unique scent—part human, part vampire, part freaky undead sex.

At the front door, Michael took the keys from me and entered first. He immediately swept through the apartment, looking for any hiding minions, I suppose. Orlando took my coat from me and hung it neatly in my coat closet. I guess chivalry is indeed undead.

Michael seated himself at the kitchen table in my most uncomfortable chair while Nelson and Orlando made themselves at home on the couch.

"Can I offer you anything?" What a stupid question. "I have a neighbor across the hall I don't like very much."

Orlando's face split into a grin. "I like you, Gia. You're funny. It will be a welcome change from the usual. Mr. Happy-Go-Lucky here is a barrel of laughs." He gestured to the stoic Michael.

In an obvious stage whisper, I said, "Is he always this much of a party?"

"No." Nelson was smiling, enjoying himself. "Sometimes he's serious."

Michael didn't move a muscle. It was just weird.

Bella rang the buzzer, and I invited her in. When she got upstairs, I hugged her to me. "Bella, did you want to talk in my bedroom?"

Orlando politely turned on the television to give us some privacy and Bella and I went into the other room. We sat on the bed and she took my hand.

"Gia, I'm so sorry." Her brow was furrowed with worry.

I waved her off. "It is what it is. Now, what's the deal with you and Daniel? Is it revenge or something? You're pissed at him for changing you?"

"It is revenge, but not for that. I haven't regretted that for years. I told you that Julius died in a fire twelve years ago and that most thought it was suicide. Well, I never did. Daniel was furious at him for taking me away from him. It made him appear weak in front of his coven. I think Daniel killed him, and I need to know for sure."

She got up and started pacing. "Seeing centuries of life go by can be agonizing. Julius told me that he thought of suicide daily, until he met me and I took away that pain. Then after almost three hundred happy years together, he ends his own life? It just seemed wrong to me. Some of the others had known of his previous wish for death, so they bought into the self-induced fire. But . . ." Her voice caught. "I just can't believe he wanted to leave me. I know it was Daniel. He would have gotten a special thrill from hunting and trapping a vampire as old and as powerful as Julius. It must have taken a lot of patience on Daniel's part—my Julius was not easily fooled."

Bella was fiercely loyal. And if I thought about it, wouldn't I do the same thing if it were Johnny?

"Gia, I need to know for sure. And I then I want to kill him."

"Just how do you plan on killing him, Bella? He's the most lethal creature I've ever come across."

"I . . . I don't care if I succeed. I hate him enough to kill him or die trying."

I wanted Bella to have her revenge, and let's face it, the world would be a better place without Daniel. But she was discounting the other dangers. "Bella. Think this through. Hate won't be enough here. He's positively diabolical. He'll tear you to shreds, and still be around and still hunting me."

Bella sank into the corner of the bed and seemed to shrink before my eyes.

"And unleashing Daniel has put not only you and me in danger. As we speak, he's probably rifling through my office looking for my Rolodex, which would give just about everyone I know a death sentence."

Guilt was clearly etched on her face now.

"Of course, I have that little prize here with me, and it's infinitely more valuable with me alive so that I can identify which clients are what, but still . . ." I wanted her to know that I was not budging on this. "Consider what you've done."

She looked up at me, pitifully vulnerable. "What can we do?"

"First of all, I think you have to give up finding out about Julius. I know that will be hard, but you're going to have to look into your heart for the answer. Knowing you the way I do, I can't imagine Julius would kill himself, and at the very worst, I can't imagine he would do it without telling you." I squeezed her hand; I knew it was going to be hard for her to let go.

"Second, I know someone. I'll take care of it. It will have to be enough for you to just know that he's dead."

"I guess it shouldn't be a surprise that you have slayers in that Rolodex of yours, as well. Anyone I know?"

"Actually, I only know one slayer—it's best if you don't know who—and I've never needed him in that way before. And Bella, I'm bringing Lola in on this. I need some daytime protection. You know he has slaves." She nodded. "And I want *you* to tell Jonathan." She nodded again.

I could tell she didn't like that part at all. Jonathan was going to be rip-shit when he found out his cousin had endangered my life. He probably wasn't going to be too thrilled with me for agreeing, either, but I could blame that on stupid human tendencies.

"Bella, I need to make some phone calls. Will you please excuse me?"

She left the room and I called the witch doctor. I told him I'd meet him tomorrow around lunchtime. He didn't ask questions; he simply took the appointment.

Then I called Lola. That was significantly harder. I explained everything and she yelled at me for a good twenty minutes. She insisted that she and Max come over right away, and I couldn't persuade her otherwise. Great. Supernatural sleepover at my place—we could have pillow fights, do each other's hair, and eat raw meat together until dawn.

Then I sat alone in my bedroom and thought about Daniel. I wasn't surprised at how much he knew about me, or how easily he had found me. There were so many times I'd felt I was being watched—some were Jonathan, but others were probably Daniel or one of his minions. The slave at lunch that day with Lola—was she one of his? How many others were out there tracking me?

And Billy. He must have been in on it, too. Or at the very least he must have talked about me. Maybe he heard me and Bella talking in her hotel room that day and called Daniel. Perhaps hearing what Daniel wanted from me made him do what he did to me. Knowing now that he had a crush on me, I'd bet he thought he'd be protecting me, or maybe allying himself with me if he changed me.

Jillian, of course, was part of it, but what about the vampire in the West lobby? Was she supposed to bring me down or learn more about my mission? Even Mr. Twenty Questions on my flight from New York to LA could have been part of Daniel's plan. How many others were there that I didn't even notice? It's a miracle I was still breathing.

But I *was* still breathing, I had friends, family, and a new life ahead of me to protect, and I'd do everything I could to keep it that way.

18

Watch It, Bitch, or You'll Be a Ghostwriter

That night was surreal.

Bella was as quiet as Michael. They sat together at my kitchen table and stared off into space. I had no idea what Michael was pondering, but I figured Bella was coming to grips with the fact that she'd never know the truth about Julius. It must have been quite a blow.

I, on the other hand, had a most enjoyable night, considering the circumstances. Lola and Max were at my apartment within minutes of my call, and they both got on famously with Orlando and Nelson. We laughed and watched old movies until about two a.m., when Jonathan called. I kept my tone light and pretended to be sleepy, after which Lola demanded that

226

she sleep with me in my bed, and we both crashed until daybreak. Lola and I left the sleeping vampires in my living room with Max, who was curled up on my area rug under an afghan, and went to work.

She hung around in my office for a while, driving me crazy. When she finally began to annoy me so much that I threw a stress ball at her head, she popped down the hall to chat with her editor.

I kept to myself the rest of the morning and made sure I didn't have contact with anyone long enough for them to start asking questions about why Lola was hanging around me like a shadow. I knew my behavior was strange. When have you ever seen a shy and retiring publicist?

Luckily, most of my coworkers didn't really pay attention. Like most publishing houses, Speculation was closed the week between Christmas and New Year's, and everyone had where's-the-party-itis for pretty much the entire month of December. I was the least of their worries.

All except for Lois, that is. She was watching me like a hawk. I managed to avoid her until just before I was going to leave for Brooklyn.

She came into my office and closed the door. I was on the phone and motioned to my guest chair while I finished leaving voice mail for a radio show producer.

When I was done, Lois said, "We have to talk, Giovanna." She leaned forward so she could keep her voice down. "I know something is up. Spill it. When is your last day?"

She was good, I'd give her that. How should I tell her? I'd been working with her for ten years, and we were friends as well as coworkers. Oh, what the hell. It would be one less thing for me to worry about, and if anyone would understand, she would.

"Lois, you can't do anything about this if I tell you." She

nodded in consent. "Friday before the holidays will be my last day. Act surprised when you hear about my untimely death, okay?"

"Jonathan?" I nodded. "I don't blame you. I don't think I could have said no to him, either. I guess that breaks number three of the four rules of a good publicist."

By the way, those rules are as follows: 1) never be in the picture, 2) never let your author be photographed while holding a drink or a cigarette, 3) never tell another publicist a secret, and 4) there's no crying in publicity.

I laughed. "You'd better break rule number four and cry at my funeral. Don't think I won't be there, watching from the shadows. Tell me, how did you know?"

"Ha! You think you're the first publicist to leave Speculation for scarier pastures? Your predecessor is currently running wild with a pack of werewolves in Thermopolis, Wyoming, and the one before her is living in another galaxy. She's very happily married with three hamsters, or children, or whatever they are—hairy little buggers; I have pictures."

"I guess I should feel lucky we don't publish Bigfoot's biography." We both laughed, at then I looked at my watch. "I've got to go, Lois. I have a doctor's appointment." Without looking up, I said, "Hi, Lola."

She had managed to stealthily come into my office and was standing behind Lois's right shoulder."

"Jeez, Lola!" Lois jumped in her seat. "I hate it when you people do that."

Lola grinned, enjoying herself. "What's the topic today?" She rolled her eyes. "Not necrophilia again?"

"Watch it, bitch, or you'll be a ghostwriter." I swung my purse over my shoulder and intentionally clipped her arm.

"You see how she talks to her authors, Lois? I think you should fire her."

"We get it, Lola," I said with exasperation. "You heard our whole conversation. Ready to go?"

"Wow, you're in a foul mood today, Chickpea. Not sleeping well?"

I gave her the finger.

Dr. Laktarnik's wife was pleased to see us until she breathed in. Then she made a huffing sound and grudgingly led us into her husband's office. How could she smell the change in me? What the heck was she?

We entered his office and he hugged Lola tightly. When they let go, she dropped onto the leather sofa and made herself at home.

"Miss Giovanna." He took both my hands in his. "How are we feeling?"

"Physically? Fantastic. But—"

"No, no, your health comes first." He gestured to my neck. "Let's see how you're healing these days."

I pulled down the neck of my turtleneck to show him the wounds. He lifted his hand to touch them but I pulled away.

"Miss Giovanna, I won't hurt you."

Lola barked out a laugh. "It's not that, Doc. She just doesn't like you that way."

I blushed and explained that the wounds held rather special qualities. He quickly seated himself at his desk and began taking notes, asking me very embarrassing questions about the freaky undead sex I'd had. Lola was grinning ear to ear, enjoying this way too much.

When he was satisfied that I had nothing more to tell him, he sat back and steepled his fingers. "Now. Whom do you want me to kill?"

Well, that was to the point.

"His name is Daniel, but he also goes by Dante, Diego, David, and several other D names. He currently lives in Providence, but I heard he also has a place in South Beach. Right now, I know he's in New York." I took out two folded sheets of paper from my purse, one with the sketch and one with his current Providence and Miami addresses on it.

Almost shaking, Dr. Laktarnik took them from my hands. He looked up at me and I swear there were tears in his eyes. "My dear Miss Giovanna. You've just given me the gift of a lifetime. We've been hunting him for many years."

"You should have called her sooner, Doc. Little Miss Nancy Drew here is unbelievably connected," Lola said. "Go ahead, tell him what you know."

I told him everything, beginning with Felix's strip club and ending with yesterday afternoon. Not knowing what details would be significant, I left out nothing.

He told me he was bringing in his associates, the professionals. This made me incredibly nervous, and he had a hard time convincing me that his friends wouldn't lay a hand on my friends.

"I can assure you. We know about your friends and if they had misbehaved, they would be disposed of by now."

That was a scary thought. Jonathan had been *misbehaving* in those weeks we were broken up. How close had he come to being destroyed?

"I also admire the way your particular group of friends always takes care of the troublemakers themselves. We've never had to intervene." I assumed he was talking about Jonathan killing Billy. "You've landed with a responsible group." I supposed this was a compliment of sorts.

"When will you do it?"

"The sooner the better. Possibly tomorrow at midday; he'll be weakest then. But we'll need time to assess his security detail. I presume he's a well-protected man."

That, I'm sure, was an understatement. "He wants to meet with me. We could set a trap."

"I'd rather not use you as bait unless it's absolutely necessary. Relax, Miss Lola—we'll only use her as a last resort." Lola had sat up protectively, her hackles raised. It was nice to have a friend like her.

"Having Miss Lola with you during the day should keep his slaves at bay. But don't underestimate him at dawn after twilight. He'll have no problem finding you alone, regardless of your many escorts."

That was a sobering thought.

"Now, let's get you outfitted with some protection." He stood up and opened the cupboard behind his desk and began removing an assortment of objects, most of them gleaming silver. "Let's start with what you already have."

"I carry a twenty-two, a stake, and garlic." I patted my purse.

"Does the garlic bother you yet?" I shook my head no. "And your stake, is she wooden or silver?"

"Wooden."

He shook his head. "That won't do. That usually only works between vampires, and you don't have the strength to drive it through the spinal column yet. It's not piercing the heart that kills a vampire; it's severing the backbone—that's why decapitation is the best method."

"Sliver is better for you. Sliver blessed by the Catholic Church is even stronger, and all my silver comes from the church. Here." He handed me what looked like a big elaborate letter opener. "I'd rather you weren't close enough to use this on him, but just in case." I took it from him. "Now, let me see your gun." I complied and handed him my .22, which was loaded with silver bullets. He looked at it, then handed me a Glock. "This is better for you; it's faster. All three safeties are disabled one after the other when the trigger is pulled. How is your aim?"

"Dead-on." An old boyfriend of mine used to take me to a firing range on dates.

"Good girl." The doctor loaded a pistol with silver bullets, then took more ammunition out of the cabinet.

I glanced over to see Lola curled up in the corner of the couch. The smell of the silver was upsetting her.

The doctor noticed it, too. "Lola, why don't you go see Mrs. Laktarnik? She's making liver and onions."

"Okay." It was almost a whimper. She scurried from the room. It made me uncomfortable to see her so shaken and vulnerable.

"Now, here's the last thing. It's the most simple, and the most practical." He handed me what looked like a dish-soap bottle.

"I thought holy water didn't work?"

He smiled. "You're very well informed. This is filled with garlic juice and silver-laced water. It won't kill him, but it will slow him down enough for you to use one or both of the other two weapons." He put a big plastic jug on the desk. "For refills."

"What about that big knife? That looks like it could do some damage." I gestured toward the gleaming cutlass-like weapon in his cupboard.

"That's rather special." He took it down to show me. It was silver with a bone handle and engraved with symbols that appeared to be a mix of Celtic, Greek, Slavic, and Asian. "It's been used by my kind for centuries. It's only to be used by us. It's mainly used for decapitation, naturally." He looked into my eyes. "You do know what I am, don't you?"

I nodded. "You're a *dhampir*."

He smiled at me. "You are an interesting woman, Miss Gia.

You could have been a great slayer." I must have slightly re-coiled, for he chuckled. "Don't worry, I'm not recruiting. I didn't have much of a choice. My father was human, a very skilled slayer, in fact. My mother was a slave, bitten several times, but never completely changed. My father was charged with killing her, but instead he fell in love and married her. Now you see why I'm such a romantic." He was smiling warmly. "Sometimes the most unlikely relationships are the strongest." He took my hand. "Now, you try to stay alive until your boyfriend gets home."

That was my plan, as well. "Thank you, Doctor." I put the weapons in my purse and picked up the jug, then I remembered what Brian had told me. "I've heard that he can be out when it's dawn or just before dusk." I relayed what my Massachusetts werewolf told me.

The doctor nodded. "He's been getting more powerful—only very old or very strong vampires can do that. But they can't be in the direct sunlight, no matter how strong they are. Miss Giovanna, you'll have to try to be as safe and as careful as you can. I'll drive you ladies back to the city, but first, let's have some of that liver."

For the first time in my life, that sounded appetizing. I think I was on an undead version of the Atkins diet.

Lola stuck to my side the rest of the afternoon. She was down-right annoying. At about 4:30, I saw Johnny come online.

BiteMe: "u there?"

"Lola, it's Johnny. What do I say to him? I don't know if Bella talked to him yet."

Lola sat in my guest chair with her feet resting on my desk, reading the latest issue of *Starlog*. She didn't look up. "Just talk to him. If she told him, you'll know within seconds."

PitchAndMoan: "Hey there. What are you doing up so early?"

BiteMe: "I have a lot of business here in DC before I come

back to NY. Hey, sorry I woke you last night. I'll call earlier tonight."

I felt like I was lying to him, and it felt all wrong.

PitchAndMoan: "Have you talked to Bella yet today?"

BiteMe: "No, why?"

PitchAndMoan: "Just wondering. She said she wanted to talk to you."

BiteMe: "Okay, I'll call her now. Catch you later."

He signed off.

I answered a few e-mails, and when Ian finally came by to say good night, I realized just how tired I was. "Come on, Lola, let's get the hell out of here." I put on my coat. "Subway or bus?"

"Cab."

"You paying?"

"You think I'm going to let you take a subway with Daniel on your tail?"

Good point.

Since Speculation was located in the heart of midtown, it was fairly easy to get a cab. Lola hovered around me protectively, sniffing the air, and thankfully it was only seconds before one pulled up. I opened the car door for Lola. "After you, bodyguard."

She climbed in, and as I was about to follow, an incredibly strong hand closed over mine on the door handle. I knew it was him.

"Your skin smells delightful." I felt his breath in my hair; he was breathing in the scent of my half-changed blood. "I love them in this phase—so tasty, but sadly, they don't put up much of a fight."

Frozen at the taxi door, I looked down at his hand covering mine. It was warm; he must have fed recently. I took a deep breath. *I'm über-underworld-publicist. I'm cool.*

Without turning around, I said, "Daniel, this is a bad time for me. Why don't you call my assistant and make an appointment?" I reached into my purse and pulled out my squirt bottle of silver/garlic water.

"Oh, I prefer to be spontaneous."

Lola was about to pounce on him, which would have meant certain death for her. Before she could move, I turned and doused him.

He staggered back and fell to the ground, immediately drawing a crowd of tourists.

I was in the cab in a second and Lola yelled "Drive!" at the cabbie. As we pulled away, I looked back.

He was standing in the halo of the streetlight and he was hauntingly beautiful. Jet-black hair, high cheekbones, piercing blue eyes—and those unbelievably powerful hands were clenched into fists as he watched us drive off.

Lola was already on the phone to Max, telling my new East 85th Street coven to meet me on the sidewalk in front of my building. I sat very still, trying to digest what just happened. How close had I just come to death thirty seconds ago?

My phone vibrated, and I answered it automatically. "Hello?"

"Just what the fuck do you think you're doing?" Jonathan screamed. Vampires could be very loud. Even through the cell phone, his voice filled the backseat.

"I—"

"You're so fucking stupid, Gia, I can't believe you!"

Lola could hear him and went to take my hand, then realized it was soaking wet. I had spilled the silver/garlic water all down my front. She found a dry spot on my knee and squeezed it for support.

"Johnny, are you driving?"

"No, I'm sitting on my ass while you try to get yourself

killed. What do you think? I'll be at your apartment in a few hours."

I knew how fast Johnny drove; he'd be there in record time.

"I don't know who to be more pissed at—you or my asshole cousin. I can't believe she put you in that kind of danger!"

"Johnny, it wasn't like that. It just—"

"Come on, Gia. You're so vulnerable now—how do you expect to deal with one of the most powerful vampires out there?"

I could understand his anger, but I was getting tired of being yelled at. I took a deep breath and spoke in a calm, soft voice. "Well, let's see: I just kicked his ass about two minutes ago. Does that answer your question?" I really did not want to have this conversation in the cab. "We'll talk about it when you get here. Drive carefully." I snapped the phone shut.

Lola rolled her eyes. "Boy, you really told him off. 'Drive carefully?' He could survive a ten-car pileup without a scratch."

"I'm not worried about him surviving a ten-car pileup: I'm worried about him causing one. You know how he drives."

We pulled up in front of my apartment, where four vampires and a werewolf were chatting it up with my neighbor. Orlando, Nelson, and Max were playing with her two French bulldogs while Bella talked animatedly about something, and Michael stood off to the side silently.

"Hello, Mrs. Battliglia. I see you've met my friends."

Bella looked like she was going to burst into tears at the sight of me, and came over to hug me.

"Careful, Bella, I'm all wet," I said pointedly. It wouldn't do to knock out Bella with my silver/garlic-sodden coat in front of Mrs. Battaglia.

"Gia, dear, you have such nice friends."

I felt Orlando's strong hand on a dry spot of my arm. "Yes, it was so nice meeting you, but we must get Gia out of these wet clothes before she catches a cold." And I was whisked off the street and up the stairs. "Gia, you smell awful," he said.

"It's my new perfume, eau de silver chalice and garlic."

"Eh, take a shower, will ya?"

"I intend to. I think I may have a date tonight." I raised my eyebrows suggestively.

Orlando opened my door for me. "I wish your apartment was ten times bigger. I don't want to be anywhere near y'all when Jonathan gets ahold of you and Bella."

"Thanks for having my back, big guy."

"Hey, I stay out of lovers' quarrels and family disputes."

I showered and came into the living room to hang out with the others while we waited for the J bomb to arrive. Max cooked rare hamburgers for me and Lola, while she arranged for Dr. Laktarnik to meet us at the office the next day.

"Good," I said through a mouthful of burger, "I may try to talk him into writing a book for us. Maybe a series of romance novels about half-changed vampire women and their hopeless attraction to strapping young slayers." Lola threw a dish towel at me. "No, it really has potential."

Jonathan rang my buzzer. I knew he was pissed, but I was dying to see him; I'd been fantasizing about him all week. I couldn't turn that off just because he was going to read me the riot act.

I ran into his arms and he held me tightly to his chest and kissed my hair, still damp from my shower. Then I felt him stiffen, and looked up to see him staring at Bella.

"Why don't I let you two talk?" I tried to extricate myself from his arms, but he held me tight.

"Oh no, you don't, you're not getting off that easy." He

guided me toward the bedroom and motioned to Bella to precede us.

"Yes, Dad." I rolled my eyes, but he was having none of my playful mood.

After the door was closed, Bella and I sat on the bed while Johnny stood glaring at us with his arms crossed. She explained how this hunt for Daniel had started, why she wanted to find him, and why she wanted to keep it to herself—that she was sure she was the only one who still thought Julius's death wasn't accidental.

I jumped in to tell Jonathan about Felix, Jillian overhearing, and Daniel getting wind of my extensive underworld contacts. By the time I got to my close encounter with Daniel outside my office, he was pacing and running his hands through his hair and giving me that same look he did in LA. However, this time I wasn't backing down.

"Listen, Johnny, Dr. Laktarnik is on the case, and he and his professionals will take care of him—they've been hunting him for a long time and they're not about to let him get away. I know you're pissed that I didn't tell you, and I'm sorry about that, but I made a promise and I keep those. You've got to calm the ef down."

He stared angrily at me. "I can't believe I left you here before you were completely changed. You're so—"

"I'm so friggin' *lucky*. Think about it: if you had changed me, I wouldn't be able to carry around that silver/garlic cocktail that saved me tonight." He had every right to be mad at me, but in all fairness, I can't believe he wouldn't have done the same thing in my place. "I promised Bella I'd help her long before you decided to commit to me. Changing me sooner wouldn't have helped. Nothing you could have done would change this situation."

He sat on the edge of the bed. "You say you keep your

promises?" I nodded. "Then promise me you won't do something this stupid again."

"I'll do my best. But I *am* just a dumb blond you know." His lips were threatening to turn up into a grin. "Don't smile, baby, your face will crack." He did smile at that. "So we're okay, then?"

"Yeah." He pulled me into a hug. "I'm okay with you, too, Bella. I should have known you'd want closure."

She was nodding, then stood and left the room.

I was worried about her, but then saw that Michael followed her out of the apartment. Jonathan had moved on and was now nuzzling my neck. "Easy—there's a bunch of beings with exceptional hearing in the other room."

He groaned disappointedly and pulled away. "Yeah. I guess you should get some sleep, too. You look half dead."

"Very funny."

19

An Awful Nosebleed

I slept badly that night.

My alarm went off at seven, and I nudged Lola until I believed her declaration that she was awake. Bella and the men were lounging around the living room.

Max was in the kitchen and asked, "Can I make you two breakfast?"

He was a pretty good cook, but I was too anxious to eat. "I'll just have coffee. Lo?"

"Make me an omelet, Max—full of onions and peppers." She came around to kiss him. Apparently werewolves were not deterred by morning breath.

I ducked into the bathroom; my breath could have knocked a buzzard off a shit wagon. I came out with my teeth brushed, my hair done, and my makeup on.

"Are you sure about going to work today?" Jonathan asked, following me into the bedroom.

"I'll be fine. I'm meeting Laktarnik there later, and it's daylight. Lola can take care of anyone he sends in the daytime." I didn't tell him about my suspicions that Daniel could maneuver around during certain times of the day; why worry him more? "What will you be up to?"

"I'll crash. I think I'll give Bella your bed, though—I don't think I could sleep if I had to smell you all day."

I was in the closet picking out my clothes when I heard the bedroom door close. He came up behind me. "Do I have time for a little breakfast?" He pushed my hair to the side and rested his lips on the pulse point on the right side of my neck. It felt as though all the blood in my body rushed up to meet him there. Dizzy, I held on to the hanger rod of my closet for support.

"I think I can squeeze in a few minutes for you." I began to turn around but he held me in place. He reached around to undo my robe and slid one hand between my thighs while the other tilted my head back to expose my neck. His finger pressed against my lips. He had bitten it for me, and I took it into my mouth to let him bleed onto my tongue. His teeth sank into my skin and although the sensation should have become familiar by now, I was still amazed at the intensity of it. It took all my willpower not to cry out.

He drank for only four or five seconds, but when he was done, he had to support me so I wouldn't crumple to the floor. As I recovered, I leaned into him. He was tense and I knew he wouldn't have an easy time dealing with my leaving.

I turned around in his arms. "Hey, you sure that door's locked?" He nodded. "Up for a little human fun?"

"What did you have in mind?"

I slid my hand into his jeans. "We human girls really suck sometimes, too."

"I—"

"Shut up and take it like a man." I winked at him before I slid down to my knees and helped him get over his—um, shall we say tension? When he was nearing his peak, I reached up and offered him my wrist for another taste. He stumbled forward with his release, and if there was any doubt in my mind that he enjoyed it, I was vindicated by our tumble onto the floor of my closet. "Well, that was very graceful."

He helped me off my shoe rack. "Sorry about that." He was still shaking. "That surprised the hell out of me."

"Ya think?" I struggled to untangle myself from the belts and scarves that had landed on me in our fall. "Now I really do need to get to work." I picked out the first turtleneck I could find, got dressed, and left for the office with Lola, who was grinning ear to ear. Stupid supernatural hearing. I think I blushed all the way to the corner as we went to hail a cab.

Then I saw him, standing in the diner on the corner, looking out the window over a cup of coffee directly into my eyes. The sun had just risen and there he was, out in the daylight. "Lola, move." I pushed her into traffic and we dodged cars until I jammed us both onto a bus that had just pulled up.

"What the . . . ?" Lola wasn't an easy person to physically move—that whole lycanthropic strength thing, you know. I grabbed her head and turned it toward the diner. Daniel was there giving me a creepy grin and a wave. Son of a bitch!

The bus pulled away and Lola and I made our way to the back. We kept silent about what just happened and got off after three stops.

"G, how was that possible?"

"Brian said he attacked his pack at daybreak. I think he's strong enough for weak sunlight."

Lola flashed me a reproachful look—I guess I shouldn't have kept that detail from her. "Where do you want to go? Home or Speculation?"

"Speculation. If I stay in my office, he can't come in. And Dr. Laktarnik said he can't come out in the midday sun." I thought about calling Michael. The doctor had also said very old vampires could stand some sunlight, but day was quickly becoming dazzling and I couldn't put him at risk.

That day was much the same as the day before. Lola lounged on my guest chair reading and I tried to wrap up as many loose ends as possible for Lois without looking suspicious to the rest of the company.

Lola was perusing a manuscript from my shelf. "So let me get this straight: giant spiders from space are really responsible for the crop circles?"

"No, this guy's a human. He has no clue." In a bored voice I added, "We all know that it was an army of Sasquatch and wood nymphs that made the crop circles. Duh!"

Lola barked out a laugh.

Dr. Laktarnik called to say he was running late for our meeting. He was supposed to be at my office by one, but now he'd be getting here closer to four. I told him about my morning sighting and he said he'd try to get there earlier, but he was bringing along several younger slayers and it depended on their schedule. I booked the conference room for a "book proposal meeting."

The day dragged on. Being confined to my office and my apartment had me feeling like a prisoner. Johnny called me at about 3:30, complaining that Orlando's snoring was keeping him up, and asked what time he could pick up Lola and me from the office. I told him that since Laktarnik was bringing a gaggle of slayers with him, he should probably hold off until after they had left the building, or maybe I'd even have them escort me home. He grudgingly agreed.

The good doctor arrived at 4:45 with an entourage that looked like they stepped out of the pages of *Fortune*. All four slayers were dressed in business suits and carried briefcases. Our witch doctor, however, looked like he always did. He wore a sweater with elbow patches over a button-down shirt and corduroy pants, his glasses were askew, and his white hair was a fright.

Ian ushered them all to the conference room and he seemed to be appalled that none of the men, other than Laktarnik, would shake my hand. I didn't think now was the time to tell my assistant that I was a half-vampire in a room full of *dhampir*. That's when I noticed their smell—or lack of smell. I'd never really thought about it, but my witch doctor had no smell at all and neither did these gentlemen. No cologne, soap, no general body scent—nothing. Weird, but I guess that was to their advantage.

We got right down to business, discussing possible scenarios, going over potential pitfalls. The meeting went on for over an hour.

We were so engrossed in our planning that it wasn't until Lola yelped that we were alerted to the fact that something was very wrong. Daniel had come to Speculation. Everyone in that room could smell him coming down the hall. I hoped he could smell only me and Lola.

I reached for my purse and its vampire repelling/killing kit. Briefcases popped open and suddenly the conference room was filled with five fully armed slayers, a crouching werewolf, and me, clutching a dish-soap bottle and a pistol.

There was a knock on the door.

We looked at each other, confused. We didn't expect him to knock.

"Come in?" What else would I say?

Confidently, Daniel pushed open the double doors—

and froze. He was paler than the night before, which made his blue eyes look electric—or maybe they were more pronounced because they were wide with surprise. He couldn't smell the *dhampir* and expected to find only me and Lola in the room.

I raised my pistol, but before I could pull the trigger, I heard five satisfying thwacks and watched as Daniel fell backward into the hallway, five cutlass-shaped knives deeply embedded in his neck and chest. As he hit the floor, his head rolled six inches to the left.

I heard the racing hearts of the seven of us who were still breathing. Lola eventually climbed down from the chair where she had crouched, ready to spring.

I walked over to Daniel's body, surprised that there wasn't a lot of blood. I was even more surprised to see a pointed shoe nudge his severed head away from behind the conference room door.

"Gia, dear, hand me that phone, I'll call maintenance to clean the carpet tonight!" Lois stepped into view. "Gregori, it's so good to see you again." She walked over to Dr. Laktarnik and hugged him fondly. "I hear Gia has been talking to you about collaborating on some books for us. I think it's a fantastic idea. Gia, the phone, please?"

I had not moved a muscle. Lois was acting like this happened every day. Okay, this *was* Speculation we were talking about, but still. One didn't see vampire heads rolling down the halls on a regular basis.

I handed her the phone, still in stunned silence. She punched in numbers and tapped her foot impatiently. "It's a good thing you did this after hours; it'll be a lot easier this way. Lola, there are garbage bags in my bottom left hand desk drawer, be a dear and get them for our friend here. Gia, get a grip and go intercept Ian before he stumbles onto this." I nodded and snapped out of my stupor. On my way out, I heard Lois still issuing orders.

"Gregori, while your friends here help Lola get rid of this," she waved her hand toward Daniel's mangled body, "why don't you call Jonathan—you have his cell phone number? Tell him Gia and Lola will be home soon. Oh hello, maintenance? I'll need the rug shampooed in front of the ninth-floor conference room. We've had an employee with an awful nosebleed."

Safe. I finally felt safe. The feeling was exhilarating. It had all happened so quickly, I was having trouble believing it was finally over. I sent Ian on a ridiculous errand (to go and buy six pastrami sandwiches for my guests) and escaped to my office to digest what had just happened and to let the adrenaline rush pass.

There was a soft knock on my open door. "Miss Giovanna, are you okay?" Dr. Laktarnik had come to check up on me.

"Yeah, I'm okay. Just shaken." That was an understatement.

"That was so . . ."

"Fast?" He smiled, "It's best to dispatch that sort of business quickly. That way no one chickens out. You and Miss Lola have a lot in common. You both behave well under pressure."

This was behaving well? The adrenaline racing through my veins was almost making me nauseous, I was trembling, and it felt like my heart was going to leap from my chest—but I'd take the compliment.

He smiled warmly and gestured to my neck. "May I have a look?" He gently pulled down my turtleneck, careful not to touch my skin. I wasn't sure if I was going to get scolded for the new bite, but he didn't say anything about it. "How are your symptoms?"

I'd been in such a state, I hadn't even noticed how I was feeling. "Okay, I guess—I haven't really been eating, but I have a lot of energy."

"You're healing better. I think one or maybe two more times before the real thing." He looked at me over his glasses. "I know this is useless, but I have to tell you: you can still back out." I wouldn't say he looked especially hopeful when he said this, but he was serious. "You'd make a nice addition to my group."

I almost laughed. "Doc, do you know how many of my friends I'd have to kill to be part of your *Fortune* 500 slayer posse? No thanks. And don't worry about me. I know what I'm doing."

He took my hands in his. "I know you do, Miss Giovanna. I know you do."

20

See You at the Funeral

I took a cab back to my apartment, which I hoped was empty except for Johnny.

He was waiting for me on my front stoop, looking delicious. I wanted to forget the last seventy-two hours ever happened and just lose myself in him tonight. I practically ran to him, and he gently held me back when I launched myself at him.

"Easy there, killer." He grinned like he was up to something.

"Nice to see you, too." I put my hands on my hips. What was he up to? "You're a little premature on the killer part; I had nothing to do with Daniel—that was all the good doctor and his friends."

"Have I told you how very well adjusted you are?" patted

the step next to him. I sat down and I noticed he had something in his jacket. "Did you have a nice day otherwise?"

"Cut the bullshit." I smiled back at him and shoved him. He knew this was just what I needed now—I'd talk about how I had the shit scared out of me another time. "Are you going to tell me what you're hiding in your jacket, or are you just happy to see me?"

He leaned over to kiss me. "I wanted to give you something that would help you get over the day you just had." He opened his jacket, and inside was a kitten. Now, that was the last thing I expected.

"Do I need a familiar?"

"That job of yours has made you really freaky, you know." He handed me the kitten. It was a very cute little orange thing. "It's part of my plan."

"I held it close to my cheek and listened to it purr.

He reached over to pet the kitten under the chin. "It's something for you to leave behind for your parents to care for." I raised my eyebrows. "No, it's not like the kitten will replace you, but it will be a welcome distraction to them. Something for them to focus their attention on, other than their grief and the estate dealings."

"That's actually a very good idea. What should we name it?"

He took it from me and held it up. "It's a she."

"How about Lola? She'd appreciate the joke." I sang, "Her name was Lola, she was a kitten . . ."

I loved to hear him laugh.

"Let's go upstairs to feed you and the kitten. You haven't been eating lately, have you?"

"Please don't lecture me. Besides having zero appetite, I've had a few things on my mind lately, not to mention working with your lawyer in all my copious free time."

"I love it when you talk like an English major." We turned to go inside the apartment.

Inside, Johnny applied minimal heat to a steak for me. I really couldn't call it cooking, considering it barely touched the grill pan before I said, "That's cooked enough for me." It was practically still mooing. While I ate my steak, I told him that all was going as planned—I had my will in order and my new ID printed up, Lola and Max had agreed to come with me to Jamaica, she had agreed to take care of my mom, and that I had already purchased my plane tickets and made my hotel reservations. I also told him about Lois, giving my notice, and all the prep work I'd been doing at work.

"I'm impressed that you have all the details wrapped up ahead of schedule, in spite of all that was going on."

"Hey, I'm a publicist. Details are my specialty," I said.

Johnny moved in and nuzzled my ear. "Damn, you smell good. Like steak. It's been good catching up, but I don't think I can wait any longer."

"I thought you'd never ask."

I wondered if sex would change after I did. It certainly couldn't get any better. I was a sweaty, limp mess when he was through with me, and he, well, he acted like a guy who hadn't gotten any in two hundred and eighty-eight years.

My new wounds weren't nearly as bad as the first time. The doctor was right, I was beginning to heal faster.

I was fascinated by it. I held out my latest, a puncture mark inside my right elbow. "Look at this one."

"Want me to kiss it and make it better?"

"You know it." He did, and I shuddered. When I had caught my breath, I asked. "How will you let me taste you for real?"

He traced my lips with his finger—it was one of the few

places I didn't have a bite mark these days. "I'll just cut myself and you'll drink. I'll feed beforehand, so you can get a good amount. I have a feeling you'll have a very big appetite."

Me, too. I had been starving, but I really had been having a hard time eating anything other than rare meat. I found myself listening to people's blood, and it made my stomach growl—an uncomfortable sensation. I was smelling humans and picking up not just scents, but emotions. I could smell fear, excitement, nervousness. Lola smelled so overwhelmingly like sex, I found her distracting.

We spent the whole night in bed. Mostly we talked—I had been through one hell of a week—but there were a few careful little tastes and a lot of attention paid to my puncture wounds in between. I mean, come on, I was lying naked next to the man I had been fanatasizing about since I laid eyes on him. I couldn't very well just let him lie there now, could I?

Johnny explained more about the physical transformation that lay ahead, and what to expect from the rest of his group. In addition to Nelson, Orlando, and Michael, he had told most of his friends what was going on, but wanted to wait before bringing me back to see them. When we went to that club last time, his friends apparently found me a little too irresistible in this in-between stage and he didn't want to put me at risk.

I asked about how he met and came to change Jillian, and he told me that she had sought him out, saying she'd been bitten by a rogue vampire on the streets of DC and needed help. She fed him a long, pathetic sob story. He felt bad for her and when she pleaded with him to change her, he did. After the change, he found out the truth. The rogue was really her ex-boyfriend—a very new convert—and it was never his intention to change her; he was going to keep her a slave. She got wind of his plans, did a little asking around, and set out to find an older vampire for protection. I was surprised Johnny fell for it, but who knows what he was going through at the time?

I asked about Michael, too. He was the oldest vampire in his group and it freaked me out that he never spoke. Johnny told me not to worry about him, that he had already given his approval. Not that it was needed, but it would make things so much easier. He told me how to act toward Michael after I was changed; to be respectful and not to go against any of the rules without talking to him first. "He's excited that you're joining us. He's intrigued by our unique relationship. In fact, I think he's even a little sweet on you."

"Jealous?"

"Damn right. If he changes you, you'll be able to kick my ass."

"Well, we can't have that." I reached over and caressed the ass in question. "I wouldn't want to damage this fine bit of you."

Saturday night was my friend Elena's Christmas party. Johnny had gone back to DC on Thursday, but made it home in time to go with me. I was having second thoughts, though I wasn't sure if I could handle seeing all my friends like that, knowing it would most likely be the last time and pretending that it wasn't. I came up with a way out. "You know, other than Lola and Max, you'll be the only nonhuman there. So if you're uncomfortable, we don't have to go."

"No, you'll be there, too, and you're not exactly human these days, either."

Good point. I hadn't begun to allow myself to think of myself that way yet, but he was right. My wounds were really beginning to heal now, so I knew I was beginning to transform. I was also becoming much more nocturnal.

We walked the few blocks to Elena's, a beautiful carriage house tucked away in the east eighties.

She welcomed us in and I introduced them. "Elena, this is Jonathan; he's the one I told you about from DC." He handed her a bottle of wine and Elena greeted him a little too enthusiastically, holding his hand a little too long. Who could blame her? He had his ol' bloodsucking charm on at full tilt.

After the introductions, she unceremoniously pulled me to the side. "Freakin' heck! This is your author's manager? He's super hot. He's got the most intense eyes." She paused. "But you know what bothers me? He doesn't make a lot of eye contact."

She didn't know how lucky she was that he didn't.

Actually, Johnny did sometimes make brief eye contact with my friends that night, using his little vampire hypnosis trick to put them under a little *Like me, I'm good guy* spell when I introduced him. Maybe I could introduce him to my parents—and maybe I would get my brain replaced by a cauliflower.

We went upstairs to put our coats on the bed, and found Lola and Max already making out on top of the mound of outerwear. I covered them up with our coats and joined the party. Elena was not the only one of my friends to comment on the deliciousness of my date. I smiled to myself every time they whispered this in my ear, knowing that he was hearing it all. I warned him, "Don't let this go to your head."

"Nah, I'm used to it." He gave me a smug grin. "It's nothing I haven't heard for centuries."

I poked him hard. "Don't be a wiseass."

As I predicted, it was hard to leave, and we stayed until about three a.m. I didn't like saying good-bye. I kept thinking to myself *See you at the funeral*, and it was depressing the hell out of me.

Johnny sensed this and cut me off.

"We should go. It won't get any easier."

He was right. I hugged my friends one last time, made false promises to see them after the holidays, and left.

Johnny left Sunday night. He had to tie up some loose ends before our vacation and I had a hell of a week in front of me. On Monday, I saw my parents off for their traditional holiday cruise—they had started spending their Christmases on cruise ships when I went off to college, and we'd celebrated the holidays the weekend after New Year's ever since. This year they were going to Greece, which worked out well for me. It would be a long and complicated trip home when they heard the news, which would give them time to think and a lot of obstacles to distract them. It was hard to keep up a brave exterior, but I tried to act as natural as possible. They were excited about Lola the kitten, and told me to bring her to their house when I came to visit in January.

In the days that followed, time had a strange habit of speeding up, then slowing down to a crawl. It was so erratic that I'd often be caught off guard by people wishing me good morning or good night. I was in a strange form of limbo and couldn't wait until it was over.

Finally, it was time to leave. I took care of all the last-minute things a human would before a vacation. I asked Elena to watch my cat, purchased a bunch of trial-size toiletries at the drug store, bought a few tank tops.

It was the day before our offices closed for the holiday week, and everyone was in a festive mood—except me. I was excited, nervous, apprehensive, scared. I tried to join in, but my heart wasn't in it. I went into the conference room where everyone was congregating. I took a glass of wine and a cookie, but the smell of the cookie was making me nauseous. I wished all my coworkers a happy holiday and played along.

When I retreated to my office, Lois followed and sat down. She'd had a few glasses of wine in the conference room and was a bit red in the face. "You going to finish that?" She pointed to my barely touched glass of wine.

"Knock yourself out." Then, in my best Gary Oldman Dracula impression, "I neeeaveer drriink . . . vine."

Lois laughed. "So." She chewed on her thumb, I gesture I knew would precede questions. "This is it, huh?"

"Yeah."

"How does it feel?"

An interesting question. I wondered if she had been offered the same opportunity at any time in her career.

"It feels right. I love him, Lois."

"Well, obviously." She drummed her fingers on the arm of the chair. "I'm going to miss you a lot. Not just your work, but you." I nodded, a little choked up. "This will be weird. Do you think you'll stay on as Bella's personal publicist—under another name, of course?"

"No, I'm going to make a clean break. Pursue my new career as a phlebotomist." We both grinned at that. When in mixed company, we often referred to our vampire authors as such. Since I would probably never see her again, I asked her, "Have you ever been tempted? You know, by one of our authors?"

"Yes, many times. It's a very seductive lifestyle, and early on in my career, I came pretty damn close—I've even been bitten twice." She raised her eyebrows at me. "Don't look at me like that. He was a very sexy vampire and I have to say, I've never felt anything like it since. But it didn't work out, and now it's too late for me. I have my children to think of."

I gave her a sly grin. "Why, Lois, I never knew you had such a wild side."

"And you never would have, if you weren't leaving."

"I'm going to miss you."

"Don't worry, I have a feeling we'll be in touch." She paused and examined her fingernails. "So, this is a pretty weird love story. Do you think you have a novel in you?"

I hadn't thought of that. I wondered if a love story between a saucy publicist and a dashing vampire would sell.

21

What's Your Poison?

What can I say about the Caribbean? It was hot and it was sunny. Temperature rarely affected me anymore, and I wasn't a big fan of the sun these days, either. Funny how something I once enjoyed so much was now hardly missed.

I flew down to Jamaica with Lola and Max in the morning and made sure lots of people at the resort saw me check in. Johnny wasn't meeting us until later that night, so Lola and I spent the day at the pool. She sipped on a frozen rum drink while floating nearby on a raft while I sat under the shade of the swim-up bar and worried endlessly about what was to come that night.

"What if it doesn't work on me?" We were barely whispering, but we could both hear each other perfectly. My hearing ability had increased exponentially.

"It's been working for centuries. What makes you think you're so damn special?" Lola had listened to me worry and complain all the way down on the plane, and now I was subjecting her to it while she was trying to relax. I couldn't blame her for getting annoyed.

"Well, I have this whole inability-to-heal thing. What if it doesn't take?" I looked at my wrists, hidden under several bracelets. The wounds were healing better and better these days, but we weren't talking about a little love nibble. This was the real deal.

"That has to be your worst and most ridiculous paranoid delusion of the day. You've been healing better each time, and now you're just being annoying." In a louder voice, "Bartender, make that woman a stronger drink!"

I kicked her raft across the pool.

"Wow, those bites look pretty bad."

What? I was so wrapped up in my own little world of doubt and anxiety, that I didn't even notice the guy sitting two stools down. "Excuse me?"

He was looking at my ankles; he must have seen them when I kicked Lola's raft. "Those mosquito bites—man, you must have scratched the hell out of them."

Bug bites. He thought they were bug bites. I relaxed. I had taken care to cover up my neck bites with makeup and my wrists with bracelets, but I could do nothing about my legs. "Yeah, apparently, I'm a very tasty morsel."

He moved over to sit next to me. "So, can I buy you that drink your friend suggested?"

"This is an all-inclusive resort." He was hitting on me. I know this will sound corny, but since Johnny and I became a couple, I really hadn't noticed other guys. This one wasn't bad; sort of an aging frat boy. He had a certain boyish charm and at the very least, he was distracting me from my apprehension.

"Well, then, can I order you a drink?" He looked at me hopefully over his sunglasses. "What's your poison?" He adjusted his backward baseball cap.

At least this should kill some time. "Vodka." Maybe Lola was right and it would help me take the edge off.

"And how do you like it?"

"In a glass." In my opinion, vodka should only be mixed with vermouth, and today I wanted to stay away from Johnny's number one turnoff.

"Just straight vodka?"

"Strong and straight, like my men."

He smiled and ordered me my drink and got himself a beer (big surprise), and we chatted for a while. I found out he was here for his brother's wedding, then he asked if I'd been to the clothing-optional beach yet—how very subtle. When I couldn't take him anymore, I excused myself and went to my room to get ready for my big night. On my way out I splashed Lola and Max, who were making out in the shallow end of the pool.

I was putting on mascara when I heard Johnny's feet on the stairs of our villa. I ran over to the door, and at his knock I called, "Who's there?"

"Room service."

I opened the door. He looked fantastic. He wore jeans and an untucked button-down linen shirt that he had managed to miraculously keep unwrinkled. I hoped that unwrinkled clothes were part of the vampire mystique; that was a trick I could use.

"Is that what we're calling it these days?" I teased.

He kissed me lightly. "Well, I did bring some champagne." He came in and kissed me lightly on the lips. "Although it smells like you've had quite a few cocktails already. What's the matter? Cold feet?"

"No, that's just your cold heart—you're confused." I was backing him toward the bed.

"You're a real wiseass, you know it?"

"Mm-hm." I was now kissing his neck and aggressively unbuttoning his shirt. I had missed him so much and couldn't get close enough to him. All the anxiety I felt earlier fueled my reaction to him; I couldn't wait to have him.

He gently pushed me away. "What is this? *When Publicists Attack?* We said we'd wait until after dinner with Lola and Max. Trust me, the sex will be even better if we do it my way."

"First of all, it can't get any better, and come on, one little taste won't hurt." I positioned my neck right underneath his chin. He couldn't resist and leaned in for a taste. My cute little black wrap dress was plastered to my back with sweat by the time he was done. If he was right and the sex got better, I had better be immortal. Otherwise it just might kill me.

I showered and changed into a different dress before we went downstairs. We double-dated that night like human couples—dinner, dancing, all very normal—except that none of us were technically human.

Other than a celebratory glass of champagne, I kept sober—I wanted to have a clear head for later. Lola, however, was getting pretty smashed on mojitos. Over dinner, Jonathan gave us all a little history lesson on the Caribbean rum trade. It was fascinating, especially since this was all firsthand knowledge.

Around midnight, Lola grabbed my wrist and told me we were going to the ladies' room. I complied. Human or not, all females need to go to the restroom in pairs.

Once there, she looked directly into my eyes. "You know that as your best friend, I have to do this. You can still back out if you want to."

I smiled at her. "Yes, I know that. And I'm sure this is what I want."

She hugged me and told me she'd check in on me at around dawn.

After Lola and Max turned in, Johnny and I took a long walk on the beach. The full moon had passed a few nights ago, but it was still big and bright enough to light up the sky. We didn't talk much, just savored the salt air. What was there to say? I knew where he was taking me and why. When we got to the end of the beach, to a secluded spot near the rocky jetty, he turned to look at me. "Are you ready?"

I nodded, unable to speak.

"Nervous?"

I nodded again.

"I promise this won't hurt a bit." He kissed me then. Gently at first, then harder, and that did it for us. We hurriedly undressed each other. When we'd talked about this, he'd told me how he envisioned this moment. He always said he wanted to slowly tease me into a frenzy, but now, neither of us could get there fast enough.

He drew me down into the sand. It was cool and soft, like baby powder on my new extra-sensitive skin. He paid special attention to my pulse points. He knew that after the change my hyper-responsive wounds would disappear, and took full advantage of them while he could. He stroked them, kissed them, and sucked from them. He bit me in new places that he wouldn't have dared before—either out of fear the marks would show, or maybe because he wouldn't be able to stop.

He was in total control when he positioned himself on top of me, while I was a writhing mess on the sand. When he took my neck in his teeth, I shoved my hand in my mouth to stifle my scream. He sucked on me longer, harder, and with a ferocity I had never felt before. I was on the edge of consciousness when he pulled away. He was kissing me on my lips when I felt his warm blood dripping onto my neck; he had cut his throat. He took my head and gently guided my lips to his throat. I pulled in and shook violently with the sensation. I felt his chest rumble and realized that he was moaning and shaking just as desperately as I was.

After what felt like hours, he pulled away. I saw blood trickle from his self-inflicted cut, but it was already starting to heal. I reached up and licked the few remaining drops, savoring the taste of it. My previous tastes had been so small, I couldn't fully appreciate its sweetness. His blood was salty, metallic, and vaguely tasting of . . . well, me.

I felt my teeth with my tongue. What did I expect, fangs in ten seconds? But then the other senses took over. After Johnny started snacking on me regularly, I'd developed a heightened sense of everything, but now . . . now the beach shone like daylight. I could hear people in the hotel five hundred yards away. I could smell everything, down to the different varieties of fish swimming offshore. It was extraordinary.

He was looking down at my face, enjoying my reaction as I took it all in. "Feel like taking a swim?"

Oddly enough, I did. "Lead the way."

Johnny took my hand and led me into the sea. We waded out far enough so the water reached my chest, his waist. The water felt otherworldly, velvety, like it matched my body temperature exactly.

"How are you feeling?"

"Incredible. Except that my vision is blurry."

He laughed at me. "Try taking out your contacts."

"Oh." Duh. I took them out and let them float away. I hadn't thought about it, but of course my vision would improve. I mean, have you ever seen a vampire wearing eyeglasses?

The salt water tickled all my bites. I lifted my wrists out of the water and watched as they healed.

"I'll miss those," he said softly.

"Me, too." As the words came out of my mouth, I was aware of my fangs growing. They felt awkward and hard to talk around.

"Let's see." He tilted my head up toward the moonlight. "I've always loved your smile." I grinned at him and he smiled back, my favorite little half smile. I'd have to work on one of my own.

"I feel like I have too many teeth."

"Let me see if I agree." He kissed me deeply, stroking them individually with his tongue. "No, they came in nice. Not too big. I like 'em."

His kiss felt different—if possible, even sexier. He didn't hold back like he did before, when he was afraid of cutting too deeply into my tongue. I wanted him again, but I wanted him in a new way. "So when do I get to use them?"

"Does now work for you?" He took my hand and placed my fingers over his jugular. "You'll want to enter here. I'll lean back a little—the blood flows better when the neck is at an angle like this." I felt his low, rumbling voice through his throat as he was positioning my hand. "It's going to feel weird, like you're hurting me, but don't worry. It's going to feel very, very good for both of us." He leaned down and gave me his neck.

I was a little timid. I kissed it first, and felt the blood course through the veins under my lips. That got me excited, and introduced me to hunger. I sank my teeth into him hard. He pulled me closer to him, and I felt his thoughts—he was loving it.

All too soon, he pulled me away. "Leave some for later."

I was trying to get my head around the fact that I could literally experience his feelings while I drank from him. "Why didn't you tell me you could taste my thoughts?"

"Where would be the fun in that?"

"Very funny." I rolled my eyes at him. "So why did you ask so many questions if you always knew how I felt?"

"It's not always the same. This time, you felt my pleasure. Next time, you may pick up something different."

"So is it later yet? I'd like to see what else is in your head."

"I knew you'd have a big appetite, but this is ridiculous."

"Come on, just a little love bite?" I began kissing his chest. He lifted me into his arms so my face was level with his. He trailed his mouth down to just below my ear and drank from me again. Instinctively, I turned to his neck and did the same. The force of our new embrace caught us both by surprise, and before we knew it, we were sliding completely under the water. I broke away first, sputtering salt water.

He laughed at me. "You don't have to worry about how long you can hold your breath anymore."

"Cut me some slack, will ya? I'm new at this." I recovered and went back into his arms.

"Well, I've got about two hundred eighty-eight years of making up to do with another activity. Let's go back to our room and see what we can do about that."

We spent the rest of that night in bed tasting each other. I could never find words to describe how fulfilling it was. He told me that after a good day's sleep, we'd go into town and he'd teach me how to hunt. I thought I'd be repulsed by the notion, but instead, I just felt hungry.

The next morning, at about an hour before sunrise, there was a knock on the door and I smelled Lola and Max.

I didn't want to leave Johnny's side, but I knew they could smell us in here and I knew Lola wouldn't go away. We put on some clothes and let them in.

They had brought us champagne to celebrate my death. It was a surreal kind of wedding reception/funeral. If possible, my life had gotten even weirder; vampires and werewolves partying together. It was like a bad Abbott and Costello movie. All we needed was the invisible man. And who knew, he may have been there, too.

22

Power Tasted Like Cast Iron

We couldn't live in New York anytime soon; it wouldn't do for someone to recognize me in the street. But Johnny assured me that as long as I kept a low profile and we were in and out quickly, one more visit wouldn't hurt. Besides, we had business to attend to, namely, my memorial service. As my clients, Johnny and Bella would naturally attend.

The night we flew back from Jamaica, he arranged a little party so we could celebrate with our supernatural friends and I could meet the rest of my new companions. We went to a club in the meatpacking district that very few humans knew about, which was why he chose it. It was good to see Bella again, and I was touched by the warm reception I got from their friends. Nelson hugged me and sniffed at me (Johnny told me that was normal, but it would still take some getting used to), Orlando hugged me and sniffed me, too, and Michael simply bowed low and kissed my inner wrist. He still hadn't said a word to me. Weird.

Lola and Max joined us, and the evening was shaping up to be a lot of fun until Jillian showed up around three a.m. She acted surprised that she had accidentally interrupted our party, as if she had no idea we were meeting there. Of course, everyone knew she was crashing to get back at me for Daniel. Not too bright, that Jillian.

She didn't seem to care that half the room snubbed her. It didn't stop her from coming right up to me, where she gave me a scathing look. "So, welcome." She stood in front of me with her hands on her hips. What was this, some kind of freaky Vampirella challenge? She was so lame.

I did want to deal with her eventually, but not tonight. "Thank you, Jillian. That's very sweet of you. Now, if you'll excuse me, I just remembered something." I started past her, but she stopped me with a hand on my arm. Even though she and I were made by the same vampire, she was forty years older and therefore stronger.

"What could be more important than getting to know your new friends? What is it that you just remembered?"

I was really beginning to hate her. "Let's see . . . Oh, I know: you're talking, and my legs work." This time I did manage to get by her.

I caught Bella's eye and she nodded approvingly. I guess I came off better in that exchange than I thought. This wasn't so bad. I didn't mind taking the high road.

Then I heard Jillian's voice again. "Who invited the mutt?" She was sniffing the air, her lip curled like she had just smelled garbage.

That was it. I knew she was just trying to get a rise out of me, but no one insulted my best friend. I turned on my heel.

Bella stepped in. "Ladies." She put herself between us. "Jillian, you should leave now. This is Gia's party and you weren't invited."

Jillian appeared to shrink at Bella's words, and slunk out of the club muttering that it was a public club and she could have stayed if she wanted to. She wasn't contrite, by any means; she was a sore loser and was just biding her time until she could have me alone. This sucked. This was a mess waiting to happen.

"She'll get over it." Bella had put an arm around me. "Michael wouldn't have it any other way."

"No she won't—I totally fucked up her life. I've cheated her out of the last two important men in her life. To be honest, I don't care what she thinks about that. It was the dig at Lola . . ." I took a deep breath. "She said that just to get to me. She's picking a fight because she knows I can't win."

"Relax. You did win. You won what counts. Now go dance with my cousin."

Bella was right. I did win where it counted, though I knew that wasn't going to hold water with Jillian. But this *was* my party and I felt like letting loose a bit. I walked over to Johnny and dragged him onto the floor. It was just like old times, except that this time, after we took a bunch of hot little bites out of each other, I wouldn't be going home sexually frustrated in a cab. This time I would be going back to our hotel room.

The party started to break up at about 4 a.m. Johnny came up from behind, put his arms around me, and kissed me on the back of my neck. "I'm going to take a walk by the water for a little pre-dawn snack. It seems that someone has been draining my energy lately."

"Now, who could that be?" I leaned up and kissed him.

"You coming with me?"

"No, I want to say good-bye to a few more people. Why

don't you take Max with you and have a smoke? Lola and I will meet you out front."

"Okay, I won't be long. I got us a great room at the Waldorf." He kissed me again and grabbed Max on his way out.

Lola and I tried to leave shortly after, but I had a lot of well-wishers to go through—it was like a friggin' receiving line at a wedding. When Lola and I finally left the club, we didn't see Johnny and Max right away so we figured they were still down by the water. We turned the street corner, and there was Jillian, standing in the alley. What a pain in the ass she was.

She snapped her fingers and whistled. "Come here, girl, come on, yeah, that's a good dog."

Lola gave me a bored look. "I'm assuming that's aimed at me?" I didn't know about her, but I wasn't so sure she could take on a forty-year-old vampire, or that my new supernatural strength would be enough to help her out. "By the way, Jillian, the name is Lola, L-O-L-A, Lola," she said calmly.

"Yeah, bitch. Your kind isn't welcome here."

I caught a glimpse of her eyes—all red. I looked down and saw two dead homeless guys in an unnatural heap against the wall. She was hazing. I felt a perverse kind of pride that I'd pissed her off enough to drive her into a blood frenzy, but I didn't have time to gloat since she was giving us the evil eye.

I tried to keep the situation calm. "Lola, you know she has nothing against you. She's just trying to get me into a fight."

Lola was pacing—a very bad sign. "Yeah, a fight she knows she'll win—not very sporting of her, is it? She must have picked up that little habit from Daniel, and just look where that landed *him*." Lola's voice was becoming more of a growl. "I'm not so sure she can kick my ass."

Was Lola about to shape-shift right here in the middle of Manhattan? I'd never seen her change, and I didn't even know if she could change at will or had to wait for the full or new moon. Either way, I knew she was strong and fast, and another advantage was that she was completely lucid. Jillian looked far from rational.

I had fed from Johnny earlier in the evening and I was pretty sure I retained some of his strength, so figured between the two of us, we could take her, but I'd really rather it didn't come to that.

"Jillian, you're not—" But before I could finish, Jillian launched at Lola.

I wanted to scream, but drawing attention to this scene was not a good idea. I looked around for a weapon, and my eyes fell on Michael standing beside me. When did he get there?

"Kill her, Gia."

What? He was looking at the fight in front of us, not at me; his face was expressionless.

I just stood there. It felt like the scene before me was unfolding in slow motion.

"She's going to kill your friend if you don't kill her first."

"I don't know if I can. I'm not as strong as she is . . ."

Michael's arm shot out in front of my face. "I can help you there."

Neither of us took our eyes off of the pair. I leaned in and bit down on the inside of his elbow. I felt his tremendous power shoot through me, tasting like cast iron, and I sucked in very hard. I felt a tap on my shoulder and realized he was signaling me to let go, which wasn't easy to do.

I moved to the loading area with a speed that surprised me. Still keeping my eyes on them, I smashed my fist into a wooden shipping pallet.

Lola was getting the living shit kicked out of her. Still in her human form, she was snarling and fighting to keep all of her body parts away from Jillian's mouth.

I gripped the wood and was instantly at their side. "Back away, Lola."

Lola was in the zone, but something in the tone of my voice brought her out of it and made her move away.

Without saying another word, I grabbed Jillian by the hair and plunged my makeshift stake through her throat. I felt the wood sever the spine as I jammed the stake all the way through. Just like that, I had killed her. No dramatic words like "Die, bitch"; no fancy fighting. I just stabbed her through her neck until her head threatened to separate from her body.

It went in easy. She looked surprised. She fell to the ground.

Lola and I stood there looking at her body. Michael still stood behind us.

"You okay, Lo?" I turned to her. She didn't look okay. She was scratched and bloodied and had trouble standing.

"Yeah, she never got a bite out of me and I'll heal up by morning." She was examining herself to make sure that what she said was true.

"Okay. Then let's go find the guys." My voice sounded very calm. Lola looked at me. It may have been my imagination, but she seemed a little awed. Of course, I knew she'd never admit it.

I put my arm around her and turned her away from the body. Chloe could come out and take care of it—that's what she was there for.

Michael still stood there rubbing his arm where I had tasted his incredibly potent blood, and I stopped in front of him. What now?

"Well done." He had an ancient accent, and his voice was far deeper than one would expect from such a young-looking man.

"Thanks. Why did you let me do that?"

"The rules for defending friends differ from those of jealous lovers."

"Oh." What did a girl say to that?

We started toward the club door, and Michael came around to put his arm around Lola's other side to support her.

"Giovanna." Michael was looking over Lola's head to meet my eyes. "I can see what he sees in you." I smiled shyly. I think I may have even blushed.

Johnny and Max must have heard the struggle and had returned to the club. We all looked up to see them running toward us. Max immediately swept Lola into his arms and started licking her jaw tenderly. She'd be okay. She should probably see the witch doctor just to be sure, but she was most likely already starting to heal—werewolves did that.

I called to Max, "You're going to take her to Brooklyn, right?" He nodded and lifted her into his arms. I squeezed her unbloodied shoulder. "You're one hell of a friend."

Lola looked over her shoulder and winked at me. "I'll call you, Chickpea." Max carried her to the avenue to get a cab to Little Odessa.

I still couldn't believe how calm I was through all of this. It must have been the Michael in me.

"I can't leave you alone for a minute," Johnny said as he took me in his arms. He looked concerned and a little frightened. "How did you . . . ?" He stopped, not wanting to offend me. "I mean, she was—"

"Good night, Gia," Michael interrupted.

I stepped away from Johnny. "Good night, Michael, and thank you." That didn't even begin to express my gratitude, but I knew he would appreciate the sincerity as well as the economy of my words.

He took my wrist in his hand as he had earlier that night.

"It was a pleasure." I thought he was going to kiss the inside of my wrist again, but he took a bite.

Jonathan stood there looking stunned. I later learned that as the eldest, it was Michael's privilege to feed from any of the group, although no one could remember ever seeing it happen before. None of his group could remember Michael ever offering anyone his blood, either.

Michael stood and wiped the corner of his mouth with his index finger, then nodded toward Jonathan before leaving quietly. He did everything quietly.

When I looked back at Johnny, I saw that he had trouble believing what he saw, but fully understood what had happened. He actually shook his head to clear it, then we both watched my wrist wound heal up.

"Wow, what did that feel like?" he asked.

"It felt . . ." I took a moment to process it. "Formal."

He put his arm around me. "Well, this was one hell of a way to start off. Are you going to turn out to be one of those dramatic vampires that you used to hate? Silk shirts and all?"

I poked him in the ribs. "Shut up. Nobody likes a wiseass."

We went to the corner to get a cab. It was almost dawn.

𝕰pilogue

Forever After

It's been three years since my change, and I've adjusted to the lifestyle with relative ease. In the very beginning I had the advantage of the lingering effects of Michael's blood, but that wore off within a week. Still, Johnny and I drank from each other so often that I did have more strength than the usual fledgling vampire. I'd have brief moments where I'd be as strong as a 291-year-old vampire, then slip back to my three-year-old self. Johnny was never weakened by my blood, which I found terribly unfair. He'd just smile and tell me I was greedy and impatient. He had a point there.

I found that hunting felt surprisingly natural, and discovered right from the start that I never had trouble holding back. I had an inherent knack for sampling just enough blood from each victim to satisfy myself. My marks never knew what hit them.

In the beginning, Johnny and I went out hunting together. He wanted to be sure I knew how to handle my prey, but as soon as he was sure I was okay on my own, we began going out independently—it wasn't as suspicious-looking that way. We'd split up at twilight, hunt individually, and meet up later where we'd taste each other's brains out, if ya know what I mean.

During that brief stay in New York, we did go to visit Dr. Laktarnik. He was full of questions and examined me pretty thoroughly. Sadly, my previously unhealable bites left no scars with the ability to send me over the edge. But I had something a lot better than that now: the sex was amazing. I told the good doctor that, too (hey, he asked).

We stayed just long enough to attend my memorial service. Jonathan and Bella naturally went as my work associates, and I hid in the shadows in the back of the room. Johnny told me I shouldn't go, but I couldn't help myself. I just wanted to be sure my parents were okay—and I selfishly wanted to see them again. Of course, he was right, and I cried for days as a result.

We moved to Johnny's place in DC, but soon decided that we wanted a fresh start together, and that it might be fun to travel around the country. Especially in the beginning, when my movement was still hesitant. As I practiced, I became more inconspicuous. I learned stealth, speed, and perfected that eerie ability to blend into shadows. It's remarkably easy when you know how. I also mastered that creepy hypnotizing thing.

We stayed in New England for a while, where I discovered a real taste for drunken frat boys. My new creepy hypnotizing skills were a waste of time with them; they were effectively hypnotized by my boobs. And by the way? The person who invented body shots totally had to be a vampire.

We also stayed in the Pacific Northwest for a bit. The constant cloud cover was nice, but I didn't much care for brooding musicians. They never wanted to have any fun; they always wanted to talk and tasted of too much coffee.

We've recently settled just outside San Diego, in Coronado. It's a good place for us. It's a resort town with lots of tourists and is situated between two military bases, so there are tons of transient residents. We weren't the only vampires in town, and we made some friends in our little bloodsucking community. The weather was great, the beaches were beautiful by moonlight, and it was easy hunting. And incidentally, I found I had a real taste for drunken Marines, too.

As I expected, Lola made a full recovery from her fight with Jillian. I learned that she could change into a werewolf any time she wanted to, but could only change back when the moon set each morning. She held back from changing the night she fought Jillian so that she would retain her humanoid form when it was over. It seemed reasonable, but the fact that she could think so clearly and remain in control that night is still impressive.

About a year after my change, she allowed me to watch her shape-shift. It was fascinating watching her limbs distort, her fur grow, her face transform. But all in all, it looked very painful. I never expected to see so much blood when she changed, but after I thought about it, how could a five-feet-eleven-inch woman turn into a wolf without bleeding? I gained a new respect for Lola and the other werewolves I knew. The day after, I asked her how much it hurt and she told me that it was kind of like what women say about childbirth. It's incredibly painful when it's happening, but forgotten by the next day. Having seen it, I'm not so sure.

Lola and Max got married about a year and a half ago. They had a wonderfully tacky ceremony in a cheesy twenty-four-hour Las Vegas wedding chapel. They scheduled their wedding for midnight the week before the full moon, incorporating the moon's cycle into their honeymoon plans—it was oddly romantic. Naturally, Johnny and I were attendants. They honeymooned partially at a casino and partially in a rented cabin in the desert. They both fell in love with the desert and moved there shortly after. It was a good place for them—lots of space for them to run wild, and easy for us to visit. Vegas was a great place for vampires, too. That may very well be our next home.

Lola and I still talked every day. In the beginning, she consoled me when I mourned the end of my life. I never regretted my decision, but she helped me through my grief over the loss of my family and friends, and all the trappings that came with a human life. She continued to keep an eye on my parents for me until she moved to Nevada.

I also popped in on them from time to time, doing my little "hiding in the shadows" vampire thing. My mom is convinced I'm haunting her and feels oddly comforted by it. She tells her friends that her daughter is a ghost. She's not too far off. My dad never senses my presence and kids my mother that she's going off the deep end. Nothing new there. And Jonathan was right. They doted on Lola the cat, and it really did help them get through a tough time in their lives.

Jonathan and I adopted a dog about two years ago, a big rottweiler, shepherd, and who-knows-what-else mix we found on the side of the road. We named her Jellybean and she became our guard dog. She watches out for us while we sleep during the day, and then she sleeps most of the night.

Bella was still writing her bestselling Von Rastenbourg novels. Lois promoted Ian as a replacement for me, and he was doing a good job with her campaign. She never did sign on for that satellite radio show; she preferred to have her evenings free to hunt with Michael. (They had recently become much closer—she always did dig older men.) But she was a frequent guest on a cable channel's paranormal program as the resident vampire expert.

Her first book was finally made into a movie, and Johnny and I attended the Hollywood premiere and afterparty (with me in disguise). The movie was kind of lame, but the party was a lot of fun. And in case you're wondering, celebrities taste like silicone.

Johnny continued to manage Bella's career and was on tour with her now. Thankfully, they were wrapping it up on the West Coast. I missed him terribly and couldn't wait for him to get back.

As for me, I took Lois's suggestion. I began writing a novel, but it's not about a saucy publicist and a dashing ex-pirate vampire—that would just be totally unbelievable. Instead, it's about a vampire female and a werewolf male who fell in love. They're totally attracted to each other and desperately want to bite each other, but they're worried about which characteristics would carry over from each condition. She treats her vampirism like a gift and he treats his lycanthropy as a disease. I have to say, it's pretty damn good so far. Of course, I've always been so terribly modest.

I was out earlier, but now I was just hanging around the house in my bathrobe and working on my book, when Jellybean barked. I had heard it, too—Johnny was home early. "Come on, Jelly, let's go get him."

I went to the door, the dog at my heels, and Johnny was there with a bouquet of flowers. Always the gentleman. He leaned in to kiss me in the doorway. His tongue caressed my fangs and my tongue stroked his in return.

"You're home early," I murmured.

He pushed me inside, threw the flowers on the table, and kicked the door closed. "I couldn't stay away another day. I rented a car and drove down here the second Bella's speech was over." He began backing me against the wall in the hall-way, undoing my robe. He nipped at my lower lip and I bled gently onto his tongue. He licked my mouth clean. I was also undressing him, needing to feel his skin next to mine.

"I had to see you," he moaned when I finally got his ridicu-lous silk shirt off. "The fans were unbearable, and LA left me with a bad taste in my mouth."

"I'll be the judge of that." I kissed him again. He was warm, so he must have fed on the trip home. "Actually, you taste like a stripper."

He shrugged and grinned. "And you taste like marines."

I grinned back at him. "Guilty."

Hey—it was in my nature.